Carrie's Quest

Carrie

Remember; every Mountain 'or Cake' that you climb most of the time there is an escalator or elevator on the other side. So says Uncle Confucius.

Dale

Carrie's Quest

By

Pam Sievers

This is a work of fiction. Names, characters, places and events are products of the authors imagination or are used fictitiously, and any resemblance to actual persons, living or dead, business establishments, events or locales is coincidental.

Cover design by Ken Dawson.

Paperback ISBN 9798633488289

Published in the USA

Dedication

Dedicated to my mother, whose courage and creativity fed my vivid imagination as a child.

Frances Waid Sievers
June, 1921 – July, 1980

Chapter 1

Carrie's temples throbbed. She could blame it on the drizzle, but she knew it was the angst of spending the next ten hours at her boss's home for a team retreat. She drove to the end of the cul-de-sac and slowed her car as she approached Marta's house.

Her goal for the day was to remain upbeat and engaged despite Marta's condescending remarks, repetitious demands, and her irritating, nasal voice, accentuated with a slight snort in the middle of run-on sentences. Carrie could not understand how the woman remained executive director of the hospital's foundation, but she was confident karma would eventually catch up with her.

Carrie parked directly across the street from the front door so she could have a fast get-away. From this vantage point, she surveyed the homes with wide lawns, spacious front porches, and tulips waiting to burst with the first promise of sunshine. Differing roof lines added contrast to the overcast skies. This was the neighborhood of her dreams.

She looked at the nearby houses and imagined what hers would look like—maybe the slate gray or the hunter green, just not builder's beige, or whatever trendy name they were calling it now. Then she eyed the house with the light-colored Lannon stones unique to Milwaukee. Yes, that's it; that's what she wanted. She liked the depth of the flat, irregular edges.

As usual, Carrie was several minutes early, and as assistant director, knew she needed to offer to help. She made the short walk across the street, up the sidewalk, and onto the porch.

The smell of coffee greeted her before the door opened and revealed Marta in a flowing red kaftan. Carrie looked down at her own black skinny jeans tucked into her boots and questioned her clothing choice for the day. Still, a staff retreat never called for a kaftan, especially when it made you look like an apple, a sour apple at that.

In the ten years Carrie had worked at St. Hedwig's, she had never been to her boss's home, but had listened to Marta talk about it, ad nauseam. The plum-colored, two-story foyer gave a casual, modern vibe to the house.

"Carrie, my friend, good morning. Be a dear and set the staff notebooks and pens around the table." Her voice dripped with saccharine.

Carrie's neck stiffened. "I'd be happy to." She ensured every notebook was in exactly the same spot, and every pen lay in the same direction. She rearranged the bowls of Nestle Miniatures so they were the same number of place settings apart. Carrie stood back and admired the table, hearing her late mother's voice.

If it's not perfect, it's not worth it.

While Marta was out of the room, Carrie ran her hand along the smooth, silky lines of the mahogany table set for 12. She stopped at the sideboard and rearranged the coffee mugs so all the handles were on the right side, but resisted placing the scones and muffins in a symmetrical pyramid. Noticing the photos on the wall, she squinted at the picture of a woman on a camel. When was Marta that thin? The art pieces and pictures that decorated the room told the stories of the many trips Marta and her husband had taken.

When she meandered into the kitchen, her attention was captured by the largest marble-topped island she'd ever seen. Knowing she was alone, she bent at the waist until her head touched the cool surface, and extended her arms as far as they could go to gauge its size. There were advantages to being almost six feet tall. In the adjoining breakfast area, she noticed the breakfast table set with two placemats, and smiled. Must be nice.

Marta continued to meet the others as they arrived, and Carrie took advantage of the time to peek out the French doors off the kitchen. A gazebo sat in the back of what she could tell was a well tended lawn, though a bit hung-over from the long winter. There were multiple tiered flower beds, and was that an inground spa?

"Are you admiring my backyard?" Carrie was startled when Marta walked up behind her.

"Your patio…."

"It's not a patio. This is our outdoor living area. We spend all summer out there and use the outdoor kitchen and bar most every night."

"Do you use the hot tub year-round or—?"

"Oh, that's not a hot tub." Marta flicked her hand as if shooing an annoying gnat. "That's our spool, and we keep it heated all year round."

"Spoo—?"

"Part spa, part pool. I may have you over when the weather is nice."

"That would be lovely." Carrie struggled to get that last word out of her mouth, but managed a smile. No way was she returning for a social visit. Working with Marta day to day was enough. Plus, she knew Marta had no intention of making good on the invitation.

Marta smiled and her chubby face obscured her eyes. "I'll make sure to save time to give everyone a tour. It really is quite splendid." She gave her head a flippant toss.

Carrie stepped in to the dining room and enjoyed talking with the other staff as they gathered and nibbled on their muffins and scones. She seated herself at the table so she could have an easy view out the window. She loved her job and the people on her team, but was often the bridge between the fresh twenty-somethings who still had fun with icebreaker games, and Marta and two others who kept hoping for early retirement incentives.

Everywhere she looked in Marta's house were pictures of Marta and her husband on the long river boats in Europe, safaris in Africa, and on the beaches of Caribbean islands. She squelched her feelings of envy.

At the end of the day, the team broke for dinner. To increase team cohesion, the staff members had been encouraged to invite their spouses or significant others. Carrie's singleness sat in her gut like her early morning bran muffin when she realized every person was paired up, except her. Even the college interns had dates. She joined the people around the table set in the family room and as each of the others were chatting with their loved ones, she looked over to see Marta's two dogs intertwined on the floor. A chorus of four-letter cuss words ran through her head. Even the dogs had partners.

Glad to be home after a long day, Carrie looked through her mail and ripped open a card from her cousin, Dana—a save-the-date notice for her wedding in October. Carrie slumped onto the couch and dropped the envelope to the floor. Dana was the only other unmarried of the 15 cousins. And then there was one. Feeling exasperated, Carrie knew she had to begin her search now. She would not show up—no, she *couldn't* show up—at the wedding without a serious gentleman dangling from her arm.

At 38, Carrie was close to the Age of Doom, according to Aunt Katharine, her pseudo-mother since her mother's death ten years earlier. *If a woman doesn't walk down the aisle by the age of 40, she'll be a social pariah. Eligible men will compare her to the day-old meat at the market—okay on the surface, but a little iffy once you open the package.* Carrie had already heard whispers at large family gatherings.

She picked up her phone and texted her sister and sister-in-law. "Know a good man I can take to Dana's wedding? I need to start looking now."

A few minutes later, her sister-in-law replied. "Your brother wants to know: are you still hung up on the brown shoes/black pants thing? LOL."

The only response from her sister was, "Online. Everybody's doing it." Same throw-away advice that Carrie had been dismissing for a couple years.

Carrie's cats kept her company in her two-bedroom townhouse, but she'd grown tired of having only feline company. For the first time, she was ready to get serious about getting serious. More than a date for Dana's wedding, she wanted a husband. She knew several friends would argue that, but they were all married. Or divorced.

By Friday evening, she opened the online match program. She couldn't imagine baring her soul to someone through her computer. She paused before she began her profile. *What is so wrong with my life that a one-week cruise wouldn't cure?* she asked her cat, Poppy, who was lying across her feet. Carrie knew the answer; no one wanted to watch romantic sunsets alone.

Saturday morning was her weekly match with her tennis friend, Wayne. With threatening skies, they were glad they could play indoors. Maybe he could give her some advice.

"What's going on, girl," he asked as they left the court. "You were hitting that ball as if it were someone's head you wanted to smack."

"Only my own," she said as she put her warm-ups on over her tennis clothes.

"Are you going to make me guess?"

Carrie led the way to a nearby bench. "I'm on a quest and I'm going online to find a husband," she whispered. She brushed off the bottoms of her tennis shoes and wiped off the smudge marks before she placed them in their own separate bag.

"Oh, this will be fun," he said, rubbing his hands in excitement.

"I just don't know what to write about myself. I've finally accepted that the formula I developed in high school is flawed. You know, *my gracious charm plus his good looks and snappy sense of humor equaled happily ever after*." She finished tying her shoes. "But seriously, how did it come to this?" She motioned her hands as if presenting herself.

Wayne became serious and grabbed her by the forearm as they stood. "You know there's nothing wrong with meeting someone online. I know lots of people who have met their matches this way."

Walking toward the exit, Carrie kept her arms crossed in front of her chest, her eyes looking down at the floor. "But I don't get it. Why should this work when all the conventional ways haven't?"

"It's all about timing." He gazed across the parking lot as mist was turning into a light rain. "And a little humility," he added, giving her the side eye. "Now let's run to your car where we can continue this."

They closed the car doors, and he did his best to face her. "You keep looking for the perfect match. Sometimes perfection is over-rated. You know what I mean? The world isn't a perfect place and neither are people. Some good is to be found in every person if you're willing to look."

"My mother used to say the same thing." Carrie continued to avoid eye contact and looked out her side window. "I know I can be a bit intimidating at times. Maybe even a bit judgmental."

They both laughed. "Good luck with that one," he said. "For the six years I've known you, you've had some old-fashioned ideas about what guys should act like and how they should look. It might be time to let go of stuff and just live. Get to know a guy first."

"My mom used to say, 'You can be fussy or you can be fun, but you can't be both, and you need to know when to be each.' I need to remember that more often."

Wayne smiled, sat there, and let her continue.

"I'm still not sure what to say about myself. I don't want to reveal too much, but enough to pique their interest."

"You're the communication expert. Let's break this down and talk about things you shouldn't say."

"I'm pretty good there. Cold-blooded competitor, control freak, perfectionist, doesn't give second chances, critical of things I don't like… I've heard all those things before."

"Now you're being a bit hard on yourself," he said. "But you're right, you shouldn't say any of those things. Let the poor guy find those out for himself."

Carrie punched Wayne in the arm. For the next ten minutes, they debated the pros and cons of her profile. Rain pounded the windshield, and the windows got steamy, but Carrie didn't care. It was as if they were wrapped in a cocoon of fog while plotting her escape from singleness.

By the time they were done, Carrie had made her list and was ready to begin the process. "Just one more thing. Should I say right off the bat that I'm a proud Amazon woman?"

"Do you want to attract guys with tall-girl fantasies?"

Carrie began to laugh. "Good point. I'm leaving it off."

When she got home, she completed the profile. She chose one picture, a head shot. Either it would work or it wouldn't. She still couldn't submit it, though.

Normally, a strenuous physical activity like her tennis match would help quell her anxiety, but that didn't happen. She played with her cats while listening to some of her favorite music, yet still felt a gnawing in her stomach. For the next hour, she rearranged her drawer of kitchen gadgets, replaced the burned-down candles on the mantle, and cleaned the plantation shutters in her kitchen and sunroom.

Finally, she turned the lights off, tuned her playlist to ocean waves, and sat cross-legged on the floor. She tucked her feet under her slender legs, sat tall, closed her eyes, and began to breathe deeply. Fifteen minutes later, she finished her meditation with one of her frequent affirmations. *I am one fine woman in charge of my own destiny and happiness*. She didn't care that it sounded like a cliché. It worked for her when she needed a boost. Opening her eyes, she stood on her tip toes, shook her arms, raised them toward the ceiling, stretched, and brought them down in a flurry. Her shoulders relaxed, and a smile crossed her face. She walked to her laptop and hit the send button.

On Monday afternoon between meetings at work, she checked her personal emails—42 matches. Her posture slumped, and Carrie questioned if she had been honest enough in establishing her criteria. She hadn't mentioned her aversion to men with long hair, gold chains, excessive tattoos; those with nasty exes or toddlers or teenagers or, really, any children; men who like tractor shows and tobacco; men who wear brown shoes with black pants. Nope, she'd let that one go.

For a week, she was overwhelmed with all the potential matches. She ignored messages sent her way, except one that arrived on Friday evening. She couldn't figure out why "REL" caught her attention. It wasn't what he said, but perhaps what he hadn't said; he never mentioned candlelight dinners, holding hands, pampering a woman, walks on the beach, or that tomorrow is never promised to anyone.

Three days later, she responded.

Two messages, a text and one phone call later, they agreed to meet in two weeks. She pulled out the paper calendar she kept in a kitchen drawer as back-up, and entered the date, in pencil at first. Then she erased it, and wrote it in pen. Next, she added it to her personal calendar on her phone. "Dinner with Rob." Then she deleted it. "Dinner with REL" was better, just in case someone saw her calendar and wanted to know who Rob was. The time was set for 5:45 with a note that it was really 6:00, just to be sure. *Wear flats!* was the final note. She double-checked her iPad to make sure it synced, then added it to the calendar on her work email. All bases were covered.

Chapter 2

As Carrie pulled into the parking lot, the blast of a car's horn caused her to jerk her head sideways. The other driver was screaming with his hands, though Carrie knew she had the right-of-way. Didn't she? She was a little uptight as she drove to what she called her social experiment, so she gave the driver her best smile and a pleasant wave. She just wanted a nice evening that would lead to a second nice evening. And maybe more nice evenings after that.

Maneuvering her car through the crowded parking lot, she finally found the right spot, far enough away and around the side from the entry so he wouldn't see her walking toward him. It was a quarter to six, almost late by her standards, but exactly how she'd planned it. She sat in her car for 13 minutes. She was never early for a first date, but she was never late either.

Looking in her rear-view mirror, she fluffed her long, thick hair to cover roots badly in need of a touch-up, and played with the soft curls until they covered her broad shoulders. She checked her lipstick. Other women could wear bright red, but she never got used to the look on herself. She tried to blot more of the crimson shade off, and it made her look as if she'd just had her lips plumped. She had to agree with her favorite morning TV host; it did look like a crime scene on her face.

As she got out of her car, she kicked off her heels from work and slipped into a simple pair of ballet flats. She hated being taller than a date. Trading in her blazer for a boldly colored, geometric-print denim jacket, she stood and realigned the seams in her bright green skirt. Having second thoughts that her outfit screamed, "Hey, look at me," she kept her head low as she sauntered toward the entrance. Her inner critic had been pretty loud lately.

People spilled out the doorway of the restaurant. The evening was balmy, finally set free from Milwaukee's gray and rainy spring. As she walked closer, she saw him sharing a corner of the entrance with a large ficus tree. She drew a deep breath, smiled, threw her shoulders back, and sucked in her stomach. She could hear her mother's advice: *always stand tall and proud. Let them know you mean it.*

"Hi. Are you Rob?" she asked, extending her hand as if this were a business transaction. After speaking on the phone and studying his profile pictures, she knew he wasn't flashy, but now he was even more dull than she'd imagined: sagging shoulders, soft around the edges; a washed out dark blue polo shirt; gray old-man slacks; and scruffy, rubber-soled black shoes that looked like he could be a basketball referee. She was still relieved they weren't brown. His nose could house a family of gerbils, and if anyone knew about big noses, all Carrie had to do was look in the mirror. Fortunately, his teeth looked straight and white. Maybe she could recommend a good hair stylist to tame his mop of dark curls. Thank heavens he was tall, probably the full 6′3″ he'd listed in his profile.

Oh, damn. She was doing it again—sizing him up, judging him on issues she knew meant nothing, and making all sorts of reasons to eliminate him before he could even say hello. She promised herself she'd be more open-minded, keep her quirks in check, and try to focus on him.

"Yes. Hi. You must be Carrie." He reached to return the handshake.

His palm felt sweaty and clammy. Or was that hers? She started to reach for her bottle of Purell but caught herself.

"So, you found this place okay? It's one of my favorites," Carrie said, smiling and resting her sunglasses on top of her head.

"Yeah, it was pretty easy." Rob continued to stand with his hands thrust in his pockets, glancing between the open door of the restaurant and the parking lot, letting his eyes meet Carrie's only briefly. He rocked slowly between the balls and heels of his feet. His tongue slid between his upper gum and lip.

"I've been here a couple of times with a ski club, and they've got a big menu. That's why I suggested it."

Rob just nodded in agreement and let out a guttural "hmm" in agreement. "I got here a little early, and our name is on the list."

Carrie repositioned herself so she was looking at the driveway as more cars drove in. "The music's a little loud tonight. Good thing I like this song." When he didn't respond, she continued. "The weather has sure been nice, hasn't it? I love the month of May when everything starts to get green and weather finally starts to get warmer. I think that's why there are so many people out tonight."

"Yep. Me too."

Carrie smiled and looked around at all the people actively engaged with each other.

A couple with three young boys stood nearby, and the middle son, probably around three, had just pulled a freshly planted red geranium out of a planter. She noticed Rob was watching him, too, with a slight grin.

Turning toward him, she said, "Do you want children?"

Occasionally, Carrie's internal filter took time off, and she didn't always recover well. It was as if the traffic light in her head turned red while the words tumbled out. She looked at the ground and shook her head in embarrassment.

Rob covered his mouth and cleared his throat to stifle a chuckle.

"Rob, party of two," the hostess announced. Carrie's shoulders relaxed, and Rob motioned for her to go first. They were seated at a quiet table in the patio area, away from the noisy families. Carrie liked that they had a window table, and they could look out at the pond with the fountain and the freshly groomed lawn if the conversation lagged.

"So you ski?" he asked, keeping his eyes on the menu.

"Just a few times a year. I used to go more often, but I don't have as much time to go up north or out west anymore, and that's where the better skiing is." Carrie was relieved he ignored her question about children.

Their server introduced himself and asked for their drink orders.

"What kind of Riesling do you have?" Carrie listened until she heard an American brand she liked.

Rob reviewed the list of craft beers before settling on an IPA.

"Ah, you're a craft beer fan?" Carrie gave her head a slight nod and smiled in approval.

"I have friends in Chicago who brew their own, so they've gotten me into it." He kept his eyes on his menu the entire time.

She was dismayed by his lack of conversational skills. "Is Chicago your home?" she asked, looking directly at him, still searching for a connection.

"No, I'm from Ridgewood, Michigan. Have you heard of it?" Aha, he looked up and made eye contact with her.

Carrie chewed her lower lip while thinking. She started to flick her well manicured fingernails. "No, I don't think so. Wait.... Is that a big skiing area? It sounds familiar."

Rob's face was buried in his menu again. "Yeah. It's pretty far north, along Lake Michigan."

Their server returned with her wine and his beer. Instead of having her usual first-date salad with grilled chicken, she opted for the garlic shrimp and jasmine rice. This was her night of trying new things, but maybe the garlic was pushing it. She didn't care. At least she wasn't home eating with her cats.

"Is the shrimp mixed in with the rice or just on top? I'd prefer it just on top."

"Yes, that's how it's served."

"With the shrimp on top?"

"Yes, with the shrimp in the sauce ladled on top of the rice."

"Good. Thank you. Now I know it says no substitutions, but can I have a small Caesar salad instead of a house salad?" Carrie smiled, raised her eyebrows, and hunched her shoulders a little as if to say, "Pretty please?"

"No, but I can give you a house salad with Caesar dressing."

"On the side please. That will be great. Thank you." Carrie smiled as she handed him her menu, while he turned and looked at Rob. She was trying not to be too picky, but wasn't sure it was working out quite so well.

"I'll have the ribs, full slab, baked potato, butter only, and the house salad with ranch," he said.

Her internal voice began to mutter. Oh no, not the ribs. Doesn't he know they are on the top of the list of worst first-date foods? He'll end up with sauce on his face, and I won't be able to say, "Excuse me, but you have a little something on the tip of your nose." His hands will be sticky. Nope, he probably doesn't realize any of this. Of course, Carrie knew this because of all the "top ten" and "never do" lists she'd read about dating over the years.

A large family group was enjoying themselves at a nearby table when a cake with sparklers was brought out to help the older couple celebrate their anniversary. "Grandma, Grandma, let me help blow out the candles," the little girl said.

Carrie noticed Rob smiling as he watched the child scramble out of her chair. "There was a time when I would have said yes, I'd like children, but that's probably a bit behind me now." Rob was smiling as he turned to look at Carrie.

She prayed he didn't see the fear in her face and was saved from further discussion of children when their salads were delivered, along with a loaf of warm bread wrapped like it was a gift from the multi-grain gods. She noticed Rob pick off the beet slice that sat on top of his salad, and she started to reach over and stab it with her fork, but caught herself in time. She withdrew and picked away at her own bed of greens.

The interrogation of Rob stopped when the meals arrived. Like the computer codes he wrote in his job for the bank, Rob's contributions to the conversation were precise and efficient. She'd need to do more work on her open-ended questions if she saw him again, but right now, it looked like her string of first dates would continue.

Carrie closed her eyes as she savored the aroma of the pungent roasted garlic in wine sauce that bathed the shrimp.

"Sorry, I lost myself for a minute. Did you say something?"

"How has your work been?" This simple question of Rob's took about 20 minutes for Carrie to answer in between bites of food. When she finished talking, he was licking the last of the rib sauce from his fingers. It may have been information overload to go into all the details of the upcoming garden party fundraiser she was coordinating for St. Hedwig's Cancer Center, but that's what was consuming her at work and all she could talk about now.

As she finished her meal, she pulled out the hand sanitizer and offered it to him after she used it herself. "I just thought maybe after the ribs…." Rob rubbed his hands with the gel, and let his shoulders relax a bit, a slight smile crossing his lips while he looked at her hands as she resumed flicking her nails.

"Oh, sorry. This is just a bad habit. Lots of stress at work lately," she responded, wondering how long she'd been doing that. When the bill came, Carrie made a good faith effort to contribute, though Rob insisted on paying.

"Thanks. I'll get the next time."

Rob didn't respond, and as they left, they paused on the sidewalk in front of the restaurant. "Thank you. Good choice. My ribs were great."

"I'm glad you liked it. I enjoyed the evening as well."

"Well, I'm parked over here. Good luck with your party," and with that, Rob shook her hand, turned and walked away.

Carrie was perplexed, and her shoulders slumped as she made her way to her car. He was okay, but seemed a bit indifferent toward her. Was it nerves? Was this his personality? Why would he put himself in a social situation like this if he had no interest in knowing much about her? Is he always this aloof? Or was he a serial killer, looking for his next victim? Oh no! Single, loner, nerdy, forgettable—wasn't that a serial killer's profile? She'd research that when she got home.

Rob was another one-and-done, she lamented to herself during the ten-minute drive home. It had been four years since her last serious relationship and almost that long a drought from the drawer holding her fancy silk lingerie sets. It looked like that would last a little longer.

She wanted to call Maggie, her older sister, but she was working another afternoon shift at the hospital, so she'd have to wait to fill her in. Instead, she took a short run along the trail near her condo. It felt good to stretch out her long stride and work off the nervous energy left over from her dinner.

Done with her run, and after a shower, she settled onto the couch with her two feline roommates, Poppy and Lila, who would have to hear another story of dating distress. "It's probably okay," she said as she stroked Poppy's head. "He doesn't like cats anyway." On cue, Poppy jumped onto the floor and skittered up the stairs.

Carrie laughed while Lila nestled in closer to her. Just as she was opening her iPad to begin the search again, she heard the ping from her phone. She couldn't have been more surprised. It was a text from Rob.

"'Thank you for a wonderful evening. I haven't enjoyed someone's company like that in a long time. I'll call you sometime."

Wanting to respond with, "Hello. This is Carrie. I think you sent this to the wrong person," confirmed she still had work to do on her sarcasm, another item on her long list of sabotage symptoms, so she turned off her phone.

When Maggie called the next evening, Carrie was ready to give her a detailed update "Oh Maggie, he was nice, but he barely talked. He was like a little innocent puppy."

"Be honest. Did you give him much of a chance? Did you let him talk at all, or did you just dominate like you easily do?"

"Of course, I did. But why can't I find the right guy?"

"Well, start by telling me everything about the evening."

For the next few minutes, Carrie described every last detail about Rob's appearance including his clean, neatly trimmed fingernails, but rough-looking hands. "I might have to see him again if he calls me. Those hands were ruddy, and had some scrapes and bruises. They just don't go with an IT guy working at a bank, and I've got to get the lowdown."

"Carrie, do you even hear what you're saying? You have had an opinion on every single thing about what he wore, his hair, his teeth, and even his hands. Maybe you need to focus on the total package. Did you ever think about that?"

"But I can't help that. I got that from Mom."

"No, you didn't. Mother was particular about her own appearance, and ours when we were kids, but not others'."

"But…."

"No. There's nothing else. And you can be a little intimidating, you know."

"But I wore flats this time, and he was tall."

Maggie laughed out loud, and soon Carrie joined her.

"I miss Mom," Carrie said.

"I know, and I can't believe it will be 11 years in November." There was a long pause before Maggie continued. "You remember what she would say, don't you? 'Don't be so shallow. It's not about the cover, but rather, the story. You have to read past the first few pages.'"

"Thanks. I feel better already."

"Now, tell me what you said when you responded to his message last night."

"I said, 'Thank you.'"

When there was no response from Maggie, Carrie looked at her phone to see if they'd been disconnected.

"Tell me you said more than that."

"I thought that was sufficient. And I've decided to try the demure route."

"Oh Carrie, promise me, you'll go back and tell him what a nice time you had, or anything if you have even a speck of desire that he'll call again. Trust me, demure isn't your strong suit."

Carrie assured her sister she would, though she wasn't sure she'd follow through. Yet, she was tired of eating alone, avoiding parties because she couldn't find a plus-one, and feeling like the odd one out at family gatherings.

Her mother had been impressed with how fast Carrie had been promoted in her previous sales job with the pharmaceutical company, but concerned for the personal cost that came with the traveling, entertaining and long hours. *Carrie, don't choose to live your life alone. Work isn't everything.* Until Carrie changed jobs and moved to Milwaukee after her mother's death, she'd only focused on building a stellar career, at any cost.

Struggling to find the words she'd use in her response to Rob's text, she decided instead to begin a new search. She had little in common with Rob. If he did call, she'd see him again, and if he didn't, she'd take that as a sign. Still, there was a mysterious quality about him that made her question if she should reach out to him, but Milwaukee was a big city. What were the chances they'd ever run into each other again?

Chapter 3

Each day, Carrie was inundated with more matches landing in her mailbox, and every day, she secretly hoped Rob would call. She didn't follow up as Maggie suggested, and as time went by, she became more absorbed in the final stages of planning for the fundraising event at work. She decided not to pursue Rob or anyone else until that was over.

For the next month, work was filled with one meeting after another to wrap up the preparation for St. Hedwig's garden party, Carrie's favorite work event. Food and musician vendors were confirmed, signage was complete, and volunteer assignments were agreed upon. Tickets were sold out and sponsorships had increased over the previous year, and if all went as planned, they'd raise a million dollars, and that was worth celebrating.

The only detail remaining was finalizing the script for the program, and the draft was in Marta's hands. Carrie was anxious to have it approved so copies could be made and distributed, and then the program would be perfect. Finally, Marta called her to discuss it on Tuesday afternoon.

Marta invited Carrie to sit across from her at her desk and looked at her over the top of the glasses resting on the tip of her nose. "Carrie, I'm going to make some changes to the script for the evening."

"Sure. I used our standard template and last year's as a guide. What do you suggest?" Carrie tried not to squirm in her chair, but Marta always made her uncomfortable.

"I'm removing Judith from the program. I'll speak in her place, then hand it over to Pete, just as you've written. And that's not a suggestion." She finished with her signature snort.

"But Judith is the volunteer chair of the event. That's customary."

Marta removed her glasses, leaned on one elbow, and stared at Carrie. "Judith is an over-bearing, haughty, social has-been who gets on her high-horse every time she has a microphone." After using her glasses to add emphasis to every third word, she placed them back on her round face and looked back down at the papers.

"But Judith is personally responsible for bringing in at least half the sponsors and many of the guests." Carrie struggled to maintain control over the emotion in her voice.

Marta continued to look down and flip the pages of the script. "They'll still support us."

Carrie continually thumbed the edges of the folder in her lap. "She gets on her high-horse because of her daughter, Rachel. She's passionate about St. Hedwig's after they worked so hard to save her life. She never wants to see another parent lose their child to cancer."

Finally, Marta looked at Carrie. "She'll get over it." She handed the script back to Carrie. "Now, make the changes I've circled here."

Carrie took the script, placed it back in the folder, and shook her head. She could feel her hands shaking and her face turn red. "Marta…." She lowered the tone in an effort to eliminate the anger seeping through her words.

"Don't worry, we'll still recognize her and the other volunteers." Marta used her hands to push herself up from the desk, indicating their meeting was over. "You'll talk to her beforehand?"

"Yes, of course."

"Good. Get this back to me before the day is over."

Carrie nodded and stood, at least eight inches taller than Marta, whose girth was almost as wide as her height. Carrie opened her mouth as if to say something, but instead just turned and left the office.

This signature event had been Judith's idea ten years ago when she ascended to the throne of the volunteer corps at St. Hedwig's. Her only daughter had died of a very rare sarcoma years earlier, outliving the original prognosis by several years. Judith and her husband had become so indebted to the Center that they'd become major supporters since, in time, money, and the other donors they attracted. Of course, everyone knew Judith, at least by reputation. The sole daughter and granddaughter of one of Milwaukee's power families from the height of its manufacturing days, and now wife of the CEO of another large manufacturing company, she was a major player in Milwaukee's philanthropic circles.

Judith was compassionate and delivered results, but occasionally that came with a cost, like increased demands on the staff. Somehow, she and Carrie had bonded over the years, and Carrie had learned how to maximize Judith's contributions while minimizing the damage, and the party's volunteer team was a picture of loyalty to Judith.

"You're a lot like Rebecca," Judith told her one time while reminiscing about her daughter. And though Judith's big, at times domineering, personality was nothing like Carrie's mother, Judith had become a pseudo-mother to Carrie and certainly, a close confidante.

Carrie knew the best thing to do was to meet with her and deliver the news in person.

She set the time with Judith for the next morning, and knew she had to focus on delivering Marta's directive, remaining professional and emotionally controlled to keep her personal relationship with Judith intact.

Over a cup of coffee at Judith's favorite neighborhood café, Carrie wanted more than anything to talk trash about Marta, but she stayed on message.

"Judith, I don't know how to say this." She took a deep breath. "Marta has asked me to…well, this is really hard and awkward, and you know I think the world of you and...."

Finally, Judith held her hand to stop. "As soon as you said Marta, I knew. She doesn't want me to speak, does she?"

"How did you know?"

"It doesn't matter. I understand, and though I'm disappointed, that's Marta. She's needing more attention these days, I guess. I happen to know…." Judith let her words drift.

Carrie maintained eye contact, but Judith looked down at her cup of coffee. She wanted to coax Judith. What did she know about Marta?

"How about I take you out of the middle? I'll take it up directly with Marta."

"Oh. Judith—."

"Trust me. I know her well. We go back many, many years in this city. Things will be fine. More importantly, how are you doing? I've gotten the feeling you're ready for some new challenges."

Carrie turned her gaze away from Judith. "I love the volunteers I work with, and my team, though Marta gives me less and less responsibility. She referred to me as a professional party planner in a meeting not long ago." Carrie frowned at the memory.

Judith winced. "Marta doesn't respect women who are confident, articulate, and smart. You're all of those things and so am I. It's why she doesn't like me. Between your connections and reputation, I know you could find another job if you ever wanted to."

"Thanks, but you know I have a soft spot for the Cancer Center." Carrie's mother's death to breast cancer had been devastating, and to be able to raise funds for research and treatment of patients was now Carrie's passion. She just wasn't sure she could wait for Marta to retire.

"We can talk more later. We will get through Saturday night just fine and have a wonderful event. You've done another outstanding job of taking care of the details the committee has wanted," Judith said.

"Thanks. I really needed to hear that today."

The night of the garden party arrived, and Carrie stayed busy greeting the guests throughout the evening. The weather was comfortable, with a clear sky and moderate humidity, about the best Milwaukee could have for mid-June. The setting sun cast a soft glow on the public gardens until it slipped out of sight. In four hours, she'd celebrate the success of the evening and be on her way home. At least, that was her goal.

"You're going to love The Professors," Judith said, reassuring her the jazz band would be a great addition for the new tropical house. Carrie liked smooth jazz, but still struggled with her own biases toward jazz musicians, transferred by her mother.

Your Great Uncle Mack loved his jazz, and never went any place without his sax. He was a beatnik straight out of the '60s and was never without his beret that sat precariously to one side. The funny little cigarettes he smoked were probably pot or some Caribbean herb blend, though we didn't know about that at the time. But mostly, he liked to go to jazz clubs and jam, as he called it. We all thought he was a kook.

Carrie trusted Judith. She also knew the jazz group attracted a more diverse audience, which made the event more successful.

The volunteer committee did a tremendous job staging the event, letting the flowers and plants be the focal point.

"Next year, we're going back to a single caterer," Judith said before the guests gathered. "I've already had to move the paella cooks away from the Asian beef folks, who don't like sharing the grill with the mini-cheeseburger team, and the salmon cake guys aren't happy they're in a corner. Jesus," Judith said as she shooed a member of the steel band team from the shrimp bowl. "Let the guests eat first. There will be enough to go around." He turned and gave her a little wave.

"By the way, I presume you know your neckline is drooping a bit," Carrie said as she motioned on her own body. "That's even a bit risqué for you," she chuckled as her friend tried to lift her top up.

"Damn tunic. I thought it would work but the sequins weigh it down. I've got the perfect solution." Judith stepped over to an arrangement of cut flowers and pinched off a white lily, planting it between her "girls," barely held in place by the navy silk.

"Oh, that's just great," Carrie said not even trying to stifle her chuckle.

Suddenly, Carla, another member of the planning committee, approached Judith and Carrie. "Just an FYI, our jazz group isn't here yet."

Carrie let out a deep sigh. Mother was right. They're all a bunch of flakes.

Judith looked at her watch. "I spoke with Mike yesterday. They had to replace the pianist at the last minute, but he assured me they'd be here. We have 15 minutes before the doors open, and I'm not worried."

"I'm headed to the rose garden to check on the string quartet," Carrie said. "Judith and Carla, I'm trusting you with the jazz boys."

After making sure the string quartet had all they needed, and chatting with her staff person, who was their liaison, Carrie returned to the main building, relieved to know the jazz band was there and ready. Judith opened the doors, and her team of volunteers helped greet people as they arrived. Carrie picked up a lone piece of pineapple from the floor, looked over where the mariachi band had gathered, and caught one of the members wiping his face. When he returned her look, she smiled, waved her long finger and said, "Busted."

She chuckled at how the dress had changed in just ten years from a formal gala to more casual, summer wear. Few of the men wore ties anymore, and most of the women wore light, breezy dresses. It was obvious straw hats had made a comeback for both men and women.

Carrie chose an ivory and white sleeveless dress that hugged her toned upper body, and showed off her buff arms and summer tan. The flared knee-length skirt hid her muscular thighs. She accented her look with brilliant fuchsia low-heeled sandals and pinned her hair up in a messy bun to expose the plunging back.

All evening long, Carrie mingled with the guests. Only once did she need to ask one of the food providers to keep his spills cleaned up. As that conversation ended, Judith found her with another issue.

"The string quartet is closing up early," Judith said to her in private. "They've had very few people to play for, the mosquitoes are too thick and the crickets are holding a convention near them."

"What are we going to do? We promised people they'd be there." Carrie's voice had a slight panic.

Judith looked around the large room where people were enjoying the last of the food. "No problem. They've got plenty of other musical and dancing options. The Professors are excellent and the tropical house has been packed all night long. Perhaps this crowd is more sax and horns than violins and cellos."

"I feel so bad for the quartet. I'm going to go apologize to them."

"That will be nice. I'm headed to hear the big-band orchestra for one dance with Richard before we go listen to a little jazz."

"Just remind the band they only have a half hour left. We must start the program on time to stay on track."

"Relax, Carrie. It will all be good."

Carrie also loved the garden party because her sister, Maggie and her husband always drove from Ridgewood and stayed with their brother, Charlie and his wife, Kim, so they could attend the event together. This year, her father and his wife, Barb, made the trip from Ridgewood as well, but made a longer weekend out of the trip and drove separately.

After she did a last check with each food provider, she caught up with her family.

"Carrie, great job," her father said.

"Thanks, Dad. I understand the mosquitoes were a little bad tonight and the rose garden was not too popular, but otherwise, it's all been great."

"We're headed to hear the jazz band. People said they're really good," Charlie said.

"Good. I'm joining you," Carrie responded.

She hadn't listened to the group yet this evening, and this was the last music she'd hear before the program. All she wanted was a few minutes of relaxation before she had to interact with Marta. She'd avoided her all night, but did notice she seemed to hold court at the wine bar. Nope, she wasn't going to think about her. She just wanted to blend in with the others and mentally prepare for the last part of the evening.

As Brad opened the door, Carrie felt the dense, wet heat, and then caught a whiff of the tropical paradise. They wedged themselves to the side of the standing-room-only crowd where the view was better.

"Oh my. Hot sultry music surrounded by birds of paradise, hibiscus, and orchids. What's not to love," Kim said as she shimmied to the beat.

Members of The Professors were from area universities and played only a few select gigs each year. They all wore dark pants with various tropical shirts. Four of the six men had hats, but there wasn't a beret in sight. At least they looked good, and they seemed to be holding up well, she thought. She'd listened through two songs when on the third, the piano player, sporting the white panama hat, took over as the rest of the band faded out.

"Oh my God, listen to him. He's unbelievable," Maggie said.

Carrie closed her eyes and swayed to the music. This was what bliss felt like.

Once the clapping and the oohs and aahs stopped, the leader stepped forward. "My friends, before we play our last song, let me introduce the band." Carrie heard a Jeff, a Bryce, a Mitchell, and a Pete. And then a Rob. "He's the best piano player in the city. He plays with us occasionally and he's pretty quiet, and we never know exactly what he's going to do, but isn't he incredible?"

Rob stood and removed his hat as he gave a slight bow. In an instant, Carrie gasped. Her eyes bulged and she covered her gaping mouth with one hand and clutched her chest with the other.

"Are you all right?" Maggie asked.

"You are never going to believe this, but that's the last guy I went out with, the guy I told you about." She couldn't say anything more and risk the chance someone would overhear them in their cramped quarters, but the facial expressions and hand gestures exchanged among Kim, Maggie, and Carrie told the story.

The piano man, so recklessly running up and down the keys, chasing the notes with wild abandonment, hat bobbing as he tossed his head, electrifying the melody with off-beat delays, was Rob, one of the most boring, uninspiring, expressionless dates she'd ever had.

The crowd rewarded him with another rousing ovation and the band played one more song.

"Hey, I'm going to slip out. I'll catch up with you later," she whispered to her family.

Standing outside the entry to the tropical house, she tried to center herself, her head still buzzing. Maybe he wasn't just the computer nerd she'd made him out to be.

As the patrons came streaming out, she thanked them and made small talk when she could. She was grasping at any excuse to avoid Rob, and couldn't imagine what she'd say.

Trailing the last of the crowd, Judith emerged from the temporary concert hall with gusto, and a bright orange orchid had replaced the lily. Her husband walked several steps behind, wiping beads of sweat from his forehead.

"Carrie, were you in there? We just heard the last two songs. What did you think?" Judith asked, her chest puffed with pride.

"Judith, you were right, they were a great addition. Richard, I hear we owe this all to you. Thank you," she said as she turned to Judith's husband.

"You've met them, haven't you?" Judith asked. Carrie shifted her feet, and reached for her neck when she felt the tendons tense up.

"I'm going to thank them in a few minutes," she said.

"Oh no, this is a great time. Let me take you back there." She grabbed Carrie's arm and led her through a door that said "Staff Only."

Carrie didn't need or want Judith to do this, but she also knew keeping her volunteer chair happy was key to her job. In 15 seconds, Carrie had to pull down her Spanx, put on her "oh, this isn't awkward" face, and figure out what she was going to say so she didn't sound like a gushing 12-year old. More importantly, she wondered how her hair looked—it had been a long time since she'd seen a mirror, and the humidity in the tropic house was its worst enemy.

They entered the storage room where the band stored their extra equipment. The musicians were already sipping on bottles of water, and beginning to put their instruments away. A plate of fresh fruit had been picked over, and Carrie was disappointed it hadn't been refreshed.

"Mike, you fellas were wonderful, but I knew you would be," Judith said. "The patrons loved you."

"Hi, Judith. Anything for you." He reached and gave Judith a hug.

Judith turned to Carrie. "I promised you a good show, and they sure delivered, didn't they?"

Mike extended his hand to Carrie. "Thanks for this opportunity tonight." He looked at each of the band members. "I think we all really enjoyed ourselves and were happy to help out." They all nodded in response.

"I can't thank you enough. You were a perfect addition to this event," Carrie said, specifically to Mike. Scanning the rest of the group, she continued until she stopped at Rob, who took a small step back. He smiled, gave a slight nod, and tipped his hat to Carrie when her eyes met his. She couldn't tell if he recognized her.

She decided this wasn't the time or place to gush over his piano playing, but as soon as she opened her mouth, the words spilled out. "Wow, you were really good," she said in her most breathless, pre-pubescent voice, looking straight at Rob. "You were all really great. Thank you."

When her staff member arrived with a plate of assorted hors d'oeuvres, it gave her the cover to invite them to stay for the program that would be starting soon, before she excused herself.

Returning to the program area, Carrie found Pete, the president of the hospital board, and Jack, the CEO, huddling over a table reviewing the program, but Marta was not in sight.

"Carrie, thanks for another great event tonight. We're ready to get the program started, but we need to find Marta," said Jack.

Carrie scanned the room and found Marta draining the last of a glass of wine. As Carrie approached her, Marta began her own version of the stroll to music only she could hear.

"Here I come. Let's get this party started," Marta said, weaving her way through the crowd.

"I think she's had too much to drink," Carrie said to Jack.

"Oh, she'll be just fine."

As soon as Marta welcomed the crowd with slurred speech and a certain imbalance that looked like an old-fashioned top that might spin out of control, Carrie's suspicions were confirmed. Marta was drunk.

Jack looked for help from Carrie, who had opened her copy of the script, and pulled out two different colored highlighters. "Here's the list of sponsors. You and Pete can easily go up and take over thanking them and then the volunteers. Pete will share his remarks and that's it."

They listened to Marta repeat a story about the hospital's support of a local clinic, and when she began to snort, then snicker while telling the story of an indigent patient who needed surgery, Jack hopped up the two steps, and took the microphone from her.

"The impact St. Hedwig's has on the city affects each of us in different ways, and Marta has been part of that for 22 years." He started clapping while Pete gave her a slight hug and walked her off the stage where he handed her off to Carrie, who had a chair waiting for her. While the patrons stood, Carrie tried to position herself in front of Marta and looked over the crowd to see who might be watching Marta disintegrate as the evening closed. Her eyes met Rob's in the back corner of the hall, and she wondered if he might stick around to talk with her.

Marta's husband strode over and stood behind her chair. He was as inconspicuous as possible as he helped Marta to her feet, and they left the room from a side entrance as soon as the program was over. He seemed too familiar with the role.

As the evening came to a close, Carrie saw Rob and the others from The Professors exit toward the parking lot. She said good night to her family and confirmed with Maggie that she'd pick her up in the morning for their 10:00 tennis match. It would feel good to whack the dickens out of the ball as she recovered from the event and bumping into Rob.

When the bands had been paid, the caterers had cleaned up, and the last of the staff and volunteers had removed all the signs and supplies, Carrie finally kicked off her shoes and sat down.

"Don't get comfortable. Wait until you get home, then you can collapse," Judith said. "Let's head out." Stopping at Judith's car, Judith pulled her in tight with a big hug. "You did great, Kid. I don't know how we're going to top this. As successful as this was, maybe we need to try something different. Or we should both leave, then we'll see what Marta does."

"Judith, I am so sorry. I could not believe her tonight. This event was perfect until that. I didn't know what to do. I am done being her caretaker. This isn't the first time, you know. Just the first time in public. It was a perfect evening until that point.

"Jack's a good guy," Judith said, "but Marta's time has got to be coming to an end. That was an embarrassment for the hospital. She's turned off too many people in the community with her aloofness, and tonight was a shame. No one can work with her anymore. When she started to drift from the script, I knew we were in trouble."

Carrie looked at the pavement, shaking her head. "Judith, she was drunk." Anger seeped out with the words.

"Regardless," Judith straightened herself and held her head high, you saved it when you made Jack and Pete look good. You were prepared, as usual, and I know the other members of the committee appreciate it as well. Thank you." Judith draped her arms around Carrie's shoulder as if she were her daughter, looked toward the clear sky, and drew in a breath of fresh summer air. "Don't worry. I suspect she'll be gone sooner than you think." And with a wink and a gentle tap to Carrie's shoulder, they said goodnight.

"Thanks Judith. I've got some stuff to figure out, that's for sure." As Judith drove off, Carrie sat in her car, threw her head back against the head rest, let her mind drift to Rob, and began to laugh.

The guy's a brilliant pianist. What other surprises does he have?

Chapter 4

Carrie slept hard, and the alarm was a relenting reminder of the morning ahead with her family. She dangled her feet from the edge of the bed and scrolled through her phone. Lots of pictures from the event, but it was the text that grabbed her attention.

"Good to see you last night. Do you like sushi? Are you free Tuesday night?"

Rob. Carrie rolled her eyes and flopped onto her back in disbelief. Finally, she sat up and composed the text.

"Free? You have the wrong woman. And I don't like sushi, but my cats do."

She smiled, then deleted the message and typed another one.

"I'd love to. It would be fun to learn about your piano playing." Blech. Too bland. Delete, again. She'd respond later when she had time to think of a perfect response.

It was an easy Sunday morning drive to her brother's home to pick up Maggie. She loved spending time with her older sister, and today, her goal was to get her advice on Rob. But as soon as she got into the car, Maggie started talking.

"Emily is driving me nuts, and I don't know what I'm going to do."

"Whoa. Good morning, Sister."

"Oh yeah. Sorry. Great party last night." She smiled at Carrie.

"I think we're both ready to let off some steam. You go first. What has my lovely, free-spirited, independent 17-year old niece done now?"

"She texted me a picture of herself this morning. Her hair is orange—like brilliant, blinding orange."

"Show me when we get to the club. Orange hair is not the worst. I think we need to go play tennis and after, we'll both be better off. Now let me tell you about the text I got this morning."

Between Maggie's issues with Emily and Carrie's confusion over Rob, their match was filled with forceful volleys and wicked serves. Both sisters had continued to play competitive tennis since high school, and today it was as much therapy as anything.

"I never know what she's going to look like from one week to the next," Maggie said smashing home a baseline drive.

"How could he not even let me know he was going to be there?" Carrie responded with a backhand to Maggie's serve. "And now he wants to know if I'm free Tuesday? For sushi?"

"Two weeks ago, she came home from the thrift store with two old prom dresses. For three days, she did nothing but sew up in her room, and the next thing I know, she's dyed her hair white-blonde and wants to go to a party dressed like Little Bo Peep," said Maggie, returning the shot.

"Did he think I wouldn't know he was there? Was I supposed to pretend I didn't know him?" Carrie said, putting too much spin on a cross-court shot. "And why do I even care?"

"Out," and with that the match was over. "She's a great kid, but I just don't get this stuff. Cosplay. They dress up like characters from books or movies, the more super-natural, the better. Brad isn't concerned. He just refers to Emily and her friends as the creative nerds. What do you think?"

"Oh no, I'm practically allergic to children, remember."

"That's right. They're 'ooey and gooey,' you used to say."

"No. It was 'icky and sticky' and not much has changed, though I do adore my nieces and nephews."

Maggie and Carrie both felt better after the physical game, but also ended with more questions, as they gathered their towels and put their rackets away.

"And what about her twin sister, and her older brother? I can't believe he's going to be graduating from college in a year."

"Kate has her own drama and David is always solid as a rock. At least, that's what he makes us think." Maggie threw Carrie a sideways look. "He might just be a great con artist for all I know."

"I admire you. You're a wonderful mom, with three great kids, but this is exactly why I never wanted kids. I don't think I'd ever have the patience. After college, you went right back home to Birchfield, spent Friday nights shopping at Target to decorate your first apartment, and became super-nurse at the hospital. A few years later, you married Brad. I don't think you ever had a wild side, did you, not even in high school?"

"Well, Mom never found pot in the pockets of my jeans when I came home from college, if that's what you mean."

Carrie began to laugh. "Yeah, that was stupid on my part."

Maggie shook her head and let out a long sigh. "Back to your dilemma. Are you going to call him, or just respond to his text?"

"I wrote a text and asked him why it took this long to call me when he said weeks ago that he'd call."

"You did not!" Maggie stopped zipping up her tennis case to stare at her sister.

"Nope, just kidding. I haven't responded."

Maggie handed a water bottle to her. "Here, you need to drink this and cool down a little."

"I have no idea if I'm going to respond. What would I say? Maybe I'll wait a few weeks." Carrie took a drink, then wiped her forehead with her towel.

The drive back to Charlie's was filled with their usual chatter and continued sister talk about vacation plans at the family's cottage on the lake, and of course, their dad and Barb. Though they'd known Barb for several years prior to her marriage to their father, it was still odd to walk into the old family home and see her there. Carrie stayed at Maggie's home every time she returned to Birchfield now and felt a bit like a visitor when she went to the old house on the corner of Albert and Williams streets.

Today, the house still held a lifetime of memories. Carrie and her friends had played many games of ping pong in the basement rec room, and as a little girl, she'd loved watching lightning dance across the skies during thunderstorms as she snuggled between her folks on the front porch swing. Maggie and Charlie had moved on and created their own families and homes, but at times, Carrie was still trapped in the memories of her adolescence. By the time she was ten, Carrie had not only the run of the large, old home, but all the time with her mom she wanted. Her dad still worked long hours as director of emergency at the hospital, but when he was around, he gave all his attention to his youngest.

"You know about the house, right?" Maggie said. "That they're selling it?"

"What?" said Carrie, as she swerved around a corner.

"You mean he hasn't told you? Act surprised when you do find out."

Ever since her father married Barb, Carrie had struggled with her relationship to him. Maggie always had a closer relationship with him from the time they were kids, and she lived just a couple miles away from him, so it made sense that Maggie was more in the loop.

Still, Carrie felt a little disappointed that her dad hadn't told her. Did Charlie know? That would be the true barometer of family connectedness.

"So how do you feel about this?" Carrie said to Maggie. "That's our family home. What about all the rest of our things there? Mom's things? And where are they moving?" Carrie was shocked, though she knew this day would come. When Barb moved in, many of the family items were divided, but much of the house remained the way it was while Barb and Carrie's dad made plans for the future.

The answers would have to wait as they pulled into the driveway. Carrie just needed to get through brunch without saying anything obnoxious to her dad or Barb, and then get back home and figure out her next step with Rob. They knew Kim would have a delicious brunch, and everyone was waiting for them. As they filled their plates with steaming egg-and-sausage casserole and fresh fruit, everyone filed in around the dining room table that was set with juice and muffins.

"These eggs are delicious. What's your secret, Kim?" Barb asked.

"Basil. I can't make eggs without a hint of basil anymore."

"Aunt Carrie, Mom said you looked really pretty last night," said Liesel, Charlie and Kim's seven-year old.

"That is so sweet. What else did she say about the night?"

"She also told us there was a cute guy there that you liked," said Hans, Liesel's 10-year old brother.

"Give me those muffins," Kim said as she took one and pretended to throw it at her son, who raised his hands in mock defense. "You know I didn't say that." She tore a bite off her muffin and chewed it while everyone laughed and looked at her. "I didn't use those *exact* words."

Carrie was glad the attention turned to Kim and loved to see the family having good times. For a moment, she'd forgotten about the house, Rob's text, and how tired she was. Maggie and Carrie helped Kim clear the table while Brad began to load the car for their return trip.

"Carrie, Charlie," her dad said, looking at each of them, "Come into the family room with me for a minute."

"I wanted to tell you we've decided to sell the house. Barb is selling her condo in Florida and we're going to divide our time between the lake and our new home in Arizona." He looked for a response from Charlie and Carrie.

"Okay, that sounds good," said Charlie, nodding while he kept his hands stuffed in his pockets.

Carrie's shoulders slumped as she continued to stare at her father.

"But what about your love of Florida and boating?" Carrie centered herself on her feet and let her hands dangle along her long torso. She released the fists she'd made and shook her fingers loose.

"I still love boating and will look forward to doing that every summer. It just makes sense at this point in our lives. You know, Barb's daughter and her family have been living in her house in Birchfield for the year, but he's taken a new job in Phoenix, so they're moving. We're selling that house as well. We decided it was time to finally consolidate homes and get our own place."

"Wow. I get it. It's just sort of a jolt," said Carrie. She shifted her weight and leaned on her right foot, with her head cocked slightly. "How soon? What about all the stuff? Can we still take what we want?" She tried to manage her impulse reactions and realized her hands were in front of her, waving like an orchestra conductor.

"Well, that's why I wanted to let you know. You'll need to come up and go through any of your personal things that are still there, and then see if there is anything else you want—furniture, TVs, knick-knacks, your mother's nice crystal and silver—all the things still left in the dining room. And then there's all the Christmas boxes in the basement. You three kids will need to make decisions about all of that. About the only thing I'm going to keep is my chair."

Charlie just stood there, hands in his pockets, smiling. "Dad, I think that's great."

"When do we have to do this? Can it wait until we come up next month? Wait, are we even still getting together like we always have for one big family weekend at the lake?" By now, Carrie's arms were crossed tightly against her chest, with an occasional flick of the hand. "What if one of us wanted to buy the house? Or all three of us? And what are you going to do with the stuff we don't want?"

Her dad stepped closer and put one hand on her shoulder. "Of course, this has nothing to do with the weekend at the lake, and that would be good timing. In addition, we're going to start renovating and expanding the cottage this fall, and we are building a guest house so there will always be room for everyone. This is why I wanted to tell you when I saw you, and not over the phone. We will work it out together. And the things you don't want? I don't have an answer for that yet. We'll see what's left."

"That's great Dad, we'll make it happen," Charlie said, as he looked at Carrie. "I'll ask Kim, but I doubt if there's much we'll take. I know I don't have any personal things there anymore."

Carrie glared back at her brother, as if to say, 'That's it? That's all you have to say?' but she knew there was nothing more to be said. She hadn't lived in that home in almost 20 years, but she had a lifetime of memories to sift through, some good, some bad. And of course, every one of them included her mother.

She waved goodbye to her dad and Barb as they drove off.

"I'm still sort of shocked, but I'm not sure why I'm surprised," Carrie said. "Between the lake and Florida, they're hardly there."

"You will always have room at our house. You know that, right?" Maggie gave Carrie a tight hug before she and Brad took off. As soon as they were gone, Charlie busied himself sweeping the garage.

"Charlie, our home. It will be gone and…" her voice trailed.

"Carrie, you're overreacting. It's just a house." He moved a bike to access the shelves. "Besides, this is my home now. And really, you want to buy it?"

"You're right. That was dumb. I'm going to say goodbye to Kim and the kids, then I'm headed home."

As she drove the few minutes to her condo, her mind was racing, thinking of everything in the house she wanted to rescue, from the rugs to the pieces of family heirloom crystal that had been passed down from one generation to the next. And the Christmas stuff? What kind of childhood goodies did those boxes hold? And then there was the snow blower; it was just a couple of years old, and she had been with her dad when he bought it. Why would she focus on that? Maybe this was her push to buy the house she'd been wanting.

Driving home, she felt the urge to knit as soon as she got back. Even after all these years, she still grieved the loss of her mom, and from the time her father started dating again, her heart ached a little more. She knew it was an immature reaction, but it was still a struggle, and knitting reconnected and calmed her, even though she'd never make the beautiful cable sweaters her mother had made for all of them.

Barb was wonderful for her father, and Carrie could not deny that she was kind to Carrie and the others, but kept her distance. But Carrie was now the odd man out on family gatherings and was more aware of the solitude of her singleness. It was a month before they would all gather at the lake. She'd have to work on her attitude by then.

As she pulled into her garage, she remembered Rob's text. Maybe he was worthy of another date after all. Plus, Kim was right; he was sort of cute.

Chapter 5

After a few minutes knitting, the events of the previous evening and that morning caught up with Carrie. Stretching out on the couch in the warm sunroom, Poppy and Lila settled in at her feet. Her cats were great company, but Carrie would be damned if she would become a crazy, old-maid cat lady. They were simply not the company she was seeking. Feeling refreshed from the nap, she realized she didn't have a lot of other social options, so she replied to Rob's text.

"Thanks. I play tennis every Tuesday and Thursday after work; also Saturday mornings. And sorry, I don't care for sushi, but I do like Thai food. Indian, too. Maybe another day?"

After a series of texts, they agreed to meet after work in a couple of weeks, at a popular restaurant in the warehouse district that hugged the Milwaukee River, with a boardwalk separating the tables from the boats that cruised in and out of downtown.

She knew the restaurant well. Her former long-time love, Kyle, was a boater and they would often tie up at a nearby marina and dine along the waterfront. Suddenly, she recalled their last conversation, when Kyle was transferred to Denver several years ago. He thought Carrie's love of skiing would be a natural for her to join him, but she wasn't willing to uproot from her job, family, and friends, and she said no. Often, she second-guessed that decision, but the relationship died when he pulled out of the city and headed west. And here she was, all these years later, still on her quest to replace him.

Carrie loathed this initial part of the dating ritual: making small talk, obsessing over saying the right thing, and wearing the right clothes. Why couldn't there just be a simple ten-question test that determined compatibility? Why did people have to go through uncomfortable dinners and stumbling conversations, grasping for whatever each of them was looking for? Maybe the cultures where arranged marriages based on parental investment and approval weren't so bad. Certainly, her dad could round up a couple of goats and a goose or two.

Over the years, Carrie had dated some iffy specimens, but no one like Rob. Dinner along the river on a warm summer evening was far better than the UFC Fight Night she went on with one date, or the walk in the woods, which turned out to be a ruse for checking on her date's hunting blind. She never forgave that man for making her walk through muck and wrecking the new pair of boots she'd just picked up at Nordstrom's. Yet over the years, she knew she had been too quick to judge and dismiss over petty differences.

But Rob? She finally had to admit, he seemed really kind and not self-centered, and worth a second date. Her goals for their next date were simple: ignore the stress from work, draw out more of his personality, and look for what they had in common. And hopefully, snag a third date.

Walking from the parking ramp at the end of the block, Carrie looked right past him as she approached the restaurant. Maybe it was his aviator sunglasses that framed his tan face, or the shorter hair. His light blue checked shirt and dark dress slacks were a stark contrast from their first date. He startled her when he waved. "Hi, it's nice to see you."

"Thank you. I hope you haven't been waiting too long." She couldn't help but notice he still wore the scruffy rubber-soled black shoes.

"Just long enough to make sure we could get a table on the water. I hope that's okay with you."

Carrie smiled and followed his gesture as he pointed to the door.

They were seated on the patio, and the glare from the water was so bright, they each left their sunglasses on. She took the menu from the hostess, and began looking it over.

"So, how's work?" he asked, glancing at her.

"Good," was all she said, her head eyes fixated on her menu.

"Did you have a hard time finding a parking spot?"

"No, I'm in the ramp at the end of the block." She smiled back at him.

"It's another beautiful evening, isn't it?"

Carrie drew a deep breath and lifted her chin toward the sun. "My favorite kind of weather, though I could do without the humidity." She could feel Rob looking at her while she returned her gaze to the menu.

"Don't forget to save room for their chocolate cake covered with ganache. You won't be sorry. It's my favorite."

"Umm," she said and just smiled at his suggestion, without looking up. She really didn't feel like talking and probably should have canceled, but she'd do her best.

"I hope this doesn't offend you, but you look lovely. That silver and turquoise is very nice," he continued.

"Thank you. I know most women wouldn't wear a bolo tie as a necklace, but I love it." Carrie held up her hands as if to say I don't care. "I bought this on a trip to Santa Fe. Have you been there?"

"No, not Santa Fe, but I hear it's beautiful."

"It is. Artsy and expensive, but beautiful."

Dressed in a nice pair of black summer pants and a crisp white shirt, Carrie played with the silver tips of her tie. They each ordered a glass of wine while they reviewed the menu, and when the server returned with their drinks, he asked for their order.

"We'll need a few more minutes," Rob politely told him. "We aren't in any hurry," he said over the sound of a parade of noisy boat motors.

Carrie looked up from her menu, smiled at the server, "I'll have the Jamaican salad with chicken, dressing on the side, please."

Rob sighed and exchanged glances with the server. When he ordered the meatloaf, Carrie covered her mouth with a napkin to suppress a smile, while she thought of her mother's philosophy about men, meatloaf, and their mothers.

It doesn't matter what else you cook. If you truly like a man, learn to make a good meatloaf. It will remind him of his mother, and he'll want to come back for more."

He raised his glass of wine toward her. "Cheers to a successful garden party."

"Thank you."

"I had a lot of fun. Your crowd was lively, and it's always fun to be asked to play an encore. Then after we were done, I met this interesting psychologist, who shared his theory of music and personality development."

She smiled and relaxed her shoulders, pleased he brought it up, because she was still dumbfounded that he was playing in the jazz band and never bothered to tell her he'd be there.

"People seemed to enjoy themselves and we met our goals. It wasn't perfect, but overall, I was pleased." She drew figure eights on the table with the base of her glass. "I'm glad you enjoyed yourself."

"People don't need perfection to have a good time," he said as he gave his shoulders a shrug.

Carrie sat up straight and shook her head. "It doesn't mean I don't strive for it, however." Carrie was surprised by his nonchalant attitude. She took a generous sip of her wine.

"But did *you* have a good time?" Rob asked.

"Work events like that are always stressful. You hope you have enough food; we did. You pray each musical act shows up, and they did. You cross your fingers that the weather will cooperate, and it did, but still, you never know what might happen."

Rob looked down and turned his fork over multiple times. "Mike, the leader of The Professors, just called me to play a few days beforehand, and I hadn't made the connection that it was your event. I should have, but until I saw you at the end, I didn't. Otherwise, I would have let you know." He lifted his face to meet hers.

"No problem." Carrie was happy the topic had finally been addressed. "Thank you. By the way, you guys are outstanding. And you, with the piano. I've never heard music like that before."

"Well, I'll have to get you to some clubs then."

Carrie smiled. "I'd like that."

"I felt bad for your team at the program, but your CEO sure managed it well."

"That was a mess, and she's my boss. That's the kind of stuff you don't expect. It was just announced late this afternoon that she's taking an extended leave. Imagine that," Carrie said, using air quotes to accent the extended leave. "I apologize. I just have a lot of stuff on my mind and I'm not as social tonight."

Rob nodded and as he was about to say something, his phone rang. "Sorry. It could be work." He looked at the number, rubbed his forehead, and slid his tongue between his upper lip and teeth in a manner he probably wasn't even aware of. He turned the volume off. "So, you like tennis?"

"Love it." She swirled the last of the wine in her glass.

"You're pretty serious about it then."

Carrie leaned her elbows on the table edge and sat forward. "Quite," she said with a crispness in her voice that sounded like a dry twig snapping.

"You just play for fun or competition, too?"

"A little of both."

"Are you pretty good then?"

She sat back and cocked an eyebrow. "I always aim to win and hate it when I don't."

He didn't need to know she was the favorite in the summer-long tournament for her division, or that she was the defending champ in the Lake Forest tournament coming up the following weekend. That would be bragging. If she won, then she'd tell him.

Once the meal was served, the mango dressing she drizzled over the salad woke up her taste buds, and there was little conversation. Her mind drifted back to Kyle and the Caribbean vacation they'd shared. Momentarily, she felt sand under her feet and tasted drinks with too much rum.

"How's your salad?" Rob asked.

She blinked rapidly as reality brought her back to the moment. and "It's delicious. Thank you."

Finally, she realized she'd been a bit of a jerk when she gave minimal responses when he tried to initiate small-talk, and now it was her turn to learn more about him. Fortunately, he had given her a couple of topics to chase, so she pursued the conversation.

"I think you told me you like to read. Have you read anything good lately?"

That match lit the fire in Rob. "Well, I'm in the middle of this great book about Charlemagne. Did you know he was at war during almost his entire reign? All he wanted to do was to convert everyone to Christianity."

Who the…. Really, he's talking about Charlemagne? Carrie could not believe what she'd unearthed, but the history lesson continued.

"Well, at least all the Germanic people, of course." She let him continue for several more minutes as he stopped only for bites of food. Finally, she lifted her right hand slightly, and shook her head, as if to surrender.

"Caroline Belle, don't you raise that hand at me and shake your head when I'm talking to you. Or anyone else for that matter," her mother used to say. "It's rude and it tells people you have no interest in what they're saying."

"But it's just my way of saying stop, you're telling me more than I can understand."

"Then you need to fake your interest. But for heaven's sake, don't wave them off as if you've dismissed them. You picked that up from your father's side of the family. Those Klamerschmidts never did know how to make pleasant conversation."

Rob seemed oblivious to the unintended wave off, so she smiled and tipped her head to the side, took off her sunglasses and focused her bright blue eyes on him, doing her best not to let on she had little memory of who Charlemagne was.

"He is still known in some circles as the King of Europe," Rob added.

When he finally took a breath, let his shoulders relax, and stabbed another bite of food, she jumped in. "That's interesting. I never knew that. But I'm curious, how did you get started at the piano?"

Rob looked over the top of his sunglasses, and finally took them off. He made eye contact with Carrie briefly before he looked down at his plate.

"My mom made me take lessons when I was about six. Like every other kid, I hated it at first, but then around fifth grade, I really began to like it. My mom worked at our church, and I'd go there after school, and they'd let me play whatever music I wanted." He paused.

Carrie kept her eyes on him, practicing her skills in listening. More pieces of the Rob puzzle began to connect. "Go on," she encouraged.

"When I started middle school, the music teacher discovered I could play better than any of the other students, so I got into the orchestra as the piano player. By the time I was in eighth grade, I began to be really good, and could play a song by listening to it, adding my own spin. My teacher introduced me to Herbie Hancock and Thelonious Monk. Do you know who they are?"

Carrie bluffed and nodded slightly. "Yep." She'd heard of Herbie Hancock, the Monk guy…, nope, didn't sound familiar.

"I'd never heard anything like that, and I started improvising on songs, giving everything a jazz twist. My teacher, Mr. Thomson, loved it and really encouraged me. I've always loved the coolness of the ivory on my fingers."

Carrie sat waiting for him to continue, but he stopped. She could tell he wanted to say more, so she waited. She kept her eyes on him while he used a roll to get his last bite of meatloaf.

"I'm glad Mr. Thomson pushed," she finally said.

Rob slid his empty plate away from him, sat back and placed his hands in his lap. He looked toward the boardwalk that followed the river and let his eyes follow an older couple walking their over-sized mutt. Then he leaned forward, shifting his vision from side to side as if scanning the room.

After several seconds, he began again. "Growing up, I was really shy and close to my mom; still am, and she probably overprotected me. I had a stutter that still comes out sometimes. Consequently, I didn't have a lot of friends."

He hunched his shoulders, then let them fall while he let out a sigh. "But music…I could listen to it for hours, all by myself, and then try to play what I heard. The piano, along with my computer, became my best friends."

This began to explain the social awkwardness that had stayed with him well into adulthood.

"One day, my dad came home from work and heard me playing these new chords and riffs. He was a tough brute, but that's another story. Of course, he loved his classical music, and I overheard him tell my mom I would never amount to anything if I kept playing that *crap*. I never turned back to his Bach and Shostakovich, and he never heard me practice again."

Rob let out a deep breath and his shoulders dropped as if he'd just revealed a deep secret. As he glanced over Carrie's shoulder toward the side of the restaurant, he seemed startled and a bit distracted. Suddenly, he hunched his shoulders slightly forward and directed his eyes downward, as if trying to shrink into a shell.

"This was great, and I had a nice time. Are you ready to go?" he asked.

"No cake?"

"No, I'm good. How about another time?"

Carrie was caught by surprise at the abruptness, but yes, she was ready. He settled the bill with their server and led their way out the back entrance of the restaurant that led to the boardwalk.

By the time they strolled to the nearby plaza and listened to the band playing '60s music, he was standing tall again, and looking more confident.

"Do you like this music?" Carrie asked.

"That's from my dad's era." Rob said. "I hate it." They both laughed.

"So your relationship with your dad, still not as much as it is with your mom?"

"That's a long story," and he left it at that.

The evening closed, and before they went in opposite directions to their cars, they made plans to reconnect in a couple weeks, but they'd talk by phone before then. They each had plans over the July fourth weekend, but neither shared what they were. Carrie was content with the evening. She liked what she was learning about Rob and that he had opened up a bit more. Maybe there was some promise here.

The walk to her car was quick, and she was disappointed he didn't escort her. Nothing a little training can't fix.

Before crossing the street to enter the parking ramp, she looked back and was surprised to see a woman grab Rob by the arm as he walked back in front of the restaurant. Carrie could see that as the woman stepped closer to Rob, he stepped away, until it appeared he recognized her.

Carrie entered the ramp so she couldn't be seen, but continued to watch. Even from a distance, the woman looked oddly familiar to Carrie, but Carrie couldn't place her. As she tried to touch Rob's shoulder, he backed away and waved his hands as if shooing a fly. Finally, he walked away from her. Carrie felt bad for the other woman, who was obviously excited to see Rob.

Quickly climbing to the second level of the parking garage, she looked back over the ledge. The mystery woman had caught up with Rob and they walked down the sidewalk together. At the end of the block, he stopped, chatted with her a few minutes and placed his hand on her forearm as if reassuring her, before he disappeared around the corner.

Carrie had no idea who she was, but she looked like a ghost of a woman, her clothes hanging on her frail frame, a bright green skirt fluttering in the light breeze. The mystery woman looked up and down the street, before she let her head drop and her arms hang to her side.

As Carrie pulled out of the parking lot and eased down the street, the woman got onto the city bus. Would she ever know about this story? Things had gone so well and Carrie wasn't sure she wanted to.

Chapter 6

At work the next morning, Carrie's attention drifted toward Marta's absence and the uncertainty within the department. It was assumed that Dwight, the other assistant vice president, would be their new person in charge, yet nothing had been announced. In his early 60s, he had distanced himself from the young associates on the communications, promotions, and events side of the department, and his leadership skills inspired little confidence among the other team members. Carrie was like a big sister to most of them and arranged to bring lunch in, so they could share and commiserate as they sorted through work that needed to be done. She knew they felt like they'd been relegated to a ship adrift at sea, and she hoped that directives would be handed down soon.

By 2:00, Carrie was refocused on her meeting with Judith later that afternoon. They would sit poolside at Judith's home, sip iced tea and eat lemon bars while they finalized the agenda for the garden party wrap-up meeting. "It's summer. Lemon is a summer flavor," Judith would tell her. Carrie would joke and remind her chocolate was an all-season flavor. They'd had this conversation before, so Carrie knew what to expect.

Judith's compassion and generosity toward others inspired Carrie, especially how she considered the children at the Northside Community Center her own. She worked diligently over time to stabilize funding for the Center and wasn't afraid to take on any politicians, community leaders and funders who didn't share her vision. Standing at 5'5", Judith was never the tallest nor the shortest in the room, but usually commanded the most attention. Short, silver curls framed her plump face, and she liked to joke that she was proud of her "Rubenesque curves." Except for her curvaceousness, Carrie aspired to be more like Judith and was honored when she was invited to serve on the Center's board.

Judith's generosity also extended toward Carrie, who was frequently her guest at the symphony or in the family's box at sporting events. In their closeness, Carrie and Judith had learned to support each other when they each needed it.

As Carrie gathered her notes a few minutes before she had to leave, her phone rang. "Hi, this is Carrie Klamerschmidt." There was a slight pause.

"Carrie, this is Rob. I don't think I knew what your last name was."

Carrie's shoulders relaxed, and she sat back in her chair. "Oh yeah, it's a mouthful. You just caught me as I'm headed out to a meeting. What's up?"

"Ah, sorry to bother you at work, but I was just offered some tickets to the Gabe Winston concert tomorrow night, and I know it's last minute, and right before the holiday weekend, but I wondered if you can go. It's part of the symphony's outdoor summer concert series on the lake, and there are fireworks after."

"I'd love to, but I've got a tournament this weekend. Let me think." She paused for a moment. "I'm in, and besides, it will keep my mind off Mindy Falwell." Carrie needed to refresh her life and not worry so much about her routine. And she loved Gabe Winston, part old-time crooner, part upbeat pop.

"Mindy who?"

"That's who I'll probably run up against in Lake Forest this weekend, and she's had my number over the last five matches."

Rob didn't have a response to that, so they confirmed they'd meet in his work parking lot, and they'd grab dinner at a Thai food place downtown very near the concert venue.

"Perfect. I'll see you then. And thanks." Suddenly, she realized she was flicking her nails again. Why did Rob make her nervous?

Rob was nice, but she'd likely run into people she knew at the concert, including people from work. Was she ready to make a social appearance with him? She knew how catty that sounded, but seriously, would he show up looking like Date #1 or Date #2? He was a subtle change from the other dates she'd been seen with over the years and didn't have the sophisticated look or the polished charm she usually went for. Maybe she'd just wear a big floppy hat and sun glasses and an over-sized jacket for warmth after the sun set, and hope that no one would recognize her.

Carrie, don't be so shallow, her mother would tell her. It's not about the book cover. You need to see how the plot will unfold.

She didn't care if he wore his scruffy shoes. So far, she enjoyed his company. He made her laugh and she was going to dinner at a new restaurant. Funky, Rob had called it. This would be followed by relaxing to the laid-back vibe of Gabe Winston, and with the summer breeze on her face. Carrie looked forward to the easy, comfortable evening ahead of her. Her annoying nail habit stopped.

Rob had been a mystery; little eye contact on their first date and trouble initiating much conversation, but when he got on a topic of interest to him, he could talk at length, regardless of Carrie's interest. If he was reading *Dating 101*, it was working. She was going on a third date with him.

Carrie pulled into the parking lot and was happy to see Rob walking to greet her. She threw the hat and baggie jacket onto the backseat of her car.

"I'm taking you to the Beau Thai. Ever heard of it?" He looked at her before pulling into traffic.

"No, but it sounds interesting."

"It's fairly close and has gotten great write-ups. It's just a notch above a dive," he said. "Every now and then, you might see a celebrity, because the owner will let them use the back door when his wife thinks it's safe. She runs the front. One time, I guess Tiger Woods was here, and said it was the best Thai food he's had since his mother's cooking."

"Hmm. Sounds fun. Is their food real spicy?"

"I usually get medium, but you can also have it plain or hot." He pulled over to park and turned to her. "Let me guess. You like it hot?"

"Oh no. I'm a bit of a sissy. Mild is good for me."

As they walked from the parking spot at the end of the block, Carrie immediately recognized a sweet, sugary smell, but couldn't place it with Thai food. She gave Rob a puzzled look. "Why does it smell like a bakery?"

"That's the French part. Beau Thai. Get it?" He pointed to the sign above the window. "They have dessert crepes that are really good, and that's what you smell."

"Oh my gawd, I love crepes, and now I'm really hungry."

No one famous was there, but Carrie recognized a popular morning radio host eating with a lovely redhead. His attempts at flirting are pathetic, Carrie thought, when he moved to the same side of the booth as his date.

"Do you know who that is?" She leaned across the table to Rob, and continued without giving Rob a chance to respond. "I know for certain that's not his wife."

Rob shrugged off her comment. "Obscure places have their benefits."

Carrie looked at him while he flipped over the menu, and wanted to ask about the woman she'd seen him talking with at the restaurant a couple nights earlier, but knew it was none of her business. He didn't bring it up, and neither did she.

After a few minutes of easy conversation, their food was delivered by the same woman who seated them.

"The cracks in the vinyl lend some class to this place, don't you think?" Rob ran his hand along the booth seat. The ambience was exactly as she'd expected, based on Rob's description, and the food lived up to its ratings.

"I don't care. It's worn, but clean. And this Pad Thai is the best I've ever had, but I really can't wait for my caramel apple crepe."

Carrie noticed a woman squeezing between the tables while Rob was focused on his metal chopsticks. It looked like the same woman who'd been talking to Rob as they departed the other evening, and now she was walking towards them. This was not a coincidence, and Carrie tried to kick Rob out of his fried-noodle focus. As the woman approached, her perfume reminded Carrie of her Grandma Klamerschmidt's old favorite, and the strong scent made Carrie's eyes sting.

"Hi, Rob. It's good to see you. I've waited a long time." The woman's voice was so shrill, Carrie expected to see a pack of hunting dogs appear. "You look really nice tonight. Who is your new friend?"

"Amy, what are you doing here?" He looked up from his food but did not stand. Carrie noticed the slight brush of his tongue between his upper teeth and lip.

"My name is Gwendolyn now, not Gwen, but Gwendolyn, and did you forget? This is our restaurant? This is where we came to dinner and it's my favorite, and I come here every Thursday night, just waiting for you." She paused to catch her breath.

Not waiting for a response from Rob, she immediately thrust her hand in Carrie's direction and introduced herself. "Hi. I'm Rob's girlfriend, and my name is Gwendolyn. That means blessed. Not Gwen, but Gwendolyn. What's your name?"

Rob slouched, kept his eyes on his plate and continued to stab at his noodles, and to Carrie's amazement, said nothing.

"Well, I'm very happy to meet you. I didn't realize Rob had a girlfriend." Carrie arched her eyebrows and flashed a Cheshire cat grin at Rob. "Is that true, Rob?"

Rob squinted at Amy.

Carrie looked at Rob, a slight upturn on her lip. "Tell me. Do you have a bevy of girlfriends I should know about?"

When Rob ignored the comment, she turned back to Amy. "I guess neither of us will know. All I know is he promised me a hot apple crepe tonight," Carrie said, licking her lips in mock anticipation.

She looked at Rob, who continued to avoid any eye contact with the animated woman with exaggerated blue eye shadow, lipstick well beyond her lip lines, and a dark red wig that was so big, it made her head look as if it would topple off her small frame. Carrie sat back down and resumed eating. If Rob didn't spring into action to get rid of the crazy woman, Carrie would have to unleash her ugly side, yet she wanted to hear Gabe Winston, so she stopped plotting.

Amy set an old, crumpled shopping bag on the edge of the table, so close to Carrie, she feared it would overlap her plate. Carrie kept her eyes on Amy, smiled, and gently nudged the bag until it sat at the very edge of the table. Amy used both hands to steady it.

Looking at Carrie, Amy continued. "Do you come here often? It's my favorite place, because I know Rob loves it." She stopped just long enough to turn and face Rob. "I'm excited to finally see you here again, Rob. Thursdays are still good for me."

"Oh, that's a shame," Carrie said, then turned her attention to Rob. "Perhaps we'll have to find another place next week." Apparently, she was more invested in him then she'd realized.

Finally, Rob came to life like a snake that had been poked once too often. He threw his napkin on the table, straightened his back, grimaced, and took a deep breath. He crooked his head.

Carrie wiggled in her seat and covered her grin with her napkin, anticipating the venom about to be spewed.

Looking at Amy, Rob quickly and quietly said, "Amy, we came here one time." He held up his index finger to Amy. Carrie noticed again his hand still looked a bit gnarly. "That's it. One time. And there aren't going to be any more times."

"But—" A burst of spit came from Amy's mouth.

Carrie used her napkin to mop her forehead.

Amy took a quick, deep breath, and shook her head. She opened her mouth to talk, but remained silent.

"I've told you that before. Now, my friend and I have plans tonight, and we need to finish our dinner." He dismissed her with a wave of his chopstick, and Carrie was enraptured by his awakened sternness and control. Take me now. Maybe it *would* happen on the third date.

"But you said Thursday nights were good for you."

Out of the corner of her eye, Carrie could see the hostess walking over to their table, her face in a scowl.

With firmness in her native Thai accent, and a fiery spice in her eyes, the hostess said to Amy "You leave now and no come back. I before tell you this."

For a split second, Amy curled the top of her shopping bag with one hand and reached for her throat with the other as if to say, "Who, me?"

The petite, well dressed hostess remained resolute, one hand pointing toward the exit, waiting to escort Amy to the door. As she turned to leave, Amy looked back and said to Carrie, "I didn't catch your name," followed by reminding Rob, "Remember, it's Gwendolyn now. Remember, I'm the same as blessed."

Carrie scrunched her nose, raised an eyebrow and scratched her head as she kept her gaze on Amy heading for the door. The shoes. They didn't add up. There was something else that was odd, but she just couldn't figure it out.

It was clear, dinner was over, and there would be no dessert crepe tonight. "That woman is one crazy.... Well, you know what I mean." Rob let out a long sigh, kept his head down, and massaged the back of his neck.

The Asian woman returned to their table. Rob stood to greet her. "This is Mali. She's the wife of the owner," Rob said as he introduced her to Carrie.

"No. I own, too, but I forgive you this time." She gave Rob an austere look. "But she no forgive," as she nodded toward the door. "She come here every Thursday and wait. I tell her she can't be here without eating."

Mali flashed a toothy smile at Rob, then thrust her thumb in Carrie's direction. "This one look nicer. Bring her back again."

Carrie waited for Rob to say something, and when he didn't, she said, "How about I buy tonight?" She took the check from Mali and rummaged in her purse for a credit card. "I'm sorry for you. You handled that well," she said when Mali walked away with the payment.

"Let's go hear some good music." Rob's voice sounded relaxed and hopeful.

Carrie was still puzzled by the woman. "I'm curious. I think I saw her at the restaurant the other night."

"Yep. I'll tell you about her sometime." He gave his hand a wave that told Carrie the topic was dismissed for the evening.

The 15-minute drive to the concert was quiet, and Carrie kept mulling over the scene with Amy; she had to find out more about her. Finally, she broke the silence. "I'm sorry for what just happened, but you handled it very well. I know I already said that, but I don't know what else to say."

"Thanks. Obviously, she's got some challenges."

"I'm not sure what her story is, but the shoes she had on were a very high-end pair of fashion sneakers. When my sister came down last year, we saw them and couldn't imagine who would pay so much for tennis shoes."

"Probably from a thrift store or something. I don't know much about her, but enough. She's just sad and lonely."

Carrie kept replaying the woman in her mind. It was more than the shoes that made the woman's appearance unforgettable. Carrie decided to shake it off and focus on Rob and the evening in front of them.

"By the way, I loved my meal. Let's just not return on a Thursday."

He laughed, and she was glad. "But you do owe me an apple crepe smothered in hot caramel sauce, slathered with scrumptious whipped cream."

Rob held her hand when they walked from the parking lot to their seats in the outdoor pavilion, and contentment swept over her, until she heard a familiar voice call her name. She had not missed that sound in the office. She stopped, turned, and took a deep breath.

"Oh, Marta, I'm so surprised to see you. How are you doing?" The vision of Marta in her bright, colorful print tunic with matching pants made her look like a giant fruit bowl. She complemented the look with lemon-yellow glasses.

"Of course. Why wouldn't I be? I simply wouldn't miss this for anything, but I had no idea *you* liked the symphony. It can be rather high-brow, you know."

With a gentle toss of her hand, Carrie continued. "You know me, I like all kinds of music, and I come often throughout the year. Perhaps we've just missed each other."

"I imagine you're here on Judith's tickets?" Before Carrie could answer, the stout woman straightened up and thrust out her chin, so she could look up through the lower portion of her bifocals and leaned back slightly toward her husband. "Now, aren't you going to introduce me to your friend here?"

"Of course. This is my good friend, Rob," Carrie said as she slid her arm through Rob's. "Rob, this is Marta, my boss."

When Marta didn't respond, Rob reached for her hand. "It's a pleasure. Nice to meet you."

"No, it's my delight, really," Marta said after allowing Rob to shake only her fingertips. "Well, I think we're in for a great concert. Enjoy the evening,"

Marta turned to leave and ran directly into Judith. "Oh my, hello. You surprised me. I didn't think I'd see you here tonight. I presumed…" and she looked back at Carrie.

"Marta, Alan, good evening." said Judith. "I'm shocked to see you. I'd heard from Janice that you were going away for a bit. Does this mean you're doing better?"

"Just a little holiday. I'll be back at work before they've even missed me." She flipped her nose toward her husband. "Come Alan, let's find our seats."

"Judith. I'm shocked." Carrie gave her friend a hug after Marta walked away. "I couldn't wait for her to see you. She's wrong, you know. We'd never miss her. Now, you remember Rob from The Professors, don't you?"

"Nice to see you, Rob. Have they asked you to play yet?" Judith joked, nodding to the symphony.

Rob blushed. "No, but thank you."

"I'll catch you later. Enjoy the music."

A few steps away, Rob took Carrie by the elbow and said "I'm sorry for you. You handled that really well." Carrie jabbed him in the ribs with her elbow, and they both chuckled.

"She's an insulting, condescending hag, and we can't wait for her to retire. Apparently, she's not in rehab like the rumors I'd heard," she whispered to Rob as they walked to their seats. "That was a little nasty. I don't talk like that about everyone."

"Sounded perfect to me."

Perfect. She liked that. Carrie looked at him and smiled. "I wanted to suggest that she certainly remembered you from the garden party, but that would have been too easy. She probably doesn't remember much of the evening. Good thing we taped it."

As they settled into their seats, Carrie caught Marta's attention several rows behind and gave her a little wave, and a wistful shrug. Ah, that felt good.

As the sun set behind them and a breeze blew in from the lake, Rob slipped his arm around Carrie's shoulders. He offered her his jacket, but the warmth of his arm was enough. With the slightest tip of her head toward him, Carrie felt a smile come from her soul. She loved how the big horns accentuated the emotion of the music. Or was that her heart? It had been a long time since she felt this comfortable with a man. She was curious to learn more about Amy, but right now, all she wanted to think about was Rob.

Leaving the concert, Rob ran into a tall, dark-haired man with a silver goatee. After they shared their appreciation of the symphony and the concert, the conversation took a turn that grabbed Carrie's attention.

"I haven't seen you out on the water for a while. Do you still have your sailboat?" Carrie watched the silver goatee move up and down like a marionette.

"Yes, but I'm helping a friend in Chicago," Rob said. "I'm on his crew for their regatta this weekend, and then I'll be back here on the water."

"Ah good. Maybe we'll still see you, then. We're just getting into some of the best sailing weather."

Carrie hoped her head hadn't actually spun around like a top, even though that was what it felt like. She waited until they got to the car. "You have a sailboat? You sail? You're a sailor?"

Rob chuckled. "Um yeah. Would you like to go sometime?"

They agreed on the next Saturday after she was done with her tennis tournament and he was done with the regatta.

When they got to the parking lot where they'd left Carrie's car, Rob jumped out, ran around, opened her door, and helped her out.

And he kissed her. Not hard, but sort of clumsy—half-cheek, half-lips, like someone out of practice.

Carrie responded with her own kiss on the cheek. She feared if she didn't pull back, they could be arrested for committing lewd and lascivious acts in a downtown parking lot, and the headline scared her.

"Thank you. This was a great evening. And good luck this weekend. Let me know how it goes. It sounds exciting."

"You, too. Is your tennis tourney the entire weekend or just Saturday?"

"Depends how I do Saturday. Hopefully I'll move on to Sunday."

"Don't let Mindy get to you. Dig deep and have fun. See you a week from Saturday, but I'll call to confirm the time after I check the weather."

She sat in her car and watched him return to his car, and when he looked back at her, she gave a little wave.

Carrie drove home, relaxed and happy, and now, the gnarly hands were explained. She still had questions over the encounter with Amy/Gwendolyn/Blessed/Nutsy that seemed days ago instead of four hours earlier. As soon as Carrie opened the door to her condo, the answer hit her. It wasn't just the crazy woman's shoes that confused her.

She threw her purse onto the kitchen counter, dug for her phone and began scrolling through her pictures. Years ago, she'd begun the practice of taking a selfie before she went on a date to record what she wore so she wouldn't wear it again. She knew it sounded dumb, but she couldn't help herself, and now it paid off.

Amy's shoes were outrageously expensive and didn't go with her second-hand store look. But that wasn't what concerned Carrie. It was the black slacks, white blouse and silver necklace, similar to what Carrie had worn on her previous date with Rob.

Carrie scrolled some more. Sure enough. The first time she'd seen Amy arguing with Rob outside the restaurant, she was wearing a bright green skirt and loud print shirt, very similar to what Carrie had worn on their first date. Carrie collapsed onto her couch. Now she remembered why she had looked familiar. As Carrie drove from the parking lot after that date, she had to stop suddenly as a woman crossed in front of her, heading toward the bus stop.

Could this be a coincidence? Maybe she'd wait to see if there were another encounter. She decided against calling Rob, because she knew he'd be oblivious to all of this. They were being stalked, and Amy was more with it than he suspected.

Chapter 7

Much to Carrie's surprise, Rob called Sunday evening. He usually texted, but she was happy to tell him she'd beaten Mindy in the finals. She hoped his sailing team had fared well, too.

"Both my matches were pretty easy on Saturday, but it took me five sets with Mindy today, and we had four tie-breakers, so you can be sure I'm exhausted. My legs are a bit rubbery, but I'll be fine."

Rob's team hadn't done well in their competition, but this was the first time his friend had entered a sailing race this big, and they were pleased with their performance. He had to make one more trip down the following weekend for a smaller race, but then he would have his weekends free. "Since I won't be here next Saturday, would you like to go out on the water tomorrow? We both have the holiday off. Maybe in the afternoon? I still have a little sailing left in me this weekend."

Carrie couldn't believe she'd never been sailing, but at the lake, they'd always had speed boats and jet skis and kayaks. She had mastered water skiing and paddle boarding and was now looking forward to her first sail. "Sounds great. What time are you thinking?"

"How's 2:00ish?"

"I'll be there."

Rob gave her specific directions and where he'd meet her at the marina.

Once she had a good night's sleep, she'd feel fresh and energized, and by that time, she hoped her legs wouldn't feel like wet noodles anymore.

It was an easy 20-minute drive from her Brookfield condo in Milwaukee's western suburbs, and she found the marina parking lot easily, where Rob was waiting for her. She liked that he was exposing her to something new, and her goal was to sit back, relax, and let him take the lead. It felt good not to be in charge of something. She envisioned a nice dinner when they returned, and likely staying around to see if they could ignite their own fireworks before the city's show started.

He greeted her by asking if she had a jacket, hat, and sunglasses, and yes, yes, yes, she had all three. Dramamine for motion sickness? Nope, she wouldn't need it, never had any problems.

"Well, I always have some stuff on board in case anyone does."

"Do I need anything else?" she asked.

"Nope, I think we're all set. I have a high-octane sunscreen if you want some for your face. I also have a small cooler with some snack stuff and water, but I didn't bring any wine this time. We'll let you get your sea legs first," he said. "It should be a good day, but rather crowded. We're looking at five to eight knots, nice and gentle," he continued.

It was a perfect day, as far as she was concerned. Seagulls looked like polka dots against the rich blue sky. She knew the boat-neck T-shirt was wasted on him, but she had to wear it anyway, along with khaki shorts and her sport sandals. She tied her long hair back, pulled the ponytail through the opening of her baseball hat, and grabbed her sturdy windbreaker, just in case it got cool.

"We're just going to sail out into the lake today and let the wind take us and see where we end up, but I want to get away from some of the other traffic. Lots of boats, as you'd expect for the fourth of July, but fortunately, the lake is big enough for all of us."

"I am along for the ride, as they say. You just tell me what to do and when to do it."

He unlocked the "members only" gate and led her down the dock, while he offered his best advice on getting onto the boat. He boarded first and reached back to help her. With her right leg swung over the side, the safety line got caught between her toes and the sandal on her left foot. She lost her balance and fell head first into Rob's chest. Before she knew it, she was lying on top of him and had him pinned to the deck. Her heart raced as she felt embarrassment and a romantic spark.

She scrambled to her feet and smoothed her hair. "I am so sorry. Did I hurt you? That was quite an entrance, I must admit." She could feel the blush creep up her neck and face. "I just realized—I brought everything except my coordination today. You didn't mention I'd need that."

"I'm good, and usually, women wait until the second sailing date to throw themselves onto me like that," he said as he stood up. "That's a joke, you know. The last time a girl has attacked me like that was…well, forever. But, how are you? How's the foot?"

"I'm good, really." She picked up her hat and repositioned it onto her head.

"My boat's pretty easy to manage, but let me show you how it works, and how you can help today, if you're willing."

Carrie nodded.

He showed her where the life jackets were, and cautioned her to duck when they were changing directions, or she'd get hit by the boom. The orientation was almost complete when he showed her the cabin and small bathroom with the portable toilet.

"Ew, that's a bit cozy," she said. Shoot. She meant to keep that to herself. She could tell by Rob's puzzled look that she needed to clarify what she said. "I'm sorry that just slipped out."

"No problem. It can be a little smelly down here sometimes from the exhaust fumes." Back on the deck, he turned and picked up the ropes. "Are you ready?"

He started the motor, and she helped him cast off the dock lines before he settled in at the helm. They waited until they got past the breakwater before he unfurled the sail and turned off the engine.

"Have you been sailing long?" she asked.

"Ridgewood has always been a huge sailing town, and I really grew up on a sailboat. I sail at least five months out of the year."

"I presume your parents sail as well?"

"My grandpa was a fierce sailor, and then my dad. I've mentioned he can be pretty demanding and sort of a jerk sometimes, but at least he taught me to sail. I bought my first sunfish boat when I was 13. It was just big enough to sail around the bay, but I never took it out onto the lake."

"Sounds serene."

"It can be rugged, but it was always something I could do by myself. Phil, my high school buddy who is my sailing friend in Chicago, also had a small boat, and we liked to compete against each other."

"Ah, is that how you moved there? Was he your connection?"

"He moved to Chicago after college and a couple years later, convinced me to come. But he and his brothers have a 36-foot racer. Our goal is to do the Chicago-to-Mackinac race some year."

"That sounds ambitious, and dangerous. I imagine that takes a couple of nights on the water."

"Yup, and we're a long way from that."

As they ventured further out, the wind picked up slightly. She marveled at how effortlessly Rob adjusted the sail and let the wind chart their course. She was glad she had her jacket and tucked her arms into the sleeves.

Carrie found it interesting that he seemed to seek out things he could do alone: first the computer, then the piano, now sailing, even the reading. Similar to the relationship Rob had with his mother while growing up, Carrie's mother had also doted on her. By the time Carrie arrived eight years after Charlie, and following three miscarriages, her mother smothered her with affection, and

Carrie thrived on the extra attention she got at home as the youngest child.

Always a social queen, and life of the party in college and early in her career, Carrie finally discovered this got in her way of forming strong, lasting relationships. She remembered her mother's words.

Never change your morals or values to be friends with someone else.

Her job as a sales rep for a major pharmaceutical company required lots of travel, long days, and frequent entertaining with clients. But it was at work conferences where booze flowed easily and men were away from their wives where she discovered it was easiest to expand her list of contacts. Those were her darkest days, and she was excited to leave them behind when she moved to Milwaukee.

Was it maturing, the career change, the move? Her values had a good test when her mother became sick and died a few months later. Carrie never looked back to the old life. The move to Milwaukee always felt like a good fit, and she welcomed the chance to start over with her big brother and family nearby. She loved trips to the zoo and overnights with her niece, Liesel, and her nephew, Hans. More than anything else, Carrie loved being close to family, and had adopted Milwaukee as her hometown.

"It's amazing to me, even though there are other boats out here in the distance, it's still so quiet," Carrie said.

"I know. That's the peacefulness I love."

The break from tennis felt good. Next week, she'd head north after work on Wednesday for the annual family weekend at the lake. This year would be different as Carrie and Maggie would spend all day Thursday and Friday going through things from the house. She could already feel the stress, but today, she'd sit back, let the sun warm her face, and the gentle wind toss her hair. Today, she didn't have a care in the world.

For the next two hours, they sailed Lake Michigan, enjoying the quiet time mixed with light conversation. Carrie helped with the sails as the wind shifted, and she willed her sore and tired arms and legs to use different muscles. The gentle serenity of the boat cutting through the waves left her relaxed in a way she hadn't felt for a long time, and she was almost overcome with emotion, until she realized she was really overcome with nausea. She looked around the boat and wondered what she'd do.

"Rob, I think I'm gonna need a bucket."

"Are you sick? I don't have a bucket. You just have to hang over the edge. It will be easiest here." He took her hand and helped her to the side of the boat.

Carrie barely made it while Rob held her by her belt loops to make sure she didn't fall in. He supported her shoulders with the other hand.

"Oh, my Lord, could this get worse? I fall into the boat and wipe you out, then I need to puke. I am so sorry." Carrie stood up and wiped her mouth with the back of her hand.

"Don't worry. You are not the first nor will you probably be the last. Here's some ginger candy. That should help. Let me grab a bottle of water for you, too."

"It just came on so fast, I don't know what happened." Carrie sat back and took a deep breath.

"How about you move back here so you're facing forward, and just keep your eyes focused on the horizon. I've got some ginger ale as well, if you'd like to sip on that."

Rob repositioned himself to trim the sails, all to the tune of several loud belches from Carrie. "Oh no, nothing embarrassing about this scene." Carrie took off her hat and tried to use it as a towel to wipe her brow.

"Here, use this." He handed her an old, dirty towel. "We'll head back."

She took one whiff of the towel and gagged. On reflex, she threw it down the step to the cabin. A sip of water calmed her. "No, I'm fine, really, the feeling's gone, and I'm still here. I'm happy to stay out longer."

"Well, we'll begin to work our way back. That's probably enough time anyway. But you really fooled me. Usually, most people will give some clues, but you were pretty talkative."

They sailed in silence for a few minutes while she sucked on the candy and sipped some water. "How do you do this by yourself?" she asked.

"It's a lot easier with help."

"Oh, I get it now. You're just looking for help." she teased. "You invited me to make your sail easier, right?"

Rob smiled as he stood at the wheel. She liked how the wind tossed his hair and framed his face. She hadn't noticed how deep-set his brown eyes were, or how the tip of his nose had a slight up-turn at the tip. The sail back to Milwaukee was comfortable, and Carrie took off her jacket, tossed her head back, removed the rubber band from her hair, and let the breeze lift it up. "If I didn't get sick, I could get used to this," she said, with her eyes closed. She thought about this for a minute, opened her eyes wide and looked straight at Rob who was watching her. "Well, wait, what I mean is, it's just so calm and I really am loving this." She continued to find the right words. "Well, maybe it's just that…oh, you know what I mean."

In the meantime, Rob's smile did all of his talking.

It was almost 6:00 when they got back and he tied up the boat. "You were a big help today, and it's a lot more fun with someone along for the ride," Rob said.

"I can't tell you how much I enjoyed it, really, despite everything. I think it was the smell of that sputtering motor we passed going out that started it."

"Then can I presume you'd be willing to try another sail? My favorite time of day is after work to unwind, if you'd want to try that."

Yes, Carrie would like that and she'd remember to take some Dramamine, but right now, all she could think about was going home. There would be no fireworks for her tonight.

"By the way, how are you feeling? Usually, when people get back on land, the seasickness goes away."

"I'm good, thanks. Feeling much better." She was a masterful liar.

"We could go to my condo for a little bit so you could rest, if you'd like."

This was more than Carrie had anticipated, yet she was curious. "How far from here?"

"I live here at Lakeside." He pointed to one of Milwaukee's most desirable waterfront condo complexes at the other end of the parking lot.

"You're kidding," was all Carrie managed to say.

"It came with the boat slip." A sheepish grin took over his face.

Good heavens, this guy kept getting better and better. That first date two months ago seemed like a lifetime ago. Who knew what lurked behind those drab clothes and quiet demeanor?

She threw her stuff into her car and helped him carry the rest of the gear. They entered the gated complex, took the path across the lawn, and rode the elevator in silence. This was her opportunity to learn more about him than she'd ever find out over meatloaf at a restaurant. Was she ready? What secrets would his condo reveal about him? She knew the truth is always told by the things we have and how we live.

She followed Rob as he unlocked the door to the condo and paused as she entered the long hallway.

"Sorry. Just step over those."

Carrie took an exaggerated step over the black, scruffy shoes she'd seen before, that sat atop a pile of other shoes greeting them immediately inside the door. Bare white walls, but this wasn't even a general builder white, instead, almost a bright blue white, and they were in sharp contrast to the dark wood floors. It looked as if he'd just landed there yesterday and hadn't gotten around to decorating. Or cleaning for that matter. An army of dust bunnies stood at attention between the runner and the shoe moulding.

They walked into the living area where a black leather, armless couch on a steel frame anchored one wall, with a silver gooseneck floor lamp on the far end. Note to self, she thought. Stay off that couch. The white walls and lamp reminded her of too many doctor exam rooms. Phew. At least there were no stirrups.

At an angle facing the balcony sat a worn, overstuffed, black-and-gray plaid chair with matching ottoman. The seat cushion sagged slightly, and the top of the ottoman had little slubs of fiber from years of use. Between the couch and the chair was an end table overflowing with a stack of books, some magazines and a couple used yellow legal pads, all under a closed laptop. An "I Love Northwestern" mug held a variety of pens and highlighters. A nondescript Berber area rug added some warmth to the room, and an open tube of Biofreeze at the corner of the end table explained the medicinal smell in the room.

"I'm a bit of a minimalist," he said.

She gave a slight smile and nodded. Minimalist? I don't think so. That implies a style. But institutional? Yeah, that's what his place reminded her off.

In the corner was a large black desk with two computer monitors, a single keyboard, and an assortment of papers and textbooks. A TV hung on the wall opposite the couch with a chest that was too small for the space underneath, yet large enough for another laptop. Okay, this guy is a tech dude, I get it. But two laptops, just feet apart?

Rob could see her crinkle her eyebrows trying to figure it out. He wanted to keep her guessing, but finally said "I don't have cable. I stream all of my TV, so I keep this laptop here, dedicated for that."

"So, you don't have to fight with the cable company every time the wind blows? I've got to get with the times."

And then her eyes spotted the piano, in what might have been called a parlor if this were a Victorian house. His condo was an end unit on the sixth floor and had a little alcove that was perfect for the Baby Grand.

"The woman I bought this condo from left that for me. I think I paid her next to nothing because she knew how much I loved it and would use it, and she had no one else who wanted it. She always called it Ernest after her husband, because it was a gift from him one year for her birthday. So, I call it Ernest, too."

"Do you play often?" Carrie knew he didn't by the film of dust on the surface.

"Not really. In return for the piano, I go to the assisted living place she lives in and play for them a couple times a year. She loves it." Rob turned the corner that had been obstructed. "But this is what I practice on. Have you ever heard of a Clavinova?"

Oh man, Carrie was about to get schooled on the piano. Rob sat down, flipped some switches, handed her his headphones, and started to play."

"It's all digital, and when I don't want anyone else to hear, I can just plug those in. Besides, the piano makes Mrs. Carlson's Schnauzer yip. She lives one floor down. I love this condo—who wouldn't—and it works for me now. But someday, I want a house with some property around it where I don't have to worry about close neighbors."

Carrie smiled as Rob turned off the music machine. She wanted to ask if the house he wanted would be of Lannon stone and have a wide, wrap-around porch with a huge island in the kitchen, but held the thought to herself. She did know her walls would never be sterile white, but instead, covered with photos of family and travels. But plain old white walls? This was the decorating vision of one boring man, yet he was less and less boring with every conversation.

"So you play the piano, sail, and read a lot. Is there anything else I should know about you?"

"One thing most people don't know—I'm a bit of a linguist."

"Aha, we have something in common. I speak Spanish. It's my reason to go to Mexico every now and then, so I can keep it fresh. How about you?"

"Well, I'm fluent in German and French, I can read and understand Russian and Italian, but my speaking skills aren't as strong, and I'm studying Mandarin. Almost fluent—that's the toughest one."

"*Nǐ hǎo*," Hello, she responded.

"Wait. *Nǐ huì shuō pǔtōnghuà?*" Do you speak Mandarin? Rob asked.

Carrie started to laugh and waved her hands. "No, no, no. The only thing I know how to say is hello. I learned it from a translator at the hospital once."

"I trade tutoring English for Mandarin with a Chinese couple every Sunday morning. Maybe you'd like to come with me sometime."

"Ah, maybe." She admired him, but studying Mandarin or any other language was not on her list of things to accomplish. He opened the sliding door to the balcony and they looked in one direction toward the lake, and around the corner, toward downtown.

"How did you get fluent in so many languages?"

"They just come pretty easily to me, and I've always enjoyed studying them."

Carrie was impressed, and, for the first time in her life, felt inferior to a man she was dating. She began to wonder what he saw in her. They walked back in and looked at the kitchen with dirty dishes and glasses haphazardly stacked on the counter. There was a jar of jelly with the lid off and a glass half-filled with an orange liquid she imagined was juice. She wasn't sure about eating anything made there and wondered how this guy was such a slob, yet his boat was spectacular.

"Nice table," she joked, as she stood in the center of the spacious, yet empty dining area.

"I know. Someday, when I need one, I'll find one. I usually sit on the balcony and eat dinner when the weather is nice, or at the couch off the coffee table. I've just never taken the time to go shopping for one, and right now, it isn't a priority. And I don't like to spend much money if I don't have to."

"Well, it does make a great dance floor," as she broke into an unrecognizable jerky move.

"Would you like a little rest? You'd be welcome to stay for the fireworks if you can stay that late. I have the best view. We can walk across the street to this great market and find something for dinner."

Just then, her stomach rumbled loud enough for both of them to hear. "I'd love to, but with work tomorrow, I think I need to get going. This has been a fabulous day. Really, I loved the sail and seeing your apartment. Thanks again."

"It's a condo with two laptops, two pianos, and no table. So far, it works for me."

"And a boat slip. Don't forget about that."

Carrie was not only impressed, but now totally into the mystery of Rob Linders. Her living room was painted a soothing dusty blue and the dining room and kitchen, a colorful paprika. She used lots of stuffed pillows on her white couch, along with wall art, and Mexican tiles she'd purchased over the years to tie the two together. She couldn't imagine what Rob's reaction would be if or when he saw it.

The next morning, after a long, hard night of sleep, Carrie woke feeling refreshed and hungry. Her stomach had tossed and turned well after she left Rob's, and was now as demanding as her cats. She stopped at her favorite bagel shop and took in an assortment for the handful of people at work. With the holiday falling on Monday, most people in the office took the entire week off, so there were just a couple others. With few people around, she'd use the time to get caught up on some projects.

By mid-morning, however, she'd been called to meet with the CEO, and though she was optimistic she'd gain more insight into the staffing plan in light of Marta's absence, she was also cautious. *Cockiness will lose the match*, her mother had warned her early in her tennis-playing days.

After the usual pleasantries between the two, Jack continued. "Carrie, we're in a critical time with our marketing campaign, and

I know you've been involved in some preliminary discussions with Marta, but frankly, we're behind where I'd hoped we'd be. I'd like you to map out a strategy, present it to me and the team, and then make it happen."

She felt her chest inflate.

"In addition, I want you to manage the rest of the staff team, except for Dwight and his assistant. He will report directly to me. Do you think you can do that?"

"I'm absolutely certain. What's the timeframe for all of this or even Marta's return?"

"I can't comment on Marta's return, but just want you to stay focused on the marketing plan and running the day-to-day operations of the unit. And we're increasing your salary to reflect your increased demands. Let's stay in touch each week."

Carrie felt stuck in middle management and was beginning to doubt her goals would happen the way she'd envisioned, so this was her chance to prove she could handle higher level responsibilities. She readily acknowledged that patience was not her strong suit. She couldn't wait to show that she could make financial decisions, manage more staff, and deliver recommendations that would impact the entire healthcare system.

She had exactly six more work days before she left for her trip to the family cottage, so she used the time to outline what needed to be done and set ambitious timelines for her team. She arranged as many meetings as she could, both internal and external, as well as media representatives, working around vacation schedules. She was excited to step up the hospital's PR focus using alternative media, and knew the young staff team would rally around the challenge.

Instead, three of her team members complained of already feeling overworked and they couldn't imagine taking on more assignments. The finance director pushed back on freeing extra money she'd need for the marketing campaign, and the communications team was already backed up and wouldn't be able to meet her anticipated deadlines. Two of her external appointments canceled with late notice. Her foray into the higher levels of executive management hadn't gone according to her plan, and she was glad she had a few days away. Self-doubt crept into her soul, and she hoped it would be gone when she returned.

Chapter 8

Most of the time, Carrie looked forward to the drive up north to her family's cottage when she'd listen to some podcasts or sing to some of her favorite music, anything to de-stress. This time though, she picked up Kim, Hans and Liesel right after work. Charlie would drive up Friday afternoon. As her niece and nephew settled in the back seat watching movies on their tablets, she worked to stay social with Kim and not dwell on work issues. Normally, she loved spending time with Kim, but today, Kim was chattier than normal and Carrie's plans to unwind would be shelved until she settled into her own room for the night.

Midway through the three-and-a-half-hour drive, Kim changed the conversation with some family news. "Hey, your brother and I have decided to take the kids and spend Christmas in Florida this year. All of my family is gathering in Orlando, and the kids will have a chance to do Disney World with their cousins. And since this is the first holiday season since Dad died, my mom really wanted to make Christmas happy this year."

"Oh what a great time you'll have. We'll miss you, but I'm excited for you," said Carrie. Kim's father had died in March after a rollercoaster bout with cancer, and when the end came suddenly, it had been hard on the family, especially Kim's mother. Carrie remembered how the first Christmas without her own mother was gut-wrenching. Traditions were lost, routines changed, and memories of what used to be flooded everyone's emotions. She was truly glad Charlie and Kim and their kids would spend it in Florida, but she was also sad her own family's traditions would be uprooted again. This would be the first holiday season Carrie, Maggie, Charlie, and their dad hadn't spent together.

"I was wondering how you felt about just celebrating the Klamerschmidt Christmas early this year. Maybe the weekend before? What do you think? I wanted to ask you before I brought it up with Maggie."

As long as Carrie could spend Christmas with Maggie and her family, and her dad and Barb, and take in the ski slopes of northern Wisconsin on Christmas afternoon like they did every year, she'd be happy.

"I'd be game, but then I can get together with your family any time before you head south, so that would work, too."

The mid-sized cityscapes yielded to acres of lush green farmland dotted with red barns and blue silos, and the rest of the drive was serene as the sun began to set.

By the time they pulled up to the cottage, they were ready to eat the pizza they'd picked up at a nearby restaurant. Carrie stepped out of the car and let her lungs fill with the cedar-scented air. She waved to the new neighbors who were enjoying a crackling fire.

Surprised when her key no longer opened the door, Carrie called to track down her dad, while Kim and the kids cleared off a table on the deck and started eating.

"Oh, hi Barb, I was trying to reach Dad. We're at the cottage, but my key doesn't work."

"Oh Honey, I had the locks changed. He couldn't remember all the people who had keys over the years, so that's what happened. I just decided to get new locks. Where are you now?"

"I'm standing on the back deck, and Kim and the kids are here with me. Didn't he tell you we were coming up tonight?"

"Yes, but I thought you were going to Maggie's first. She has a key."

"Wait. Maggie has a key and I don't?"

"No, Maggie has your key. Sorry about the mix-up."

"Okay, thanks. I'll call her now." Carrie took a deep breath and knew better than to take it personally.

Thirty minutes later, Maggie was there with the key, a bag of fresh fruit, bagels and cream cheese, and a bottle of wine. "I have no idea what they have, but I knew you'd like this, waving a bottle of Carrie's favorite Riesling."

Carrie thanked her sister, and agreed they'd meet at their old home by 9:00 in the morning. Kim was already pouring the wine when Maggie left.

"Here you go," Kim said to Carrie. "I think you should relax before the fun of sorting through your parent's things tomorrow. I'd help, but I'll stay here with the kids. And I'll keep Barb away from the two of you. I think things will go better without her help."

Carrie reached over and clanked her glass with Kim's. "Here's to family time at the lake."

After a couple slices of pizza and one glass of wine, Carrie was ready to head to bed. She was frustrated she and the family had waited so long to help her dad sort and purge, and now tomorrow would be tough as she and Maggie opened boxes, cleaned out drawers, and sorted through memories. She was looking forward to a good night's sleep, yet as she was getting ready for bed, her mind drifted to Rob. She'd seen him a few times, and each date diminished the negative, uninspiring first impression she initially had. She couldn't help but recall what her mother had once told her about men.

They are sort of like onions: all different shapes and flavors, and they all have lots of layers that can be hard to peel at times. They can make you cry when you least expect it, they can be stinkers, and some can be so sweet, they'll take you by surprise.

She was slowly discovering Rob's layers. She wondered if anything got more stinky than his housekeeping. Her start to the long family weekend hadn't been without some hiccups, but she relaxed thinking about Rob.

Carrie slept a bit longer than she planned, and hoped she'd be on her way before her dad and Barb arrived, but as she was finishing her bagel, she heard their car pull into the driveway. After a few minutes over a second cup of coffee and getting caught up with each other, Carrie headed out on the 30-minute drive to her old family home in Birchfield.

"We've been gathering boxes, and most of our things are already packed, so the two of you should be all set. If you have any questions about what's what, just call, okay? And I can always come back in to help. Otherwise, we'll stay out here for the day." Barb said.

"Will do." Carrie wanted to remind her that it was her family home they were dismantling, and thought she'd remember what had been there before Barb moved in. "I think we will be just fine."

"Remember, everything has to be gone. And there's a fresh pot of coffee for you and Maggie."

Carrie gave her a slight nod, feeling the coolness of Barb's words, and pulled out of the driveway without saying anything further. This was going to be a long day, and she and Maggie would have to work hard not to take too many trips down memory lane.

Maggie pulled into the driveway right before Carrie, and as soon as both women were out of their cars, Maggie caught Carrie by surprise with a big hug.

"I've been waiting to see you alone, and I couldn't tell you last night. I've got to tell you before I tell the rest of the family. The kids don't even know this yet," said Maggie.

Carrie reached over and grabbed her hand like she'd done from the time she was a little girl when she had big news to share. She was so excited, she couldn't imagine what it was, but if Maggie was happy, Carrie would be, too.

"You are not pregnant," Carrie said matter-of-factly, convinced her sister would not be this excited if that were the case.

"Oh no, please. But Brad and I just made the reservations. We're taking the kids and going skiing in Colorado over Christmas!"

Carrie dropped Maggie's hand, pulled away, and immediately bit her lower lip.

"I know we'll miss Christmas with the family, but we realized this was David's last year in college and the girls are seniors in high school. If we don't do it now, we may not have a chance to take one last family vacation together."

"You're right, and it all makes sense. I'll miss my Christmas holidays skiing up here with the family, and I knew it would happen eventually, but I'm happy for you and Brad. You deserve this. I'll just miss it."

"But Charlie and Kim…."

"Nope. Kim told me on the way up that they're headed to Florida for the week of Christmas this year. She suggested we have a family celebration before they go, but I didn't want to. It sounds like a great plan now, I guess."

"Carrie, you should go to Aunt Christina's Christmas Day party this year. You know it's legendary, but it's just too far for any of us to go from up here. For you, though, it's an hour away. You'd have a blast, and she'd love it if you came, and Dana and Kevin, and the rest of the cousins? They'd love to see you."

"Christmas is a long way away, and I'll see everyone at Dana's wedding. I'm sure something will work out. In the meantime, I say it's time to attack this stuff. Where should we start?"

"Let's start upstairs and work our way down."

Carrie started on a storage area built high up in the wall in the wide hallway, and began pulling down old bedding. She tugged on something on the top shelf, out of view, and stopped to get a step stool.

Climbing up onto the stool, she reached to pull down the weighted object wrapped carefully in an old sheet. "Maggie, did you know Mom had another porcelain doll? That must be what this is." Carrie brought it down carefully, stepped off the stool, and unwrapped it.

She looked down, closed her eyes, and shook her head. "Maggie…."

Maggie walked from a bedroom. "Damn," she said in a forceful tone. She took the partial bottle of vodka from Carrie. "There were a couple of times I wondered if she had started drinking again, but I guess I didn't want to believe it. Then she'd be fine and I'd forget it."

"How do you know this isn't an old bottle? From before her rehab? How do you know how old this is?"

Maggie turned the bottle over. "See the Surgeon General's warning? Those didn't start appearing until 1989. She went to rehab in '85."

The sisters stared at the bottle, neither saying anything. "I'll go dump the rest out," Maggie said. "And Carrie…" she paused until Carrie's eyes met hers. "Let's not tell Dad."

"I always wanted to think she was a perfect mom," Carrie said, feeling like she might cry. By this time, Maggie was in the bathroom emptying the bottle. "There wasn't anything she wouldn't do for me," Carrie said.

"You had a different life with mom than I did, remember? It was the summer between my freshman and sophomore years in high school when she went to 'camp' for the summer." Maggie's voice rose and she sounded agitated, using air quotes around camp. "You were just five and got to go stay with Aunt Katharine in Atlanta. David and I were left alone, because we were old enough to take care of ourselves, Mom said."

Carrie folded the sheet. She had seldom seen her emotionally calm sister like this.

"That was bullshit. We still needed our mom," Maggie said as she walked back to the bedroom where she'd been working. "Let's get back to work and see if we find any more bottles today."

For the next eight hours, they sorted through more bedding, glassware, knick-knacks, and framed photos as they went through the arduous process—and emptied two more old bottles of booze they discovered. Carrie had a hard time not getting bogged down with making some decisions, so she took a box marked "Family Memorabilia" directly to her car. Someday over the winter, she'd sort through everything.

On Friday, they returned and dove into the boxes filled with holiday decorations. They laughed over childhood ornaments and sorted things into bins labeled for each of the three siblings. "Charlie's getting some stuff whether he likes it or not," Carrie said.

While pulling out the last box of ornaments, Carrie noticed an old wooden crate that was pushed back under the shelving. She retrieved it and they began to carefully unwrap the items.

"That's odd," Maggie said. "This is one of David's old Spiderman sheets mom kept on a bed for him here." They peeled off the sheet to discover another bottle.

Carrie sighed and let her shoulders drop. "She was good, I'll say that much. I'm beginning to think that's why she was such a neat freak—so none of us would discover these."

Maggie grabbed the sheet and looked it over. "I think she was fighting it to the very end. David refused to sleep on these sheets the day he turned 11. 'Kid's stuff,' he said."

Carrie looked at her big sister, who was clearly disgusted.

"That was six months before she died." Maggie wadded the sheet and threw it into a trash bag.

They finished the last holiday box, and moved everything upstairs to the garage. All that was left was the furniture to try to figure out.

When Carrie took a good look at the dining room table, she had an idea. Even though it was 20 years old, its clean, Scandinavian lines were classic, and would look great in a certain Milwaukee condo. She snapped pictures of the table and matching buffet, and was ready to send a text to Rob, but decided to call him first. She'd been with her mom when she bought the set. Her condo didn't have the room, but she hated to see these leave the family. Would he want either the table or buffet? Or both? Did she want him to have both? He wasn't even family. Many meals and conversations happened around that table, and the memories tugged at her heart.

When he answered the phone, her throat clenched.

"Hey, hi. I'm up at my dad's and he has this dining room table I thought would look good, I mean maybe it would work, wait, I mean…." She caught her breath. "We're getting rid of my folks' dining table and buffet. There are six chairs, the set is made out of teak, and in great shape. Would you like me to send you pictures, and, if you like it, we'd just have to figure out how to get it to Milwaukee."

"Sure, sounds good. I'll let you know later today. Will that work?"

Carrie texted the pictures, and within two minutes, Rob called. "The table is perfect. I can't come this weekend, but would next week be all right? I'm sure I can borrow a friend's truck."

Carrie agreed they could work all of that out, wondered if there was anything else he might want, and could she throw some stuff into the truck as well?

Carrie was stunned by the time she ended the call. She was helping this guy furnish his condo, and didn't even know what his needs or wants were, or what his taste was. Well, she had to admit she knew that part—his taste was simple, and his needs were basic.

By the end of the day, she also salvaged three Oriental rugs of various sizes, two plant stands, a Georgia O'Keefe framed print, the old desk lamp with the Tiffany art deco shade that her father got for payment from a cash-strapped family early in his career, and her mom's yellow-apple cookie jar, which was always full when Carrie was a child. Carrie still remembered when David dropped the lid and put the chip in the apple stem, and tried to blame her. But the real joy was that the cookie jar had belonged to Grandma Belle, and they didn't have much from the Belles, so this would find a place of honor in Carrie's small kitchen.

She also packed up three boxes, including the silver set that her parents got as a wedding gift from her dad's sisters. She really thought that needed to stay in the family—or save it until the price of silver was high and sell it. Whatever, it was hers now. And then she nabbed her dad's snow blower. Maggie and Brad didn't want it, and Charlie had thrown his hands up, saying he wanted nothing, so she took it. She knew she had no need for a snow blower now and would have to navigate room in the garage, but it was like new and when she had a house, she'd want one. Maybe she was closer to a house than she thought, and her old soul was furnishing it already.

Her last take was the mission oak desk and chair. The chair would need reupholstering, but the desk was where her Grandpa Klamerschmidt graded his papers when he was still teaching. She carefully ran her fingers over the brass plate with his initials—ASK—Albert Stephen Klamerschmidt. Carrie had sat on his lap when she was a little girl, and he'd helped her learn to write at that desk. That plate was a reminder that she could always ask him anything. Her father was the only son with four older sisters, and when they divvied up her grandparents' items, the desk was left for her dad. Carrie was excited to have it going to her home.

She had no idea how she'd fit everything into her condo, but she'd find a way. She just wasn't ready to let these things go, so there was one more call she had to make.

"Rob, we're gonna need a bigger truck."

Chapter 9

Early the following Saturday morning, Carrie met Rob as he pulled into her driveway. She was in for a long day and hoped they could bring back everything she planned. She'd sent him pictures of what she hoped they'd have room for, and Rob still thought his friend's truck could carry everything. Carrie had brought as much as she could fit into her car when she returned from the trip home, so it was primarily the furniture and rugs. And the snow blower. Rob was still a bit confused by that, but he was happy to help.

She also hoped her family would have a good impression of Rob, though that couldn't be planned through the sending of pictures.

"Good morning. Did you have any problems finding the place?" She liked the seclusion of her condo development, but it was hard to give directions.

"No, but this is tucked away. How'd you ever find it in the first place?"

"Actually, I bought it from a friend of Charlie's. Charlie and Kim live just a couple miles away. I keep telling myself I'm going to get something bigger, but the timing hasn't been quite right. I love flowers and I really want to get a house with a nice porch."

Rob let a brief smile cross his lips. "Is this why we're bringing a snow blower back today?"

"I know, it's a bit crazy. But yep, this may be my motivation. Or at least I'm getting closer."

Rob stood with his hands in his pockets, rocking back and forth on his feet like he did on their first date. This time, he grinned and looked right at Carrie.

"And besides, the thing is almost new. I just couldn't let it go."

They settled into the drive when Carrie told Rob about the family he was likely to meet. "Just don't be surprised if my niece has blue hair and a ring through her nose."

Rob shrugged his shoulders. "You know in banking, we're a pretty wild group. Nothing surprises me much anymore." They both burst out laughing. "It's why I can't get out of black or gray. Sometimes, I live on the edge and wear navy."

"Well, whenever you're ready, I'm happy to help you break free," she said.

Rob kept his eyes on the highway, smiled, and drove on.

"Speaking of work, in another week I'll be working out of the Chicago office for the week. A bunch of meetings they want me to sit in on, and guys from all of our international operations will be there, so I'll just stay down there."

"Are you excited?"

Carrie knew Rob loved everything about Chicago and was an ardent Northwestern fan from his time earning his MBA there. She was happy he'd grown to love Milwaukee as well.

"Yeah. I'll have dinner at Phil's one night. He's got a great wife and kids. I think we'll take their boat out another night, and I'll catch a Cubs game with some of the old team at work."

"Sounds great. I'm not as familiar with Chicago as I should be, but everyone says it's a great city." She tried to keep her voice upbeat, but wasn't sure she succeeded.

"It's my favorite." After a brief pause, he continued, "So what's going on at work for you? You mentioned they were going to make some changes, right?"

As if on cue, Carrie started to click her nails.

Carrie caught him looking at her hands and suddenly became self-conscious. "Oops. Sorry."

"Did I bring up a sensitive subject? I shouldn't have brought it up." He paused. "I didn't mean to make you uncomfortable."

"Oh no, that's fine."

"So, have you been following the Brewers? They're on a bit of a hot streak. Want to catch a game?"

Carrie chuckled. "Ok, now you're just grasping at straws. I'm not thinking a thing about work today. You're the first guy I've introduced to my family in a very long time. I just don't want them to get the wrong idea."

Rob cocked an eyebrow, nodded, and twisted his lips, but said nothing.

"Oh, don't take that the wrong way. I just mean.... It's nice to have a friend who could help me, right?"

"Right." Rob looked at her hand, his face in a smirk. "But that fingernail is about to fly off if you don't stop." They both laughed.

"You asked about work. We just heard about some merger rumors this week." The speculation about St. Hedwig's had just started, and if anything happened, she assumed she'd be safe, but didn't know what the final picture would look like. She feared Jack Stewart would retire, as had been speculated. He was such a supporter of Carrie's, and she didn't want to think about it. Was Marta coming back? She wouldn't leave easily without a big incentive, and even though it was a healthcare system, no one needed a monitor to know the relationship between Jack and Marta was on its deathbed. Depending on who survived would determine Carrie's outcome.

"It's too much drama for me, so I just try to stay focused on what I'm doing."

"Hmpf. Do you think you'd be affected?"

"Oh no. I'm sure I don't have anything to worry about." After several seconds of silence, Carrie reached toward the radio. "How about some music?"

He tuned it to the station playing music from their teens and college years and began laughing when she started to sing along with one of the era's popular boy bands.

When Rob joined her in the chorus, Carrie stopped and held out a fake microphone for him. For the next few miles, they swayed their shoulders, snapped their fingers, and discovered their love and familiarity with the same music.

"I wouldn't have guessed." Carrie just kept looking at him while shaking her head and smiling.

"I knew them all." Rob smiled and kept singing.

Carrie interrupted his singing to provide directions to her family home, and gasped as they turned the corner and drove down her old childhood street. She hadn't anticipated the "For Sale" sign, yet she knew that was the plan. They pulled into the driveway, and Carrie was glad to see Maggie and Brad there, in addition to her dad and Barb. Everything had been placed in the garage, which somehow took Carrie by surprise.

"Is this everything? If so, this should be fairly quick," Rob said as he got out of the truck.

Carrie managed the introductions and led Rob to the table, chairs and buffet. She lifted off the blanket that had been covering the table. "So what do you think? Do you like it?"

Rob ran his hand across the top and examined it as he walked around it. He said nothing. He picked up one chair, tipped it over, set it back down and sat on it. Six chairs in all, no upholstery. Carrie was sure she had spent less time buying her last car, but she could tell, he would not be rushed. The buffet then caught his attention as Carrie and Barb uncovered it.

"Well?"

"This is beautiful. You helped pick this out?" His eyebrows arched, like the wood that framed the glass.

"Well, I was with Mom when she picked it out. I've always loved it. So you like it?"

"I love it. I need to talk to your dad. Maybe I can set up a payment plan if he knows I work for a bank." They both laughed as Carrie led Rob to the end of the driveway so he could talk to her dad with some privacy.

"Dr. Klamerschmidt, I'd like to…."

"Please call me Ed. I'm sure we can strike a good deal."

Rob and Brad planned the strategy for loading the truck, and Barb shouted directions from the garage. "Now, that should go in first, then set the buffet…."

"Honey, I think these two fellas have a plan in mind," Carrie's father said.

Carrie was also tempted to jump in, because after living on her own for so long, she also knew exactly how things should be done. Always.

Instead, the two sisters took a final walk through the house, heeding Barb's advice to stay on the plastic sheeting on the floor. Tomorrow, the realtor would have the first open house, and in the past week, the house had been given a fresh coat of paint and the carpets cleaned, and now it was staged to sell.

They started up the stairs of the large two-story home that belied its size from the street. Her parents had added on twice from the time they first bought it on its oversized lot, so today, with its mature landscaping, wide front porch, and updated kitchen, Carrie thought it would sell quickly. And when people discovered it had both a formal staircase in the front and a set of back stairs near the laundry room by the back door, they would love it.

Carrie and Maggie stood arm in arm while they stopped near the hallway built-in closet and laughed, remembering the times they'd climbed in and hidden behind the extra bedding. "Best hide-and-seek place in the house," Maggie said.

The odd-shaped closet in the corner with a window was the next stop. "Remember how Mom would hide the Easter baskets in here every year until she figured out we always knew where they were?" Carrie said.

"Yet somehow, Charlie always seemed to find them first," Maggie added. "We need to get downstairs before we both turn into a pile of tears."

Their last stop was at the mantle of the large stone fireplace in the family's favorite gathering spot off the kitchen. This had been their wonderful family home, but that time was gone. Maggie was already anticipating the change in their lives after the girls left for college in a year and Carrie was now focused more than ever on finding a house she could call her own. Even she was ready to move on.

"I think by next spring, I'll be able to make a decision about a house. There's stuff going on at work and I want to see how that unfolds, but I think the timing might be right then."

"How about Rob? He seems like a nice guy. Better than you thought at first, right?" Maggie said.

"He's always been nice, but I don't know."

"Could he be the one?" Maggie said, staring at her sister, waiting for an answer.

Carrie shot her a sideways glance. "Too soon to tell. I suppose if I want to hear about Muammar Gaddafi and everyone else like that every night at dinner, he'd be a good fit."

They both burst into laughter. "Can't you say anything?" Maggie asked.

"I don't know how. Or what. I tried the hand flip, but that didn't even work."

"You did not! You tried to brush him off with your hand? Oh Carrie, that is so you. And so rude."

"He didn't even notice."

"Carrie, you've got to give him a fair chance. So what if his reading list is different than yours? I think you're just afraid, that's all."

Carrie squinted at her sister and took a slow, deep breath as if she wanted to unleash her own sermonette. Instead, she started toward the door. "We've got to get back outside before Barb has them rearranging the load."

By the time they'd made it back outside, the Munsons had come over from next door. Carrie always loved Mr. and Mrs. Munson, and they'd been neighbors as long as Carrie's folks lived there. Monty was using a cane these days and Lorraine, a walker, but they came to "help supervise," Monty said.

Carrie shared a warm hug first with Monty, and then Lorraine. She was shocked at how frail Lorraine had gotten. "You took such good care of our mother in her final weeks, and you were always a grandmother to us. I'll miss seeing you when I come back to visit."

Finally, she remembered Rob who was standing next to her. "I'd like you to meet my friend, Rob," Carrie said. "These are the best neighbors ever, and no one bakes an apple pie like Lorraine."

Rob extended a hand, but Monty pulled him in for a hug, practically knocking Carrie down as he swung his cane. "Any friend of Carrie's is a friend of ours," he said. Turning to Carrie, he added, "We're sure going to miss your dad next door, but he seems happy with that Barb gal, so that's good. Promise me this, though. The next time you come up, stop over just like the old days. We may not have any pie, though. Her hands just aren't so good anymore."

Carrie assured them that, indeed, she'd stop by. When she bent down to say goodbye, the old woman pulled Carrie's face close, "You've been such a great daughter. And such a wonderful young woman. I know your mother would be so proud." She brushed Carrie's hair back from her face just as Carrie's mother did when she was a little girl. "Our own kids never come to see us anymore. They live too far away, and they can't be bothered. I don't know what we did wrong...." Her voice trailed off.

"I doubt you did anything wrong. People just get too busy these days, and when you move farther away, it's even harder. I'm sure they mean well." Carrie let it go at that. The Munsons' son in New York City and daughter in Connecticut were both in their 60s, and Carrie didn't know them well, but she wanted to track them down and scream, "Go visit your folks. Don't you know you only get one set and have only one chance at knowing them?"

Instead, she turned and found Barb showing Brad exactly what kind of knot he needed to tie down the final corner of the tarp. Carrie did well to control her inner voice that was saying, "Thank you, Barb. Because neither Brad, the camper, nor Rob, the sailor, know the first thing about knots."

With the truck loaded, they headed to Maggie and Brad's for a quick lunch before they headed home. "Kate isn't off until 5:00, but Emily gets done at 1:00, so she's hoping she'll make it home in time to see you. The kids' group at the art center love her, nose ring and all."

Brad and Rob took their sandwiches into the adjoining family room to watch the baseball game, while Maggie and Carrie sat at the kitchen table. After a few minutes of conversation, Carrie and Rob had to be on their way.

They had a full afternoon and evening ahead of them, and besides, Carrie didn't want them to get too familiar with Rob, so they slipped away before too many questions could be asked.

As they drove off, Carrie got tears in her eyes. She heard her mom's advice about moving on….

Moving on isn't always easy, and you can never look back. New places, new challenges, new people—it makes a far better story than staying in one place forever.

She also realized for the first time, she didn't know her mother as well as she thought, and she felt betrayed. Carrie clung to the image of a helpful classroom mom, prom-party organizer and personal advisor every time Carrie called, clawing her way into adulthood, but unloading the house had been a reality check for her. Her mother was no longer the definition of perfection, and Carrie began to wonder if there were other secrets she'd missed throughout the years.

Maybe it was Rob, maybe it was the sale of her family home, or maybe it was the job. Carrie didn't know exactly what it was, but she felt restless and ready to map out some moves as she took a closer look at her own life.

"Are you okay?" Rob asked.

Carrie wasn't even aware she'd been sniffling. "Just a big chapter that's closed. Sorry. I loved that house."

"I'm sure it was hard to go through everything."

"That's the understatement of the year."

"You have a very nice family. Especially your dad. He was very gracious when I accepted the dining room set as a dowry."

Carrie erupted into laughter. She was glad he had a great sense of humor. And optimism.

They dropped off the furniture at Rob's first, then drove to Carrie's. As he wedged the snow blower in her garage between her bike and the gardening tools she'd previously brought back, he turned to her and said, "I think you're going to need a bigger garage." She was tired, but could still smile. Because it was late, they unloaded everything into her dining and living areas. "I can still get to the kitchen, so can I repay you with a nice meal? How about dinner tomorrow night?" They agreed he'd come over around 4:00 and he'd help her finish putting everything away.

Carrie laughed at the look of her condo and took a deep breath. "This clutter will get the best of me. I appreciate you coming back tomorrow. Thanks."

She was the old soul of the family and couldn't let things go, but the feng shui was out of whack, and she was eager to get it under control again.

As Rob put his hand on the door, he paused, turned around, and faced her. "This has been a wonderful day. Thank you," and before she could say anything, he slid his hand around her waist, pulled her close, and kissed her.

"I'll see you tomorrow. Thanks again." And he was off.

Carrie watched as he walked down the walk, and got into the truck, and found herself waving even after he'd driven out of view. Turning, she picked up Lila and said, "I think he's more than a friend."

Chapter 10

This was the first-time Carrie had made a full dinner in a long time. She had worked side-by-side with her mother in the kitchen, but Carrie got lazy along the way and relied on too many carry-outs and ready-made foods. She was glad Rob was coming over, which gave her a chance to test her cooking chops again. She had a good sense of what he liked and felt pretty confident.

Yet she was nervous. Please don't let him judge me when he sees all the stuff I've already tucked into the condo, she prayed. And will the cake be over-the-top? She was trying to stay cool with Rob and not force their relationship, but after yesterday, she was ready to move it along. She also remembered what her mother had told her.

Now remember, a relationship is a lot like cooking. You have to have patience, you're going to have some lumps, don't forget to stir it constantly, let it start on low and build to a simmer and if gets too hot too fast, turn down the heat.

When the doorbell rang and Carrie saw the flowers and wine, she was impressed. He could have taken the price sticker off the cellophane the flowers were wrapped in, but he was trying, and she appreciated it. It was a nice touch that he'd remembered she liked Riesling.

"These are beautiful, thank you." The stargazer lilies with their raspberry-colored stripes were beautiful, but long ago, she learned to avoid this extremely fragrant flower at any length. Today, she just had to tolerate them for a couple of hours.

"Have a chair while I trim these and get them in a vase."

Rob took five steps in, stopped, and looked around.

"Be careful. You sort of have to step over the rugs and around the boxes like it's an obstacle course."

"Wow. I've never seen a place so orderly."

"You're kidding, right? Once we get this stuff moved, it will be better."

"No. It just looks really nice."

"My mother was a neat freak, and she was always my hero." She placed the carefully arranged bouquet on the table. "I used to think she was the perfect mom and wife."

"Used to?"

"It's complicated." Suddenly, she realized her hostess skills had gotten lost. "I wasn't even thinking—what would you like to drink? I'd like to save the wine for another time, but I just made some iced tea. I also have some Blue Blade Ale. I think you like that, right?

"Uh oh. You already know me. I'd love a bottle."

She turned her back to him and a smile crossed her face while she pulled his beer from the refrigerator. She saw the cake and couldn't wait until she served it.

"This was some of the stuff I was hoping you could help me with," she said, with a weak smile crossing her lips, as she handed him his beer and a coaster.

"Sure. Where's it all going?" he asked, looking around, noticing there wasn't much space.

"Let me show you around first, and where I'm thinking I want things to go." The tour of the condo was brief: two bedrooms and two baths upstairs, a finished basement with her laundry room, a storage room, and a small open space, but her favorite part of the condo was the sun room off the dining area on the main floor that led to her patio lined with a beautiful flower bed. "My mother grew beautiful zinnias every year, so these are my homage to her."

"Beautiful. I don't see a single weed."

"And you won't. I work really hard at that."

Lila and Poppy were getting some late afternoon sun, stretched out on the couch near the window. "Let me officially introduce you, but don't expect them to get up or anything. I know you don't like cats, but these two will stay here until the sun goes down and shouldn't be any bother." Neither cat moved to acknowledge the stranger in their home.

Rob and Carrie then began by carrying several boxes to the basement. She shifted each box to make sure they were all lined up exactly the same, label facing out. "This way, they're in a neat line and I can see exactly what's in each box."

Rob nodded "Sure, makes sense to me."

She marveled at his strength when he picked up the rugs and threw them over his shoulder, carrying them to the spare room upstairs. Next came the desk that got wedged in a corner in the same room, with the rocking chair next to it. She stooped to align the chair with the front of the desk, suddenly rocking the chair over his foot. “Oh, I’m sorry. Did I hurt you?”

“It’s nothing a good meal won’t take care of.”

He mocked limping as they went back down to the living area where he spotted a Sudoku book on the coffee table. “Do you like to do this while you watch TV?”

“I tend to play games on my tablet, but yes, I still like to do these when I sit outside.” She picked up a bag with knitting. “I like to knit, too, but not as much when the weather is warm.” She saw him chuckling. “What’s so funny about knitting?”

“I bet you play Words with Friends?”

“Yes. Is that funny?”

“Oh, it’s the knitting, the games, the flowers outside, the cats—you could be my mother.”

Carrie straightened up and took a slight step back, and Rob could tell he’d offended her.

“Well, I just mean a little old-fashioned. But there’s nothing wrong with that.”

She’d been compared to a lot of people, but never anyone’s mother. Suddenly, she felt old. She forced a smile and said, “Well then she must be a wonderful woman. And are you just like your dad?”

Touché.

"You mean Bob," drawing out the one-syllable name sounding a bit like a wayward sheep. "Nope, I hope not. Anyway, I just meant you and my mom share some of the same interests."

"Do you always call your father by his first name?"

"Only when there's a great lake between us."

She knew the influences of his mother on him, and now she wondered about the ways in which his father had left his mark, beyond a love of sailing. They picked up their drinks, retreated to the sun room, and enjoyed the late afternoon warmth.

"You asked about my dad. He's not a bad man, just stubborn, and he's always been long on criticism and short on praise. He said it prepared us for the real world, and he was a true believer in "the early bird gets the big contracts" theory, so it was always about getting the work done before playtime.

Rob took a long drink and continued. "The biggest challenge was that he didn't often see the point in play, so the list of chores that needed to be done was long, and they often needed to be redone to meet his expectations. Same with homework."

"Do you ever think back about how you were raised and translate that into your life today? I find myself doing that all the time."

"When I was younger, I worked hard at not being like my dad, as often as I could. Yet, he did treat others well, and he was a hard worker. I still like to get up and go to work early in the morning, just like he does. It's my quiet time. How about you?"

"My mother was fastidious and that rubbed off on me—at home and at work. She liked to be in control, and I'm finding after a lifetime of being like that, it's a challenge to back off sometimes." Carrie took a long drink from her iced tea. She hoped Rob would see she didn't want to talk about it much more.

"I told you my mother really protected me. Then in the evening when Dad was home, I would tend to just go to my room. It was easiest that way. He was a good provider, and I guess I felt loved, just unappreciated, if that makes sense. My mother is a saint, by the way, and early on, she found her ways to tolerate him, and carve out her own life. He has always treated her very well. How about you? Your dad seems like a nice guy."

"You mean Ed? Or Eddie if you are in his inner circle. He's a great guy and dad. My mother was Rita. I think I told you she passed away several years ago, and we were very close. She was my best friend and I talked to her every day until she…." Carrie's voice broke. "I look back now on my life and realize how fortunate I was, but I didn't always see it that way at the time."

Carrie was going through a tilt-a-whirl of emotions since they'd dismantled the family home, and she couldn't bring herself to talk about her parents anymore. Instead, she decided it was time to pull the meal together.

"I've made a spaghetti salad, and I just need to heat the garlic bread. Are you ready to eat?" She pulled the lid off the salad and scooped it into a serving bowl.

Rob took the bowl from her, and as he carried it to the table, enjoyed the savory aromas. "I can smell the garlic, basil, and oregano, 'the Italian trifecta,' my grandma would say, and I can't wait to taste it."

"I'll just get a couple glasses of water, too," she said as she reached into the cupboard. "Do you like to cook?" she continued to fill the glasses.

"I can do pasta pretty well, but that's about it. My mom comes from some Italian roots, so I learned how to cook it at an early age," he said. "Beyond that, I just throw together what I have on hand and call it a meal. Cooking for one is sort of boring, so I end up picking something up on my way home or at the market across from my place."

"Now that I know you can handle your way around the kitchen…." Carrie stumbled over her words and felt herself blush. "I love cooking, especially this time of year when there's so much local produce. The cucumbers, peppers, tomatoes, all fresh. Then add some olives, a little salami and mozzarella cheese, and it's a meal."

"This is excellent. Magnifico!" He exclaimed as he kissed his fingertips. "Thank you." The crunch of the warmed bread's crust was a nice contrast to the cold, silky noodles.

"Just let me know when you want to cook together someday. I think it would be fun, and we'd both learn something."

Rob nodded and smiled while he held up his glass. "I'd like that."

When they were done, she took their plates to the kitchen. "I've got dessert, and I hope you like it."

When she placed the ganache-covered chocolate cake in the center of the table, she was certain she saw a bead of sweat form on Rob's forehead. They made eye contact during the brief, awkward moment when he looked up at her before he turned his eyes back on the cake. “Oh, my.”

“I remembered you saying how much you liked it.”

Carrie enjoyed every moment, even while he licked the last of the cake off his fork. Suddenly, she admitted, she found herself interested in getting to know him better. She’d never made such an elaborate dessert for anyone before.

“We’re in some great sailing weather. Interested in trying it again? Maybe some night this week after work?” Carrie agreed like a child grabbing at cotton candy, and Friday would work, but she also knew she’d take the sea-sickness drugs he’d recommended.

Rob helped clear the table, and accepted her offer to take some leftovers home, but Carrie insisted she would finish cleaning up. “I don’t mean to eat and run…” he said.

“No problem. Yesterday was a long day, and you’ve really helped me get things in order here. We can do this again sometime.”

As they walked toward the door, Poppy wove her way around his ankles. He bent down and patted her on the head. The cat responded with a purr that seemed to say both thank you and I approve.

“It’s not that I don’t like cats. They just don’t usually like me. It looks like yours is the exception.”

Without thinking about it, Carrie reached up and gave him a quick kiss on the cheek. “Thank you. This has been very nice.”

Rob smiled, but didn’t return the affection. Instead, he turned and walked to his car in the driveway. Before he opened the door, he pulled his phone out of his pocket, stopped, checked a message, and shook his head. Without looking back toward Carrie, he got into his car and drove off.

Not a kiss, much less a wave. That wasn't quite the goodbye Carrie had hoped for. Her mind flashed back to when he walked away from Amy at the restaurant, and she must have had the same dejected feeling.

Carrie was mystified by Rob. There had been no mention of Amy since she broke up their dinner, and Carrie certainly wasn't going to bring her up. But even as she found herself looking forward to spending time with Rob, she couldn't be sure he felt the same way. Tonight was the perfect opportunity for him to respond to Carrie's kiss, but instead, he thanked her for the food she sent with him and walked away.

Through the years, Carrie had taken many different approaches to dating. In some cases, she hit it out of the park on the first date. Other times, she'd waited until the third date for sex, the industry standard. Rob would require a different approach and could tax her patience.

She wanted to stay home on Monday and continue unpacking and putting away items from the boxes, but she also knew going to work would take her mind off Rob and the status of her life. For the first time, Carrie heard more serious talk at work about a merger with another healthcare system located in Michigan. Or was it a buyout and, if so, was St. Hedwig's the shark or the bait? They'd been the shark the other time Carrie had been through this, and knew she'd survive again.

Throughout the week, there was much speculation and hearsay, creating anxiety for everyone. At least she had her Friday night sailing date to look forward to. She would ride out the storm again, but it still made work more stressful, with a new team, potentially, and new bosses to adjust to. If it were similar to previous experiences, it would be complicated by an absence of communication from the top, and a fluid timeline that could either drag the process out over years or complete it in months. She hated all of it, but she knew she could manage. A couple of places had told her they'd find a place for her, but she never knew if they were serious. And if she did leave St. Hedwig's or the healthcare field, what did she want to do? Just as long as she stayed in Milwaukee, she'd be fine.

Friday morning, her phone pinged, and she saw a text from Rob. "I can't go sailing tonight. How about tomorrow?"

She agreed to Saturday, late morning after she was done with tennis, but the flatness of his text made her wonder what other plans he had Friday night. Rob had gotten her wrapped up in an uptight mess, and part of it was the mysterious aura that hung around him occasionally. He was a true Renaissance man, and his awkwardness in the beginning had mostly disappeared, but his emotional inconsistency was unsettling to her after having dated for several weeks.

With an unplanned free Friday evening, she joined her brother and his family for a trip to the Brewers' game. Carrie knew she could rely on Kim for some relationship advice.

"Oh Carrie, you know men aren't always the most dependable, and he may be sorting things through, as well. You met him online, right? Maybe he's checking out other women he's met. Did you think about that? You're not the only woman out there looking."

"But it's been three months since we met and two since we've been seeing each other regularly."

"Oh stop. If you like him, give him time. That's all I'm saying. Relationships don't always follow the plan we create in our minds, and you might have to loosen up a bit. Stop trying to control a schedule you've created." Kim paused, kept her eyes on the field, and took a sip of beer. "I had to wait until football season was over for your brother to pay much attention to me. And that was in 1998 when the Packers were in the Super Bowl, so it was an even longer season." Kim looked down the row to see her husband enjoying the game. She turned back to Carrie. "The good news? They lost, and I was there to comfort him."

"You are so bad. I need to learn some of your tricks."

"Just patience, Girl, patience."

"To be honest, I don't know if I want to be that patient. He's had lots of chances, and I keep getting matches sent to me. Lots of those guys look pretty good. Maybe I should message a couple of them."

Kim dropped her head and shook it. Finally, she looked at Carrie, opened her eyes as wide as she could and looked at Carrie. "Seriously? Why be in such a rush? Give it some time."

Suddenly Carrie heard her mother's voice. *A relationship is an investment and you're in it for the long run. You're looking for someone you can love truly and with all your soul.*

"I'll have a better feeling after tomorrow, I guess. But you know, I have to have a solid date for Dana's wedding this fall. I cannot face the aunts and uncles alone."

Both women laughed, sat back, and enjoyed the game, even though they hadn't followed it much, when suddenly, Kim sat up and looked at Carrie. "I have an idea. Why don't you wear one of your cute little workout outfits tomorrow? See if he says anything."

"Really? I just got a new set and I loved it as soon as I saw it."

"It sounds perfect. Just take another shirt so you don't get fried by the sun."

"Maybe I should have listened to more of your advice over the years," Carrie said as she rolled her eyes. They lifted their plastic glasses of beer toward each other and smiled.

Chapter 11

In the morning, Carrie checked the weather before she went to play tennis, and even though it was partly cloudy, she thought it would still be good for her plans for the day. By the time she met Rob, the clouds had rolled away, the sun was high, and the wind was perfect for another sailing date.

"Hey," Rob greeted her at the marina. "Are you all set?" Again, he was dressed in olive-green cargo shorts, an old, worn out T-shirt, and a wide-brimmed canvas hat with a drawstring under his chin. Again, he looked like he should be on a hiking trail instead of a boat.

"I'm great and all medicated up, so it should be a better ride for me today. Before we go, would you mind putting some lotion on my back?" She took off the windbreaker she'd worn over the workout top and handed him the sunscreen.

Rob slathered her back, shoulders, and neck, and wiped the rest on his arms, but said nothing.

They untied the boat and glided through the harbor into the wide-open waters. Carrie knew they were headed south, toward a favorite place of his between Milwaukee and Chicago, for a late lunch. "I invited Phil and his wife to join us for lunch."

"Oh, wonderful," Carrie said, silently cursing Rob for not telling her ahead of time. Thank heavens she'd showered after tennis, but now it was too late to worry about her last-minute decision not to wash her hair. That's what she had a baseball hat for. And she would never have worn black-and-green legging-shorts and an elongated sports bra to meet his friends for the first time. She couldn't worry. They were already too far out for her to jump overboard and swim back.

Rob was preoccupied while he maneuvered the sailboat among several fishing boats coming back into the harbor, a couple of speed boats and another sailboat working their way out, when he finally finished. "Anyway, they couldn't meet us. They're headed to the zoo today with some friends, but it's no big deal. I'm going early tomorrow, and Phil and I will go out on his boat, and I'll see the rest of the family during the week sometime."

Carrie smiled and relaxed a bit. They rode in silence for ten minutes, with Rob managing the controls the entire time. When she attempted conversation, he responded with one-word answers.

"You seem pensive today."

"Just a lot on my mind about work. I'll be glad when this next week is over," he replied.

Carrie hoped that's all it was. "Is work stressful when you're in the home office?"

"It's not that it's stressful per se, but the days can be long, and there's some ambiguity about my role right now. Mostly, I sit in these meetings and just try to remain engaged, so I'm ready when they call on me for my opinion about the reality of implementing their tech vision. Sometimes, I have to bring them back to the real world, and sometimes, I have to help them stretch."

"Do you think they'll move you back to Chicago sometime?"

"That's almost guaranteed, but I'm not sure what they have planned. I'll probably know more by the next time I see you."

The lake was smooth, and Carrie learned more about handling the boat as they zig-zagged west and east to move south. By the time they moored the boat and had a short wait, she was hungry for a burger this place was known for.

"You want a drink to wash that down?" Rob asked.

It was the levity Carrie needed. "With my track record on the seas, I'm not going to push it. I'll just have water, but go ahead and grab a beer. I can be the designated sailor on the way back."

"Ha. Now that's a good one."

Rob hadn't initiated much of any conversation, so by the time the boat was headed back toward Milwaukee, Carrie was grasping to fill the void. "How's the dining room furniture working out? Do you like it?"

"It's great, and I love it. Thanks."

"Well, you can thank my mom, but I'm happy you have it." Carrie said. A few minutes later, the silence had gotten the best of Carrie. "So, I've been wondering about Gwendolyn or Amy. I wonder how she's doing, poor thing." There it was, out of the blue.

This snapped Rob out of his wind-induced, Lake Michigan trance. He shook his head as if not hearing the question correctly, but continued to look straight ahead. Carrie noticed the Adam's apple bulge in his throat as he swallowed hard.

"She used to work in the adjoining building to mine, and I'd see her around a bit in the café they have in the basement. She was always alone and usually reading a book. I sat down at her table one day when it was crowded, and there weren't other spaces available. Shortly after that, I didn't see her anymore until I bumped into her one day as I was going to lunch. She was in the plaza, reading again. She jumped right up when she saw me coming her direction, and we chatted a bit. She caught me off guard and asked me if I'd like to meet her after work the next night for dinner, so we agreed to the Beau Thai. This was right after I met you the first time."

Carrie continued to look at him. She hoped her serious look concealed a smile.

"It wasn't five minutes into our meal—no actually, it was before the meal had even been served—and I knew this woman was…." He struggled to find the right words. "She has some serious struggles."

Carrie slurped as she took a sip from her water bottle while stifling a laugh.

"It gets better. Then I learn, she worked as a temp in the county offices in, get this, mental health services, and she was on a medical leave to get some help managing some issues. Every now and then, she appears out of nowhere as if she's following me. It's just weird. She's harmless, just a little cuckoo, I think. I actually feel sorry for her."

"Have you seen her since the night at the restaurant?"

"Some of us worked late one night, and I'm sure I saw her waiting for the bus near the office, but she didn't see me."

"Do you have any idea what she had on? Would you remember?"

He looked at her questioningly. "I don't even remember what I had on. But her shoes caught my eye, because they weren't the shiny tennis shoes like you'd remembered. Instead, she had this pair of shoes, no, more like sandals, that laced up her legs. I remember them, because I couldn't imagine who would wear shoes that took that much effort, and they reminded me of something like gladiators wore." Rob snickered. "Only *I* would know what gladiators wore, I imagine."

Carrie gasped. "Rob, they're called gladiator sandals, and Rob, I think she's stalking you. Or maybe us. I wore a pair of those the night we went to the concert when she saw us at the restaurant."

Rob looked at her, but his sunglasses covered up what his eyes might be saying. He opened his mouth, but didn't say anything, and turned back to motoring the boat into the slip. "Here, I'll hop out, then you toss these to me," as he picked up the ropes. It was obvious to Carrie that he wasn't going to talk any more about Amy.

Carrie helped him tie up the sails and secure the boat. He was careful to remove everything and cover it, knowing he wouldn't be back on it for a week.

"How about we take a little walk, then call it a day. I have to finish getting ready for next week," Rob said.

"That's fine. I'm working at a fundraising picnic tomorrow for the Northside Community Center and should take care of some things tonight as well."

As they began to walk, he slipped his hand into hers. "Did you enjoy the day?"

"I loved it. I love anything on the water and, of course, I didn't get sick this time," she said, and then laughed.

"That's a good sign. And you're a great first mate. You caught on really well and knew what to do when the wind shifted. I hope I didn't make you work too hard today."

She smiled in return. "I had a good teacher," and looked at him. "Good luck this next week and, if you have a chance, call me. Just to touch base and catch up, okay?"

He'd try to remember, but at the very least, he'd text her. As they returned to her car, he bent down and gave her a quick hug that felt distant and unemotional. "I've enjoyed today. Thanks.

"Good, I'm glad." Carrie took a step back, dropping her arms to her sides.

"We'll go sailing again when I get back, if you'd like."

"Sure. I'm sure it will work. Just depends on my schedule." She spoke quietly, and her words carried a tentativeness that surprised her.

"Dinner still on for Friday night?"

"Great." She didn't mean to have the crispness like the first bite of an apple.

"And about Amy. I'm not worried about her, and you shouldn't be either. I promise. She's just sort of a nuisance." Rob looked toward the ground and kicked a few pebbles.

Carrie wasn't so sure about Amy. That was the third time Amy had appeared dressed in clothing similar to hers, which was more than a coincidence. But her primary concern was Rob. She punched in Kim's number as she left the parking lot.

"Hi, Car…."

Carrie cut her off before she could continue. "I did what you said, wore my cute little outfit and even asked him to put lotion on my shoulders. Nothing. Not a single comment, and when he walked me to my car, he hugged me like we'd just met. He just reached over, and gave me the thinnest of hugs. Our shoulders didn't even touch. It was over before I could even put my arms around him. What is up with that?"

"Oh, Girl, I don't know what…."

Carrie cut her off again. "Don't worry. I'll figure something out."

The Northside Community Center's annual picnic was held in the parking lot and adjoining green space of the center. It was part celebration for the kids and families served by the Center, and part fundraising event that helped provide weekend meal kits for the center's qualifying families. "It's a shame with all the food waste in our city that people go to bed hungry," Judith had said when she approached the staff about starting the program several years ago. Each year, Judith and her husband managed to get all the food donated for the picnic, and all available board members were expected to take turns cooking the hot dogs and burgers, helping the team who catered the rest of the meal, or working the ticket tables. The staff ran events for the kids and families who attended.

Fortunately, the sky was slightly overcast, which prevented the temperature from rising north of 90 degrees. Carrie arrived around

10:00 to give Judith a hand organizing the tables before she worked the family ticket counter from noon to 2:00. The blacktop of the parking lot kicked up enough heat to leave her feeling wilted, and she was glad she was under a tent. As soon as she was done, she grabbed a burger, and joined some of the other board members at a table under a large oak tree at the edge of the lawn.

She was eager to head home to enjoy a short bike ride on the trail near her home before she relaxed the rest of the day. Dating had taken a chunk of her time, and she hoped she'd talk to Rob throughout the week before their date next Friday evening. If not, she didn't know what she'd do. She'd already canceled her online dating application and wasn't up to trying another match anyway.

She had just finished eating and was headed to toss her plate in the trash when she heard her name called.

"Carrie?"

She knew the voice, and before she could control the shaking in her hand, her plate dropped to the ground as she turned.

"Kyle Saunders. I'd know that voice anywhere. What the…?"

"Here, put your drink down here." He took her glass and set it on a table before giving her a hug that lifted her off the ground.

Over the years, she'd regretted her decision that she didn't move to Denver with him, and replayed the "what if" game over and over in her head. Yet something had gnawed at her gut when she was deliberating, and she finally found peace months after he left. Now here he was, standing right in front of her. She could barely catch her breath.

"I've been transferred back here, and LeRoy Johnson is my boss. He suggested I support this today, and I'm glad I did. Great crowd."

"LeRoy? The board chair of Northside Community Center? I'm on the board with him. Great guy."

"Yep. I've just been back for a month and I knew I'd look you up when I got settled. This is perfect timing."

"Well, let's get you something to drink and some food, and you can fill me in a bit."

"That sounds good, but Carrie? I've got to say you haven't changed a bit. You're just as beautiful as when I left." Kyle's green eyes peered deeply into her soul. They weren't everyday green, but reminded her of emeralds streaked with flakes of gold that glimmered in the sun. She'd forgotten about the lure of his eyes. His shirt showed off his broad shoulders and well-developed biceps. His sandy-colored hair was a bit shaggy, and still looked like he'd just gotten off the slopes, but stylishly cut to accentuate his million-dollar grin and dimples.

"You always knew exactly what to say. And I see you're still working out," she said as she touched his upper arm." He responded with a mock flex. "Now you go, say hello to LeRoy, grab some food, and I'll sit and wait here." Carrie wasn't sure her weak knees could hold her, but that was the impact Kyle always had on her. She sat at the first table she could find, smiling at the large family gathered at the other end.

A couple minutes later, Kyle returned without food. "Carrie, can we find another time to touch base? Several of the people from work are here, and I really need to hang with them. New kid on the block, you know."

"I totally understand. But let me give you a card. And call me sometime."

Carrie wobbled back to her car, feeling a bit flushed. She really wanted to call Rob, to get a read on the Rob-o-meter of love, but knew he was with Phil on the lake today, so she'd have to trust her own instincts. But why was she so quick to give Kyle her card? And encourage him?

Her bike ride took her an hour, and by the time she returned, she had to push the cats off the couch in the sunroom. She tried to read, but thoughts were darting around her head like shooting stars. Finally, she flipped on the TV and scrolled through until she found a movie to watch. *Love Lost.* Perfect, just perfect, she thought.

When Kyle called her later that night, she couldn't bring herself to answer, or even return the call. Her heart raced and, suddenly, she began flicking her nails. She took a shower before she went to bed to try to relax, but when she last looked at her alarm clock, it read 1:19. She dreaded work the next day.

Chapter 12

After ten years working for St. Hedwig's, Carrie had assembled a team of younger employees who had learned to work well together. At times, she regretted having to nurse a couple of them into the world of professional work and help them weave their way into adulthood, but she knew others had helped her along the way. She relaxed after their regular Monday morning team meeting, feeling confident the team was making great progress on the new pieces for the marketing plan.

"Carrie, can I see you for a few minutes," Jason, one of the young associates, asked as the others left the meeting room.

"Sure. Let's go to my office to talk about the app you're working on."

"About that." Jason closed the door to the meeting room, then handed her an envelope. "This is my letter of resignation."

Carrie sat down and invited him to do the same.

"Jason, you're my right hand with events. Tell me all about it."

By the time he was done telling her about his move to Florida, she was crushed he was leaving, and that she'd not had any inclination.

"I'm thrilled for you, but sorry you hadn't warned me, considering how close we've worked for these last couple of years."

"I couldn't until I knew for sure."

"I'm happy for you. I really am."

By the time Carrie arrived home from work, she was still frustrated Jason was leaving. But she was also envious that it was so easy for him to pick up and leave, and that he was taking the leap to try to do something so different, so far from his home area.

She was about to pull a leftover chicken breast from the fridge when instead, she grabbed the green onion dip and found a bag of chips in the cupboard. Tasting a chip and discovering it too stale to eat, she also realized the dip was months old. Both got pitched. She checked the freezer—yep, tucked behind some veggies, she eyed the ice cream. She was all set, but dutifully ate the chicken breast first.

An hour later when Kyle called, his smooth, deep voice soothed her. They only talked for 15 minutes before he had to end the call, but it seemed as if four years hadn't passed.

"Tomorrow night sounds great, and I love Mancinucci's," she said, twirling a lock of hair between her thumb and forefinger.

"I'll see you then, and I hope Giovanni is still there playing the violin." She recognized the clicking sound he made with his tongue and knew there was a wink at the other end of the line. She never did tell him he sounded like a cowboy summoning a horse to move faster.

Carrie ran her hand through her hair and shook out the long waves. This was the same restaurant where he'd asked her to move to Colorado with him. It wasn't a proposal and he wasn't interested in getting married then, but maybe down the road, he would. She wasn't as confident.

She had exhausted so much energy trying to impress and please Kyle when they dated that she didn't want to put any effort into what she'd wear when she saw him immediately after work. After all, she was a changed woman. Plus, she had Rob—maybe—and his sensible rubber-soled shoes, and his contentment with a night at home reading or playing the piano or letting the wind guide him on the lake. At least she had him. Didn't she?

Before she went to bed, she carried out her usual routine of planning her clothes for the next day. Memories of Kyle caused her to dig through her stash of silk and lace undies until she exhumed the brilliant red thong and matching bra. She threw them back and closed the drawer. Her black everyday Jockey French-cuts would be just fine.

Four outfits later, she settled on her dark brown pencil skirt with matching silk blouse. Were the pearls too much for work? It felt good to be back in her high heels after spending so much time in summer flats and sandals, and the leopard print stilettos looked great, but would lead to questions from her coworkers, plus they fought with the pearls. She'd wear her favorite pair of nude pumps to work and save the spikes for dinner. The pearls were replaced with a simple gold and amber teardrop necklace. Nope, she didn't want to get too fussy for Kyle. She wasn't even sure there was any fire left for him, or if he had any for her, but the dinner would be a good indicator.

Mancinucci's was busy, but somehow, Kyle had been able to secure a booth toward the back. He was always a wink and big-tip kind of guy. The place was known for their low light and booths with tall seatbacks to afford extra privacy. Table candles added to the ambiance. "Whenever I've been here, I've wondered how many of the women were wives or mistresses or somewhere in between," Carrie said, looking from booth to booth.

"I never thought of that. Just a great place for a good meal," Kyle said. Carrie ignored his foot against her leg and wrapped her feet under the seat of the booth.

"So tell me about your job. And certainly, you found someone else?" Carrie asked, noticing he wasn't wearing a wedding band.

"I've been really lucky at work. No complaints there. And I met Kristin right after I got to Colorado, I knew it was sort of a rebound relationship because I always loved you, ya know, but she was a snowboarder like me and we just connected, and then she got pregnant, and we got married. Our son is almost three, and you should see him on skis already. I love him, man. Then our daughter came fifteen months later, and now, she's entered the princess phase."

"So, are they here with you?" The upturn of her voice was part curious and part anticipation.

"Kristin and I are having a hard time, and she wouldn't move back here with me. Wanted to stay near her family. Where have I heard that before?" Kyle pulled out his phone and showed several pictures of his children. Carrie was sad there were none of Kristin.

"They're darling. Your son looks just like you."

"What can I say? Lucky kid." His voice dropped with the disappointment of a lonely man.

"I'm sorry it didn't work out with Kristin. Maybe it still will someday."

"Thanks," he said, giving his shoulders a shrug and looking aside to the next booth. I'll go back once a month for work, so I'll be able to see the kids." He drew a big drink from his martini. "And how about you? I don't see a ring, so I take it you're not married."

"I have a wonderful life. I love my job, I'm still in the same condo, I'm still the reigning tennis champ, so life is good."

"No man in your life?"

"I've been dating a great guy, but it's too soon to tell if it's going anyplace."

"You know, I bought a boat as soon as I came back. Wanna go out with me on Saturday?"

"I have tennis at 8:00, but I could be ready by 11:00. Would that still work?"

"Perfect."

Carrie smiled at his response. She liked perfect. By the time the evening was done and Giovanni had serenaded them, Carrie was more relaxed than she'd been since she'd run into him a few days earlier. The wine, no doubt, helped as well, but she stayed with her two-glass limit.

Always the gentleman, Kyle walked her to her car and opened the door for her. "A kiss. Just for old times." Carrie felt his tongue explore the inside of her mouth, while he held her tight. She didn't pull away.

"I'll pick you up at 11:00 on Saturday. I think I can still find the place."

Carrie drove home with her head in a bit of a fog. That was the impact of Kyle, and she knew it. She had such conflicting feelings for him and wasn't sure why she had accepted the boat ride invitation so quickly, but he was decisive, and she loved his attention.

By the time she got home and out of her dress clothes, it was too late to do anything outside, so she sat on her floor and did some stretching, much to the amusement of her cats. She was missing her yoga and excited to get back into it after Labor Day.

It was just Tuesday, and Rob hadn't called or even texted yet, and she wondered if he would. He wasn't very good at that, but maybe she would text him just to let him know she was thinking of him. She really needed to know how he felt about her and whether he was thinking of her as much as she found herself thinking of him.

After putting on her workout clothes, she lit the candles on her mantle and got into the lotus position on the floor of the living room. The room began to fill with the scent of a lemony lavender as she began her breathing exercises, taking long, slow breaths in through her nose, filling her lungs. She exhaled slowly through her lips, working to relax the muscles in her face, jaw, neck, shoulders, arms, and stomach. Suddenly, her phone rang and shook her out of her meditative state. She tripped as she reached for it, hoping it was Rob. Instead, it was Maggie, and they talked for almost an hour.

It was the perfect way for Carrie to put a wrap on this day, and Maggie helped her erase the tinges of guilt she felt for seeing Kyle. Yes, she could have dinner with Rob one night and go boating with Kyle the next day. Rob had barely kissed her, then Kyle showed up after a four-year absence and did a tonsil search on the first date. Oh Kyle, why did you have to come back, and Rob, where are we? She'd know more about that on Friday when they had dinner.

She loved talking to her sister, but Maggie was no Rob.

By the time Carrie went to work on Friday morning, Rob hadn't called or texted, and hadn't responded to her text. She was ticked and hurt, and she'd work on her attitude before they met for dinner later that day.

At 10:00, Kyle called and canceled their boating trip Saturday. "Hey, I'm sorry, Babe. I just scored some great tickets to the Brewers game with a couple of guys from work. Maybe another time?"

Carrie relaxed her shoulders. "Sure, that's fine, no problem. But Babe? You called me Babe?" She tapped her pen against her desk like she was a drummer in a band.

"Sorry. Old habit, I guess." Carrie used her free hand and brushed her hair back behind her ear. After they ended the call, she sat back in her chair and sighed. Now she could focus on dinner with Rob.

An hour later, Rob sent her a text. "Going to stay here and go sailing with Phil tonight and the crew tomorrow. Can we do Sunday afternoon?"

Carrie scrunched her face, closed her eyes, and shook her head slightly. Two men and both canceled. After several minutes, she sent a return text. "Nope, won't work. Helping Kim throw a birthday party for Hans."

"How about dinner Sunday night?"

"We'll see," she responded. Carrie felt used and remembered her mother's advice. *Never make a priority of someone who considers you just an option.*

She wasn't sure she wanted to end things with Rob yet, but this wasn't the first time he had canceled.

By the end of the work day, Carrie had mapped out her weekend, and was looking forward to some alone time. She was beginning to second guess the time she'd devoted to dating. Meanwhile, her to-do list had grown, so she'd focus on things around her condo. After tennis, she'd start by attacking the boxes in her basement and sort through everything that had come from her parents' home.

With an open court after her scheduled 8:00 time, she and Wayne played until 10:30. After the vigorous game, she opted for a relaxing massage at the club, and the masseuse focused on her legs. She was going into her final week of match play for the area-wide tournament, and so far, she had a slim lead in her division and wanted to end the season with another title.

By all standards, Saturday was a gorgeous late-summer day in Milwaukee with a warm sun high in a cloudless sky. Temps were in the low 80s with low humidity. Carrie knew they wouldn't have many of these days left, so she scrapped her plans to work in the basement. After a light lunch, she slipped into her bathing suit, loaded up her bag with towels, lotion, and a book, grabbed her sunglasses and hat, and headed to her condo's pool. She walked in her jeweled flip-flops with more purpose, with a little kick in her step, her shoulders back, and confidence leading the way.

Remember, it's better if you leave something to the imagination, her mother had said each summer when Carrie picked out a new swimming suit.

Most days, she heeded her mother's advice. Today wasn't one of them. As she peeled off her cover-up, it was obvious she'd shaken off the two canceled dates when she revealed her sexiest bikini—tangerine orange with string ties.

Several minutes after adjusting her chair and reading a few pages, she tilted her head back to enjoy the warmth on her face. Closing her eyes, she felt relaxed for the first time since Rob had canceled. Kyle's blow-off wasn't as significant, but this was Rob's second offense in a month, and she didn't like it. She was still perplexed why he was in such a funk when they'd gone sailing the week before, and then disappointed when his only text during the week was the cancelation notice on Friday morning.

"Excuse me, is anyone using this chair?" The deep voice shook her out of her melancholy funk.

"No, I don't think so," she responded, then realized, she'd left her bag on the chair. "Oh, sorry. Please," she added, motioning the man to sit down after she tucked the bag under her chair.

"Thanks. By the way, I'm Lorenzo."

Carrie sat up straighter and crossed her legs at the knees, slightly embarrassed at how exposed she felt. She kept that bikini on hand for trips to Mexico, but usually wore something a bit more modest at the cabin or when she sat at the condo pool. "I'm Carrie. It's a great day for the pool."

"Sure is. I've just moved in and glad I could still use the pool this year."

"Welcome. Where'd you move from?"

"Houston, Texas." His voice was smooth and had a southern charm that reminded her of hot caramel on ice cream.

"Well, it's a perfect day for the pool, but wait a few months."

"Are you kidding me? More than anything else, I'm really excited to experience my first snow. I can't wait to ski."

"You've never seen snow?" Carrie had asked.

"Oh, I've seen it. I've never lived with snow."

Carrie and Lorenzo let the conversation between them dance for almost two hours. It was faster than a waltz with your father, but not as hot as a tango with a lover. Finally, after a dip in the pool to cool off, and half an hour sitting on the edge, dangling her feet while she talked to him, she excused herself. By the time she left, she'd agreed to meet him for dinner at 6:00.

Carrie scuttled back to her condo, flopped down on her bed and let the events of the afternoon race through her brain. A sales rep who wanted to learn to ski who exceeded her minimum height requirement—she couldn't wipe the smile off her face. He was a little older than her norm, but it was just dinner.

By the time she showered, washed her hair, and tried on five different tops with her white, ankle-length skinny pants, it was 5:45. She had decided on the light turquoise, gauzy, off-shoulder number that fell just below her waist. Her skin glowed from the sun, and the curls of her hair framed her face and settled on her bare shoulders. A smudge of eyeliner and mascara was the only makeup she needed, except for a swipe of a pale lip gloss.

The doorbell rang, and Carrie felt her eye twitch. Inhaling a deep breath, she opened the door to welcome Lorenzo. They each burst out laughing.

"What would be the chances that you'd wear white Bermuda shorts and a dark turquoise-and-white striped, button-down shirt? This looks too planned," she said as she invited him in. "I'll run up and change."

"We're fine. So what if we look like we should be together."

Carrie swallowed hard and curled her lip as if to say, "I'm not so sure," but settled on a slight shrug and said, "Let's go."

Lorenzo had old-school manners as he opened the door to his sparkling white SUV and held her hand as she got in. She wrinkled her nose slightly to whiff the scent that reminded her of the pine-scented cleanser she used on her kitchen floor. The car whined quietly as he opened the sunroof.

“Let me know if this gets too windy, okay?” His smoky blue-gray eyes were almost as brilliant as his smile. Specks of gray hair peppered his sideburns and temples, and she noticed a pronounced widow’s peak for the first time, as the rest of his dark brown hair fell back into medium-length waves. She wondered how old he was, and didn’t want to ask, but she’d never dated an older man before.

Carrie smiled at him and nodded in agreement.

“I’ve heard about this new seafood place downtown that’s supposed to be really good. Would that be okay with you?”

Carrie hadn’t been there, but was eager to see if it lived up to its reputation. She nodded.

The drive downtown was uneventful and, for that, Carrie was glad. He inquired about her family, and filled her in on his. She hoped her game-face didn’t flinch when he mentioned the ages of his adult children, and by the time she did the math, figured he was almost 20 years older. She had to convince herself it was just dinner, and was glad when they were seated quickly at the restaurant.

“So, I’m sort of a wine snob. How about you?” he said while reviewing the wine list.

“Ah, slightly,” she said chuckling. Actually, she used to be, but these days, two glasses were her absolute limit, and she wasn’t as picky.

“I know this place has a large selection, and I was interested to see the list. I like a nice French Chardonnay.”

Carrie raised her hand to cover her smile and tucked her chin to her chest. The similarities continued, though she wasn’t sure he wasn't just trying to impress her. It was agreed, they'd get a bottle, and it lived up to Carrie's memory. Chardonnay used to be her wine of choice until she discovered it had a higher alcohol than Riesling. The smooth dryness was a great complement to the king salmon crudo they enjoyed, but Carrie wasn't sure she needed to eat raw seafood again.

By the time they were done with the bottle, Carrie was beginning to feel a little light-headed. She excused herself to the women's room, in part to see if she'd heard from Rob. Still no message, and she was disappointed. Of course, she hadn't committed to seeing him on Sunday and knew her "we'll see" response at his request was a bit passive-aggressive. Still, she was disappointed that he hadn't called or texted.

Soon after she returned to the table, the sommelier uncorked another bottle of wine, and Lorenzo raised his glass for a toast. "To a new city and new friends."

Carrie returned the gesture, and felt the warmth of the wine slide down her throat. She used to teeter with drinking too much wine, so she'd been monitoring her consumption over the past couple years. Carrie slowed down, so she could enjoy her phyllo-wrapped whitefish, but the drink was catching up to her.

"Rob, this is delicious. How's yours?" She carefully picked up another bite of food.

Lorenzo held his fork in midair as he looked at her.

Catching his look, she suddenly realized what she'd said, and covered her mouth with her napkin. "I am so sorry. I don't know where that came from, except you remind me of a guy at work named Rob."

"Is he tall, dark, and handsome, as well?"

"Exactly." Carrie continued with her meal. "And modest, too."

"Well, since you asked, my scallops are great. This place lives up to its stars. How about we share some strawberry shortcake for dessert?"

"Oh." She paused. "I couldn't." She stopped to take a deep breath, realizing her words were slightly jumbled. "Really."

"Well, we have to finish this," he said as he held up the half bottle of wine.

Carrie held out her glass for a refill, knowing she'd regret this in the morning.

When they finally left the restaurant, he put his arm over her shoulder to help steady her as they walked to the car. She began to giggle when he reached across her and helped her with her seatbelt. Slowly, he turned right out of the parking lot, and began driving north through the city instead of getting onto the freeway and heading west, as she'd expected. She wasn't sure if it was the wine or her own naiveté, but suddenly, she felt a clenching in her stomach.

She was drunk, in a car going the wrong direction as the daylight faded, with a man she had only met a few hours earlier. She rode for three more blocks doing her best to orient herself with the city she knew very well, but tonight, nothing looked familiar. Her giggles turned into fear. Her head was spinning, and she felt like she might throw up. She gripped the passenger door and tried to put the window down, but it was locked. "Wait, where are you taking me?" she suddenly shouted as they passed Wisconsin Avenue, then Wells Street.

Lorenzo looked panic-stricken as he pulled over into the right lane. "I'm just getting onto the freeway up here. Remember our ramp is closed for construction, and I don't know another way."

"Oh," was all Carrie could say. "I need to go home."

"And I'll take you straight there."

"Can you put the window down a bit for me?"

"Sure, but you control it with that top button."

They rode the rest of the way listening to some classic love songs, while Carrie continued to maneuver her seat between forward and back, reclining and sitting upright, in an attempt to get comfortable. He helped her to her front door and used her key to open it. She took one step inside and assured him she'd be fine.

"This has been a wonderful night, and I'm sorry I got so confused. I don't know how I'm so drunk and you're fine. Thank you, again. Good night, Rob." Her words spilled out, and the last thing she saw was the look of confusion on his face when she closed and locked the door.

Chapter 13

Twelve hours later, Carrie woke to a ringing sound. She hoisted herself up onto one elbow and realized it was her phone, but it wasn't on the charger on her nightstand. She held her head as she fell back onto her pillow, and finally realized the phone was downstairs. Poppy sniffed around her face, and Lila pawed at her hair, trying to get her up. Shielding her eyes from the morning sun, she winced when discovered she was just in her bra and panties. She could see her pajamas hanging in the closet. Her clothes sat in a pile on the floor, neatly folded, but there was no sign of her shoes.

Sitting on the edge of her bed, she rested her elbows on her knees while she cradled her head in her hands. The taste in her mouth reminded her of what Poppy's last hairball smelled like. Mustering the strength to stand, she grabbed her robe and shrieked when she saw herself in the mirror, puffy eyes and smeared makeup. She finally wobbled downstairs to feed her cats, find her phone, and flip the coffee pot on.

Her head throbbing, she worked at remembering the events of the evening, what she ate, and where her shoes were. Suddenly, her phone pinged with a text. It was Rob, and she was overcome with relief. He made her feel so safe.

"Are you okay? I've left messages last night and this morning. I'm worried. Where are you?"

Then she scrolled through the messages he'd left.

6:13 p.m. "Just wanted to say hi. Sorry I didn't call earlier. Hope you had a great week. Looking forward to seeing you. Tomorrow?"

7:37 p.m. "Do you like to go shopping? Would you go with me sometime?"

It just struck her as funny. Do I like to go shopping? "OH, HELL YEAH," she wanted to text back, but showed some restraint. Plus her head hurt. She kept scrolling.

9:14 p.m. "Are you okay? I'm sorta worried."

11:38 p.m. "I'm hoping for the best and that you're alright and didn't find anyone to replace me with. Dinner Sunday?"

She texted back. "Sorry I missed your messages. I'm home. Where are you?" She prayed he was still in Chicago. Not having the strength to call him, she wasn't in a position to even talk to him before she went to help Kim.

"I'll be home by 5:00." By the time they were done texting, it was confirmed he'd come to her condo, and they'd figure out the evening from there. He sounded excited, and more than anything, Carrie hoped she'd feel human by then. She didn't know how to read Rob, or her own feelings, for that matter.

Before she jumped into the shower, she listened to the three voicemails he'd left. A single tear rolled down her cheek. She couldn't remember the last time anyone had expressed so much concern about her.

Running a few minutes late after her nephew's party, Carrie was glad she got home before Rob arrived. While upstairs changing her clothes, she heard the doorbell ring and flew down the stairs to welcome him. Instead, it was Lorenzo, her sandals from the previous evening dangling from his fingers. She thanked him and quickly grabbed the shoes just as Rob was getting out of his car. Unsure how to camouflage the awkwardness, Carrie tossed the shoes into her dining room, and walked Lorenzo to the driveway where she introduced the two men.

"This is my friend, Rob, and Rob, this is Lorenzo. He lives in the condos here."

"Rob, huh? Nice to meet you." Lorenzo reached to shake Rob's hand. "I need to be running along now. Enjoy the evening." Carrie hoped Rob didn't see his wink. Or the shoes.

"New neighbor," she said as she looped her arm through Rob's and led him to her front door.

"So he said."

"Met him at the pool yesterday." She paused as they entered. "Can I get you something to drink? Are you thirsty?"

"No, I'm fine. He had your shoes?" which came out more as a question than a statement. She motioned for him to sit in the living room.

"I know. I left them under my chair at the pool. How stupid of me." As he attempted to sit in the chair, Carrie rushed to move two throw pillows before he sat down. "Those are just for show."

Rob watched fluff the pillows under the window before she sat cross-legged on the couch.

"So, tell me about Chicago. And how was sailing? Did you and Phil have a good time? And did you get to do everything you wanted to do?"

"Chicago is always great, and work is good, but I need some new clothes. Would you like to go shopping with me sometime?"

Carrie closed her eyes and gave her head a slight shake as if trying to comprehend the question. "I'm not sure I follow. How did we jump to that? Should I start making my list?"

They both laughed and the tension disappeared.

"I've been invited to present at the bank's annual meeting, and I need to look more upper management-worthy," he said.

"Are you getting a promotion?"

"Not yet, but when I do, it will definitely be back to Chicago. I'm almost done with what they'd wanted me do in Milwaukee."

"Well, that's exciting. Something to look forward to." She tried to hide the reservation in her voice.

"But for now, I need some new clothes." His voice rose with the excitement of a child.

Rob seemed more self-assured, and what she liked best about him was his calmness, the slowness in which their relationship was developing, and that he demanded so little from her. It was refreshing for her and a change of pace, though her patience was getting a little thin. In the past, she was too quick to form relationships and quick to dismiss them, but Rob was a different guy from any she'd ever dated, and she liked him. And he expected little in return, which pleased her even more. It reminded her of what her mother told her.

Don't lose yourself in a relationship with someone else.

"I'd love to go with you sometime."

"Thanks." Rob sat on the edge of the couch and took one of her hands in his. "I'm sorry I didn't call you last week and then canceled dinner on Friday."

"Thanks. I was hurt, because this is the second time you've done this to me."

"Ouch. You're right. It won't happen again."

"I just don't know where we are," she said, removing her hand from his and sitting back to put some distance between them. "I don't hear from you when I think I'm going to, and you leave me hanging."

Rob slouched and turned to look out the window for a brief moment. His eyes softened as he faced her. "I love spending time with you. You are bright, articulate, kind. You are passionate about your work, and committed to whatever you're going after."

While he paused, Carrie looked down and began to fidget with her hands. She waited for the "but".

"And you're beautiful. It scares me."

They sat in silence for several seconds. Carrie felt a heat rush in her face. She wanted to reach over and kiss him just as she had longed for him to do, but instead, she sat composed.

"I've never had to think about someone else." He dropped his chin, then looked into her eyes like a five-year-old asking forgiveness. "Have patience with me?"

Carrie reached over and hugged him, and held his forehead next to hers as she spoke, her fingers laced behind his head. "This is what I think. You are a great person and have so much to offer. You're just not the best boyfriend." She winced as soon as the words came out.

Rob sighed. He struggled to find the right words. "Does this mean it's over?"

"No, absolutely not, and that didn't come out exactly right. Now let's go get pizza. I'm starving."

His smile was the broadest she'd ever seen, and then he pulled her close for a long, smoldering kiss. Oh yes, she was not letting him go, no matter how much patience she'd need.

As they finished the last of their thin-crust pie, Carrie checked her calendar for the next day. "I'm going to be downtown tomorrow morning for a meeting. Can you do lunch?"

"That would work out. I have a meeting at 2:00, but my morning and lunch are free," he said. "Let's meet just outside my building in the plaza, and we'll find something within walking distance. Will noon work?"

"Noon is perfect." Now she was the one with the wide smile.

Carrie's head still had a dull ache as she lay down for bed that night, but one thing was sure—she and Rob were a thing, and their relationship was moving forward. No more Kyle, and no more Lorenzo, or anyone else, she told herself, only Rob.

After a full morning of meetings on Monday, Carrie looked forward to her lunch date, even though she'd just seen him the night before. It was a short walk from the parking ramp, and just as Carrie was about to take the steps up to the plaza, she saw Rob exiting his building. Immediately, she saw Amy/ Gwendolyn leave her seat at one of the patio tables and quickly approach Rob. What was she doing there? Carrie tried not to be annoyed, but the immediate image of the crazy woman set off alarms in Carrie's head.

Fortunately, neither Rob nor Amy had seen her, so she stood out of sight and watched the exchange. Clearly, Rob was taken by surprise and tried to move past Amy, but the delusional woman thrust a package toward him. He pushed it right back to her, and looked around the plaza.

Carrie decided to make her move, and it was time for her to rely on her chutzpah and take charge of the situation. She hoisted her purse onto her shoulder, lengthened her stride, and scattered the pigeons as she crossed the plaza.

Rob noticed her first and looked either afraid or relieved, Carrie couldn't tell.

Then Amy looked in her direction. Carrie sidled up next to Rob, put her arm through his, pulled him close, reached up, and planted a big, wet kiss on his lips.

"Hi, Amy, I'm Carrie, Rob's girlfriend." She slid her arm to his waist and noticed the shirt Amy was wearing. "Did you go to Minnesota?" Carrie couldn't remember when she'd last worn her shirt like that, but knew she often liked to wear it running near her condo.

Amy smiled at Carrie and replied, "It's Gwendolyn, remember?" She turned her attention toward Rob, ignoring Carrie's question. "Rob, is it true? I thought I was your girlfriend. I bought this present for you. It's a pink shirt, because I thought you'd look really good in pink."

Rob stood there, no words coming from his mouth, as he ran his tongue across the top of his teeth.

Carrie relaxed and let her arm sit looped in his while he kept his hands in his pockets. She tightened her grip and pulled him closer. "You and I both know what a kind and compassionate gentleman Rob is, right? I believe he had dinner with you one time, and it would be easy to think he cared a great deal for you, because that's the kind of man he is—warm and genuine, and he wouldn't hurt a cockroach."

Rob looked like a bobble head. "That's right," he said. "I've tried to tell you that many times. There's nothing romantic between us."

"But I thought...."

Carrie reached out to touch Amy's forearm to reassure her. "It seems like you're a very nice woman, but Rob and I are together now, no matter how much you try to dress like me."

Rob still stood there motionless, but Carrie was convinced he was standing taller, with his shoulders back.

Amy looked toward the ground, dropping her hand with the package to her side. "But I thought maybe if I looked like you…."

"Amy, I'd be happy to give you a ride to your doctor's office or maybe home?" Carrie offered, softening her voice.

"No. I have a bus pass. I'm not sure what to do with this shirt now."

"Where are you living?" Rob asked. Carrie raised her eyebrows and looked at him in disgust and elbowed him in the ribs.

Amy looked up with anticipation. "Why? Will you come and visit me, Rob? Do you want to come to my apartment? I would like that so much. I knew my plan would work, I just knew it. I could cook for you."

"Gwen-do-lyn, Rob and I are going to lunch now, because we both have to get back to our jobs."

Amy slouched and looked away. Turning to look at Rob, her eyes welled up with tears. She said, "But you really would look good in pink."

"Good luck, Amy. Or Gwendolyn," Rob said.

Several steps away as they left the plaza, still with Carrie's arm looped in his, Rob stopped and just massaged his forehead. "I cannot believe you." He let out a big sigh with a small snicker. "You are incredible."

"What is so funny?" Carrie asked. "You didn't say a thing except to ask where she lived."

"I couldn't help it. I was transfixed on the fact that two women were fighting over me. Me! That hasn't happened since second grade when Stacey Larusso and Nikki Beechman both wanted to sit with me, because my mom had thrown an extra bag of Skittles in my lunch. For a minute, I was stuck back in second grade when two girls liked me for my Skittles."

"Well, let's go before I run back and grab that shirt from her. Did you see it? Brooks Brothers shirts aren't cheap." She took him by the hand and led him across the street. "We're going to the Irish Pub just down the street."

"It's too early to drink, you know," he said with a laugh.

"I know, but the minute I get home, I'm having a glass."

"Sounds good. Do you have a second glass?" Rob asked. "Or is it rude to invite myself over?"

"I'll be home by 5:30, and will get two glasses out. And by the way, I agree with Amy," she paused and winked at Rob. "You would look good in pink."

Rob arrived shortly before 6:00, and before he even said hello, he wrapped Carrie in his arms, and they kissed long and luxuriously. Carrie's body tensed, then felt like melting ice cream in his arms.

She led him upstairs into her bedroom. She began to unbutton her blouse and turned to help him with his belt before they fell onto the bed.

It was awkward and clumsy at first until they found the rhythm, but fun and spontaneous, and left both with smiles they couldn't shake.

They lay there for several minutes, her head on his chest, arm around his belly, while he stroked her bare back with his warm hand, neither speaking.

"Do you like to dance?" Rob finally asked.

"Do I like to dance?"

Carrie felt her face freeze as if she'd had too much Botox. For all of her dating life, she'd had men that loved sports and drinking, usually at the same time. She'd endured dances at weddings and was good with the Hokey Pokey, the Chicken Dance, and a drunken Polka, but that was her limit, so no one ever noticed her total lack of coordination. And now, Rob wanted to know if she liked to dance. She shivered as she knew where this was going.

"I love to dance," he continued. "How about you?"

"You love to dance?"

"Yep. I was in a swing dance group at college."

"You were in swing dance?"

"Will you be repeating everything I say tonight?"

"Let me tell you about my dancing. In college, they mocked me. They called me Elaine."

He chuckled with the reference to the *Seinfeld* show. "You can't be that bad at dancing, as good as you are in tennis."

"One does not relate to the other, trust me. Matter of fact, my parents started me in tennis early to help with my coordination. Remember when I tried to dance my way onto your boat the first time? These big feet serve me well on the tennis court, but little else."

"You are so graceful in how you carry yourself. I just imagined you were the same way on the dance floor."

"When I was 11, my mother tried to teach me the Twist, and I tripped and fell over the coffee table. Two days later, I had surgery on my elbow and, to this day, I still wear a brace on that arm when I play tennis. All from my attempt to dance." Carrie broke into her herky-jerky moves to a made-up beat, while lying on the bed.

"Seriously," Rob said between laughs, "Phil and his wife, Ann, have invited us to an end-of-summer party at their boat club on Labor Day weekend, and I thought it would be fun. Would you like to go?"

Carrie repositioned herself so she was propped up on her elbows facing him, wrapping herself in the sheet. She drew a deep breath. "I'd love to. Thanks. It sounds like fun."

"And if you'd like, we could spend a couple of nights downtown, I can show you around…."

Carrie finished his sentence, "And we can do that shopping you mentioned?"

"Michigan Avenue? Downtown Chicago? Not sure if there's any shopping opportunities there."

"Oh, the possibilities. I'm sure I can find some options for us."

"I'm going to be working out of the Chicago office on Mondays and Tuesdays right now, and I need to step up my look. I've been my dragging my heels on this, because you know I don't like to shop or spend money."

"When do you think you'll be back there full-time?"

"Soon. But I'll still be here to teach on Wednesday nights. At least this semester. We're beta testing the last piece of a project I've been leading here. After that, I'm not sure what I'll be working on, but the good news is technology isn't going anywhere, and every week, there's a new issue, so my job security is just that—pretty secure."

Carrie was excited at the prospect of spending the weekend with Rob, but before that, she had an important tennis match on Tuesday. After defending her title, she'd be ready to meet his friends and go shopping, so she could remake him… no, she caught herself. The old Carrie would have continued down that path of thinking she could change him to meet her standards. Now she knew. She wasn't remaking Rob, but merely enhancing the package, at his request. She knew that sounded only slightly better, but Rob was a decent guy who didn't need changing.

Chapter 14

Carrie had made the 90-minute trip from Milwaukee to downtown Chicago only a handful of times, and each trip had been on the train. She'd seen a Cubs game at Wrigley Field, *Wicked* at The Oriental Theater, and visited the Shedd Aquarium with her niece and nephew. She'd never spent a weekend just visiting the sights, shopping, and indulging in deep-dish pizza. When she boarded the train at the station in Milwaukee, she questioned why she'd been content to live her life in and around Wisconsin's largest city, or the family cottage up north. Chi-town had always seemed a bit intimidating to her.

She found a place to sit down at the station and checked the time on her phone, 2:15, 50 minutes before the train left. Closing her eyes and taking a deep breath, she tried to relax, but the shuffle of people hustling past her wouldn't allow it. 2:20. Maneuvering her large suitcase in front of her, she began to slide her feet back and forth. Her phone pinged—a text from Rob. She covered a slight smile with her hand, as if she'd been caught.

"Can't wait to see you. So much to do. We're going to need a longer weekend."

"At the train station, listening to music on my phone. Practicing dance moves."

"Are people staring at you?"

"LOL! Just my feet. Am sitting down."

"Don't tire them out. Big dancing night ahead."

"It will be a sight, but I'm ready." The truth was she wasn't ready to meet his friends at a dance party. Not only was she meeting Phil and his wife, but also his brothers Doug and Tommy, and their spouses, all long-time friends of Rob's. She didn't care who else was there; she loved spending time with Rob and she *was* ready.

By the time the train pulled into Union Station, Carrie realized she had agonized too much over what to take. Struggling to pull her suitcase down the platform and into the station, she caught sight of Rob, hands over his eyes in mock avoidance. "You're just here until Monday," he teased her, laughing as he took her bag.

"I can't help it. I couldn't decide." He stopped her from talking by planting a kiss on her lips.

"Let's go, Gorgeous. I've got a big weekend planned. The hotel is just a few blocks from here, so we're walking."

Carrie fell in step with him once they hit the sidewalk as they slid in with the rest of the people scampering to begin their holiday weekends. She held onto Rob's hand as he led the way, but moved to the side and paused on the bridge crossing the river to enjoy the view.

By the time they got to the hotel, Carrie had a good taste for the walking they'd be doing over the weekend. As Rob opened the door to their room, and she saw the roses and bottle of champagne next to the king-size bed, and the thick terrycloth robes waiting for them, she knew what else they'd be doing. And smiled.

"So now you see my home away from home when I'm down here. Well, the room doesn't usually smell like roses, and I don't have champagne on ice. The bowl of salty nuts? Those I have." His sense of humor helped both of them relax. "I don't exactly have a lake view, but as soon as we step outside, we're near great theaters and restaurants. And I'm a five-minute walk to work." The lightness in his voice told Carrie how much he liked it there.

Carrie spied several brochures on the nightstand and picked one up. "Hmm. Is this on the itinerary this weekend?"

"Remember, I told you I was planning everything? Well, tomorrow morning, I thought it would be fun to do a Segway tour. It takes us along the lakefront, down near the museums, and through Grant Park. Then tomorrow night, I have tickets to Second City. What do you think?"

"Forget what I said before. I think you're the best boyfriend." She threw her arms around his neck. "But I just need to know. What about the shopping?"

Rob laughed. "Oh, yeah. After the Segway, we'll hit the stores. I won't disappoint you; I promise. But now, we need to think about tonight. It should be a fun evening."

"I'll do my best to stay off your feet, I promise."

Carrie began to unpack her suitcase and hang some clothes in their shared closet. "Now I know this might sound crazy, but what are you wearing?"

Rob chuckled. "Are you afraid we'll wear the same thing? Remember, I said it was casual. That's all Phil said."

"Yeah, well, I've seen your casual, and it's slightly different than mine for a boat club dinner party."

"That's fair. I just have navy slacks and a light blue shirt. I have a light-colored blazer in case I need that." He pulled out the blazer from the closet to seek her approval. "Does this work?"

Carrie nodded. She knew her choice of a bright navy pair of pants with a navy and white stripe bias cut V-neck sleeveless top would be safe, regardless of what others might wear. A long, white casual jacket completed her look, and she felt tall and empowered. Letting go of clothing judgement was hard.

Her self-imposed rule for Friday night was to limit herself to only two glasses of wine, and then she'd switch to tonic water with a lime. She could have no repeats of the evening with Lorenzo.

Other party-goers had already filled the private dining room at the boat club when they arrived a few minutes before 7:00.

"There's Ann and the others," Rob said, pointing to a rather non-descript, brown-haired woman who was still carrying the extra baby weight from the three children she'd given birth to. Ann welcomed Rob with a gentle hug, and quickly took Carrie's arm in hers. "And you must be Carrie. We are so excited you're here. Rob has talked about you so much, and it's about time we've met." She quickly commenced with the introductions. Clearly, Ann had the social savvy in that marriage, as Phil stood back, smiled, and said nothing.

Carrie was caught by surprise. Really? What had Rob told them about her? And why did she still feel in the dark most of the time?

"Glad you could make it this year. It should be a good time," Phil said to Rob.

"Looking forward to it." Rob smiled and arched his eyebrows.

Carrie wasn't sure he meant to nod in her direction, but it warmed her, and from that moment, Carrie had a wonderful time throughout the evening. Rob, Phil, and his brothers spent a fair amount of time talking about the racing boat the brothers owned, and she thought it was cute that they named it "We Three Kings," since their last name was King. When the topic changed to a Bears versus Packers football discussion, the brothers ribbed Rob for bowing out.

Ann and the other two wives engaged Carrie about her work, how she and Rob had met, and hobbies she had. They all loved to craft and hoped Carrie did, as well. When Carrie mentioned her love of skiing, one of the women spoke up. "I grew up in Ridgewood with Tommy, and I wish we'd move back just for the skiing every winter." The woman also had a lively career in sales and no children, and Carrie felt more of a connection than with the other two.

As dinner was served, she savored the grilled steak.

"When did chimichurri become a thing?" one of the brothers asked. "What's wrong with just steak?" The other men agreed.

Carrie didn't care. She just loved how the sauce exploded in her mouth.

By the time Monday morning rolled around, Carrie and Rob were both exhausted and ready to make the drive north, even though he'd have to return in the morning. She'd managed not to embarrass either of them on the dance floor, they'd survived their Segways, shopped on Michigan Avenue, and laughed at the improv show on Saturday.

They'd walked hand in hand under the L train, accompanied by its clickety-clack, while nibbling on Garrett caramel corn. On Sunday, they sailed with Phil and his family before ending the day with a barbeque at the home of Phil's other brother, Kevin. It had been a great opportunity for Carrie to meet Rob's hometown friends and their wives and children, and by the time they parted, she felt she'd known all of them a long time.

As they drove through the quiet downtown, he reached over and held her hand. "Next trip, we'll do more sightseeing and, of course, the Northwestern campus, but I'm ready to get back now." Neither talked as they made the drive north, but occasionally, he looked her way and smiled.

"This has been a wonderful weekend. Thanks," she said.

"I sense there's more?"

Carrie chewed on her lower lip. "I hate that you'll be working down here, and I won't see you as much."

"We'll work it out. And I'll make sure I keep my weekends free." He tightened his grip on her hand. "Do you feel like going back out on the water with me when we get back? Make the most of the time?"

She simply smiled, returned the squeeze on his hand, and nodded.

While her love life with Rob was warming up, Marta returned to work the week after Labor Day, earlier than anticipated.

Immediately, Carrie's stomach started to churn as she prepared for her first meeting with Marta on Wednesday, but was well-organized and excited to share the progress on the marketing plan. She wasn't sure how Marta had taken the news that the CEO was keeping the project with Carrie, along with the staff needed to implement it. Marta's new responsibilities were significantly less than before her leave of absence, and Carrie wondered if further reorganization was in the works.

Something was different as she entered Marta's office. The shades were drawn, letting in a filtered light rather than the bright afternoon sun. And instead of perching behind her desk, Marta sat in a chair at an angle with Carrie, as if they were friends gathering for tea.

The lines around Marta's round mouth were softer, but that could have been the lovely rose shade of lipstick she wore instead of her trademark vampire red. Her simple black pants and matching tunic were in stark contrast to the sometimes loud and garish prints she liked to wear. Even her hair, which she'd worn in a dark-brown bob for years, had been stripped of its unnatural color to show some gray highlights and was layered nicely to flatter her apple-shaped face. And she looked thinner. Carrie was now questioning if she'd actually gone to alcohol rehab or maybe a fat camp that included a total makeover. Carrie shared the work she'd done on the marketing campaign.

"This is impressive. Does Jack know about the arrangement with Tillerson's yet? He'll be impressed that you got the area's largest grocery chain to buy into the campaign." Carrie was caught off guard by the praise.

"No. I'm waiting for their VP to give me a proposed roll-out date, so I'll have the entire plan in place to present. Plus, Jack was gone most of last week, and that's when they finally agreed to the proposal." Carrie tried to sound upbeat, but her history with Marta made her suspicious of her superior's recognition.

Carrie had run ideas past Jack throughout the process and he continued to give her the green light, but he hadn't seen or signed off on the final agreement. She knew it was a gamble to present it as a complete done-deal to Marta, but her own confidence had grown over the past few weeks, despite the hiccups she'd had along the way.

"I'm sure this will get his attention. Well done. I presume this copy is for me?"

Just when Carrie had given up all hope, she realized Marta did have some grace. Their conference ended, and Carrie was about to leave her office with her hand on the door.

"Oh, and Carrie?"

Carrie turned to face her.

"I'm sorry things didn't work out between you and your friend from the symphony." The comment dripped from Marta's mouth like sap.

Carrie's face froze. "Ah huh," was all she could say.

"I ran into him at this cute little Thai place a couple of weeks ago."

Carrie could feel her eyes blinking rapidly. "Small, petite woman? Rather animated?"

"Yes, you know her then?"

"Oh yes, he was meeting a long-time friend there." Carrie smiled. "But thank you for mentioning it. We're still good friends." She closed the door behind her.

Carrie couldn't get back to her desk fast enough, and she almost ran the mail delivery guy into the wall as she rounded a corner. "Oops, sorry," was all she could mutter.

For ten minutes, she was consumed with thoughts about Rob. Was that the night he told her he was working late and couldn't do dinner? Now, she knew it was Amy or whatever she was calling herself.

Carrie then shifted her anger toward Marta, and couldn't figure out why the soul-sucking woman would even mention the encounter. She hadn't changed one bit, only her appearance.

Carrie simmered in anger toward both of them.

She ended her day and went home. Luckily for her, Rob was teaching tonight, so she wasn't tempted to call him. She needed to take some time and think about what she even wanted to say.

Carrie had to develop a plan to figure out his relationship with Amy before she saw him Friday evening, and then figure out her own relationship with him. Was she becoming too clingy? She hated women like that and wondered if in her eagerness to land a man, she was a little possessive.

His suggestion to pick up dinner at Wang's on his way to her place Friday was a good idea. She knew it would be better if she brought the topic up at home, but she wasn't quite sure how.

While upstairs changing from her work clothes to her into her favorite pair of jeans and simple pullover, she heard him enter the condo. "Hey Carr, it's me. And your phone's ringing."

"No problem. Just let it go. I'll be right down." She knew she'd left it on the kitchen counter and would check it later. All she wanted to do was spend the evening with Rob, and get a sense of where they were.

Her goal to remain coy and slightly aloof fizzled as soon as she got downstairs; Rob was waiting for her with roses and an inviting embrace and kiss. "I missed you this week. More than I had imagined. It's really good to see you."

Carrie took the carry-out and placed it on the table, while Rob grabbed a beer from the fridge. The garlic from the Kung Pao chicken made her eyes water, and she was excited to eat.

There was finally a lull in the conversation as they filled in each other with their week's events. All of a sudden, Carrie blurted it out. "Hey, Marta told me she saw you and Amy at the Beau Thai a couple of weeks ago." Carrie had meant to wait and put more thought into it, but there it was, out of her mouth.

Rob continued to eat without looking up. "Yeah, I knew she saw me. I should have said something, I guess. I thought Amy was serious about getting help, so I offered to meet and drive her. I was the fool." Neither said anything.

"Umm. I was just curious." Carrie looked at him. "Was this the night you told me you were working late?"

Rob looked confused. "No. It was a night you had something for work." He kept eating. "I have no interest in her. I just feel sorry for her, because she has no one else, and she needs help. But she's still in denial, and I can't do anything about that."

"So, do you talk with her often?"

"Occasionally, I did. This was right after the 'pink shirt on the plaza' scene."

"I was just wondering."

Rob placed his napkin on the table next to his plate, took a long drink of beer, and looked at Carrie. "Are you suggesting I should have let you know? Or asked your permission?"

Carrie shrugged. "Not at all. I'm just thinking that Amy hasn't given up trying to win your heart and maybe you haven't closed the door on it."

"Come over here." Rob stood up, walked around the table to her chair and led her to the couch. "You can't tell me you're jealous of Amy?"

"Wait, let me move this. I don't want it to get dirty." She reached and removed a decorative throw, so they wouldn't lean against it.

Rob responded with his own eye-roll, then pulled her down next to him and put his arm around her shoulders "I don't care for her at all. I do, however, care a great deal for you. I may not say it enough, but I do. But you have no reason not to trust me, I promise." He nuzzled the top of her head with his chin. "Can you promise the same to me?"

She sat up and looked at him with a questioning look. "Of course. Why?"

"Because that was Kyle who called and left a message on your phone." His voice was low and filled with doubt.

Carrie sat back and cuddled into his arm and shoulder. “Kyle was an old friend, and he left the area several years ago, but has come back to Milwaukee for work. I ran into him at a work function, but there’s nothing there. Besides, he’s married and has two kids. Nothing to worry about. No interest.” She hoped Rob didn’t feel her heart flutter.

“Umph.” Rob didn’t sound convinced, but the subject was dropped, and Carrie was glad.

Chapter 15

When news of a potential merger grew stronger, Carrie had held back on the new marketing campaign, and didn't panic when her contact at Tillerson's was slow to respond. She knew how business worked. But when the marketing director called to confirm in mid-September, Carrie quickly arranged a meeting with Jack for his final approval on the plan.

Surprisingly, when she arrived for the meeting, Marta was already in the office sitting at Jack's conference table, with her copy of the plan Carrie had given her. Jack invited Carrie to sit at the head of the table, and he sat in the chair directly across from Marta. Sitting as tall in the chair as she could, Carrie gave a copy of the plan to Jack. He studied the colored charts and graphs showing anticipated revenues and expenses, target audience projections, and long-term benefits for the hospital.

"Carrie, I'm slightly confused. Except for great visuals and a couple of other things, yours is very similar to the plan that Marta gave me last week. I didn't know the two of you collaborated."

Carrie was glad he kept leafing through the proposition. She felt her spine compress and her left eye begin to twitch, as she covered her throat with her left hand to hide the tendons that were about to pop from the stress. She took a deep breath and cocked an eyebrow as she looked at Marta, who remained focused on Jack. Finally, Carrie took a deep breath, straightened up, and exhaled.

"I started working on this in July as soon as you handed the project over to me. I touched base with you on a couple of the items back throughout July and August, but I didn't have the timetable or final financial figures in place then."

Marta squirmed in her chair, and gave her hand a slight wave. "I don't know that it matters who did what. This plan has many moving parts and will take everyone's best efforts to implement it. I spoke with Tillie on the phone about the partnership just last week. You know, our families are friends and go way back since our kids were in school together."

"Carrie, who was your contact? And did you ever call Mr. Tillerson yourself?"

"I began working with their marketing director, who I know. But no, I never spoke to Mr. Tillerson on the phone." She looked at Marta, then back to Jack. "Instead, I met with him, along with his top people in finance and external affairs. When I was finished, he asked me to meet with his wife, since she runs the family foundation, and I did earlier this month. They were looking at different options to support the plan, and also wanted to run it past legal, and I've just been waiting for their VP of Marketing to call and confirm the proposal."

Jack looked between the two women, and then back to the plan Carrie had presented. "Tell me about this app you're suggesting. Is that in addition to the one we already have?"

Carrie elaborated on her team's effort to design a new app that included both a children's nutrition game as well as a donor option. "I worked with our tech team and an outside source to come up with this price. It can be a stand-alone or we can upgrade the hospital's current app."

"The hospital's average donor is 78 years old. I highly doubt they'll be attracted to an app," Marta said.

"I'll look this over, Carrie. Thanks for your forward thinking, and I'll be in touch. I have to hand it to you, you really took me for my word when I gave you the assignment and told you to run with it. I like that. Now, Marta and I have some other business to discuss."

Carrie thanked Jack and felt good about his comments, but was furious with Marta as she returned to her office. Never had anyone blind-sided or undercut her like that. She hoped her face hadn't turned as red as she felt. It seemed the God of Career Changes had struck her, and despite everything else on her calendar that day, she logged on to her professional organization's website as soon as she sat down at her desk, and began to search for other jobs. She was immediate past president of the group and had numerous connections, both local and national. She was not going to wait out Marta's departure and couldn't work for someone who had such little regard for her.

She was eager to tell Rob about this when they met later that day for their weekly dinner. If only she could hear Jack's discussion with Marta.

Carrie was glad she'd gotten to the pub before Rob did. It was already crowded and noisier than she wanted, and, in the future, she'd remember this was "burger and beer special" night. Fortunately, she grabbed one of the last booths away from the door and the bar.

She continued to replay the meeting with Jack, and Marta's reaction to his suggestions. As soon as Rob arrived, she began regurgitating the story, pausing just long enough to place her order with the server, adding a side of testiness.

"I'd be happy to come back if you're not ready."

"No, I'm sorry. We're all set," Carrie said, as she placed her order with laser focus. "And I'll stick with the water." The server smiled to acknowledge her order and looked at Rob.

"Umm. Do you recommend the big chief burger or the double decker?" He continued to look at the menu.

"Well, it just depends on how hungry you are and what you like on your burger."

"Oh gosh, I'm just not sure...."

Carrie tipped her head down and looked at him.

He returned her gaze. "I had a roast beef sandwich for lunch. I can't decide. My mother always said not to have—"

"Would you like me to come back?" the server asked again.

Carrie kept her stare focused on Rob, and began to flick the nail on her right index finger. Finally, he looked at her, then to the server.

"Nope, I'm good. The chief burger it is, with the works."

"Will that be all?"

"That's good," Rob said. "Wait, I need a Blue Blade Ale as well."

"I'll get this right out for you."

"Sorry. Now back to Marta," Rob said, his voice apologetic. Sitting taller in the seat, he continued. "I'd be ticked, as well. She's a self-serving woman who stole your work."

"But it's not just that. She never gives me the recognition. Even with the financial success of the garden party, she gave credit to Dwight for the donors that were there." Carrie tried to hide the resignation in her voice. She sat back in the booth and sighed, but had her eyes focused on the table.

Rob kept his eyes on her, but she remained silent. "She's threatened by you. Are you serious about looking elsewhere?"

"I don't know."

The server delivered his beer, and Rob took a long draw from the bottle.

Carrie shook her head and turned her gaze across the restaurant. "I'm not sure what I'm going to do. It was a perfect position, but now… I'm not even sure "perfect" exists. Or is worth it. I mean, some days she'll…."

Rob leaned on the table with both forearms and stared straight at Carrie. "First of all, what she did to you stinks. But…you've got to think this over." Rob's voice trailed until Carrie finally looked at him. "You've said you don't think she's going to be around much longer. On one hand, I'd tell you to ride it out, knock this marketing campaign out of the park, and then look for a new job. On the other hand—"

"On the other hand, what?" Carrie was close to argumentative as she interrupted.

"Let me finish." Carrie could tell by his tone, he was perturbed. "On the other hand, I say expand your search to Chicago."

Carrie looked at him as if he was practicing his Mandarin.

Rob squinted back at her, but said nothing.

Carrie was glad the server delivered the food, and they ate in silence for several minutes. Finally, she spoke. "Chicago? All my connections are in Milwaukee. I wouldn't even know where to start." She ate another bite. "Chicago? Hmph."

"Well, no job is perfect, and besides, you know how I feel about perfection. It's vastly overrated," Rob said. He had lowered his voice, making it hard for Carrie to hear. She leaned closer. "You can chase it forever, and miss what's in front of you. What makes something perfect to begin with? And what happens when something's perfect today, but imperfect in a week?"

"Good questions. I'm not sure I can answer. I used to think I knew what perfect was, but I guess now I can just say what perfect isn't sometimes."

Rob reached over and held her hand. "Let's just try to enjoy life and trust things will work out." Rob drained the last of his bottle of beer.

By the time they finished their dinner, he walked her to her car, and they kissed good night. Carrie was no longer distressed about the scene with Marta and whether she should look for a new job.

She noticed some of the trees beginning to change colors as she drove into her neighborhood. "Chicago?" she said aloud as she pulled in to her garage. Shaking her head, she couldn't imagine leaving Milwaukee.

The following Thursday night, they met for dinner at Fran's, a good neighborhood diner a block off Bluemound Road that was about halfway between the two of them. They sat in their vinyl upholstered booth unbothered for a couple of hours while she enjoyed her Greek salad and he savored his chicken pot pie.

"I'm not sure if I told you, but I'm headed back home next weekend," Rob said. "Matter of fact, I'm taking Friday off. It's my annual trip back to help my dad take his boat out of the water for the season."

"You don't sound too excited."

"It's my penance for leaving Michigan, and every trip home, it's the same old discussion. Why don't I want to take over the family business? Why didn't I take pride in being the fourth generation of Linders in the engineering firm?"

"So why don't you?" Carrie was curious. She'd read up on Ridgewood since she'd met Rob, and it sounded like a vibrant, charming Midwestern college town. With its miles of shoreline along Lake Michigan, it attracted thousands of tourists in the summer to walk the miles of sandy beaches, swim in the lake, and climb the nearby sand dunes. The winery tours especially appealed to her. Cozy shops and restaurants lined the main street, and large, old homes sat majestically atop the ridge. She had envisioned Rob learning to sail when she looked at the pictures of the bay, and could see the setting sun when she read about their amphitheater that overlooked the lake. She attributed it all to photojournalism at its best, but it still looked like a nice town of 40,000, about the same size as her hometown of Birchfield.

His story spilled out easily. If it weren't for his dad, he may have been content to stay in Ridgewood, but he'd worked for three years at the company and decided that wasn't his future. Besides, he just couldn't work for his dad. Rob's father and grandfather were the hard-working, tough, negotiating type. They didn't tolerate excuses, demanded the best of their employees, and weren't hesitant to sever ties with business partners or employees who didn't meet their standards. They were also generous to Ridgewood with numerous gifts over the years, active in community affairs, and recognized loyalty and hard work among their employees. They just liked to hold their compassion close to their chests, so close they often forgot to reveal it to their children.

"Besides, I'm a tech geek and needed to move to a bigger market, so I headed to Chicago at the urging of Phil."

Carrie sensed there was more by the way he looked off in the distance, the lapse between sentences, and the gentle glide of his tongue between his gum and upper teeth, but she didn't push.

"I've always been grateful the bank took a chance on me just as I was beginning to focus on cyber security. They even supported my Master's at Northwestern, and when they promoted me and transferred me to Milwaukee, it was a strong vote of confidence."

They both sat in silence, and Carrie didn't want the evening to end.

"Sometime, maybe you could meet my family. How do you feel about that?" he asked.

"You mean, as in go back with you for a weekend?" That seemed like so much more of an effort than a two-hour encounter while loading furniture into a truck, she thought. And it implied a real relationship. Was she really ready for that? Wait. Yes, they were in a real relationship.

"Well, not for a while. I have to sell them on the idea first that I have a girlfriend." Rob raised his eyebrows and chuckled. "They won't know how to react—it's been a while. But maybe this winter, and then you could check out the ski hills in that area, see if they're up to your standards."

"I think that sounds like something we can talk about," Carrie said as she squelched feelings of anxiety in her stomach.

"You and my mother will really hit it off, I'm sure."

Slowly, Carrie found a big smile cross her lips. She liked the idea, the more she thought about it. "By the way, my cousin is getting married at the end of October in Green Bay. Would you like to go with me? It will be crazy and fun."

"Sure. I've not been to Green Bay."

They paid their server and walked toward her car. The yellow glow of the lights in the parking lot illuminated their way.

He pulled her tightly, kissed the top of her head, and held her. "I'm a changed man, Carrie. And all for the good. Thank you.

Even the guys at work say I'm a different guy. More assertive. Even more outgoing. Maybe I just needed to hang out with a beautiful, talented woman."

"Well, I'm not going anyplace."

She returned his kiss, and let her lips linger on his longer than in the past. It was a perfect ending to her day.

Chapter 16

With a cool breeze coming off the lake, Carrie knew the fall weather would soon yield to biting temperatures and snow. It was a quiet Saturday for her with Rob in Michigan and Charlie and his family at the Badger football game. Carrie had put away her tennis racquet after she'd aggravated her elbow at the end of the tennis season and knew only time would heal it, so for the first time since June, she had the entire weekend to catch up on reading and knitting and watching sappy movies on TV. She loved dating Rob, but did miss some of her own time.

Late Saturday afternoon, she called her Aunt Katharine in Atlanta. The two of them had been close when Carrie was a little girl after Carrie spent the summer with her when she was five and her mother was at "camp." For the next several years, Aunt Katharine would visit Carrie's family for a month at their home in northern Wisconsin to escape the hot Georgia sun. During those visits, Aunt Katharine introduced Carrie to Scrabble, and together they'd read classics like *Anne of Green Gables*.

Mostly, Carrie remembered the lessons her aunt taught from the finishing school she ran in Atlanta, and the tea parties they'd have with fancy finger foods and desserts. She especially liked the cheese straws and cucumber sandwiches on the dark bread. "Cocktail bread," her aunt said, with an air of sophistication not often found in Birchfield. By the end of the first summer, Carrie drove her family crazy when she responded, "Yes ma'am" or "I'd be delighted" any time they asked her to do something. "That would be divine" came two years later.

When Carrie was 11, Aunt Katharine's advice took a turn toward Carrie's future. "You can be whatever you want as long as you're a lady first and a good wife, second."

When she was 12, Carrie's mother who had tired of having to tame her youngest daughter after every one of Katharine's annual visits, overheard her unsolicited advice. "Enunciate each word. We have to make sure you are ready for the finest of families, so when you meet the right man, you won't embarrass yourself."

Carrie's mother launched into her older sister. "My youngest daughter will never be an embarrassment to anyone." She wrapped her arms around Carrie's shoulders, whose mouth dropped open as she witnessed the zigzag between her mother and aunt.

"But she needs to be ready by the time she's 20 or the good ones will most likely be gone, and she should never be willing to settle for second best."

"Where on earth did you come up with that?" Carrie's mother asked, clearly annoyed with her sister. "Grandma Belle would be appalled at you."

"I have many Southern friends who assure me that still today, a woman should be walking down the aisle by the time she's 24. Heaven forbid, one of my friends has a sister who still isn't married at 40. Bless her heart. That's just not right, and something must be wrong with the woman. I am merely teaching your daughter to be particular and ready."

"I think it's good that God never blessed you with children."

Aunt Katharine winced, and Carrie's mother tried to apologize as soon as the words left her mouth. Like a lady, Carrie left the room.

That was the last of Aunt Katharine's summer visits, and it wasn't until Carrie's mother was losing the battle with cancer that the two sisters spent significant time together. They were friendly over the years, but it took almost 15 years for the bond of sisterhood to be strengthened again.

Upon the death of Rita Belle Klamerschmidt, Carrie and her Aunt Katharine reunited, though by now, Carrie could shrug off most of her aunt's subtle suggestions and inquiries. Carrie liked to call her every month to stay in touch, to check on how she and Uncle Tony were doing, mostly because she was the last connection to her mother's family.

"Oh, Honey Child, it is so good to hear your voice. How is my precious niece?"

"Aunt Katharine, exactly how long have you lived in Atlanta?"

"Why, Sweetie, we've been here 40 years. Why do you ask?"

"Because your Southern drawl gets stronger every year," Carrie said. They both started laughing.

"Oh, Sugar, it's been part of me for a long time now. But enough about that. How are you doing?"

Carrie filled her in on the challenges at work, and the possibility that she might look for another job. "Your mother raised you to be strong and independent, bless her heart. I know whatever you do, you'll be fine."

Carrie ignored the subtle stab at her mother.

"Now tell me, are you still seeing your gentleman friend?"

Ah. To the heart of the matter. "He's a wonderful guy, and yes, we are still together."

"Any closer to walking down the aisle? Should I be shopping for the perfect dress to wear? It will be a *very* special occasion, worthy of celebration."

"If and when that happens, I'll send a hand-delivered message. Will that be sufficient?" Carrie finished with a light laugh.

"Now, Sweetie, I'm just concerned."

"Don't worry about me, Aunt Katharine," Carrie snickered. "My mother raised a strong and independent woman, remember? I am just fine."

"All right, then. But I do hope it's in my lifetime."

Carrie was glad her aunt couldn't see her stick out her tongue at the phone in disgust. She made sure her 74-year-old aunt's health was still excellent before she ended the call. Her aunt had worked hard at dismissing her rural Wisconsin roots, which always confused and disappointed Carrie and the rest of the family.

Saturday evening, Maggie called, and they needed an entire hour to catch up with each other.

"With everything that's going on with Rob, I still hear some hesitation in your voice," Maggie said.

"I love my life," Carrie responded. "Sometimes I just feel like it's a little too routine, a little mundane. Maybe I'm too unrealistic about relationships, but I just feel ours could use a little pizazz. Some spontaneity."

"Be careful what you wish for, Carrie, and remember, you like to be completely in control. There's nothing wrong with a dependable, stable relationship. What did mom used to say? 'Be happy when the horse is in the barn. You know he's not out playing the field then.' It didn't quite make sense, but I knew what she meant."

"You're right, and I don't know why I'm being so picky."

"I know why. You're falling in love with this guy, and that scares you."

Carrie didn't respond, and scratched her head as she processed what Maggie had said. When she ended the call, she continued to ponder the suggestion, and asked herself why she could be scared. And *why* was she still single? Was that so bad? Of course, it wasn't, but she was ready to try the alternative. As relationships got a little more serious, she feared the intimacy—not the physical kind, but rather the emotional. And the fear of losing her independence.

Carrie, do not change who you are to make someone else happy. But don't expect a perfect man, either—we all have flaws, including you.

Recalling her mother's advice reminded her that every man comes with flaws. And so did she.

She looked around the condo as if its comfort would quiet her restless soul. Soon, she realigned the table runner, cleaned the tall, glass cylinders around her candles, and dusted every surface, making sure everything was in perfect order. Before she went to bed, she fluffed the pillows on the couch and arranged the magazines on the coffee table until the room looked like a furniture showroom.

She started up the stairs, paused, and turned to look around the first floor. Thank you, Mother, for this focus on order and perfection, but ultimately, it's a waste of time and energy.

Carrie was settled on the couch to watch her favorite football team and looking forward to the late afternoon and evening with Rob as soon as he got back from Michigan on Sunday. The sky looked threatening, as the trees rained leaves of reds, golds, and oranges from the stiff breeze. She hoped he'd get there in time to go for a short walk along the trail. Ever since they were last together, she'd done a preliminary job search and wanted to bounce some ideas around with him. His calming disposition always helped her feel more at ease about work.

When Rob finally called about 3:00 Sunday afternoon, he was less than an hour from her place. "You won't believe what I bought. You'll be so surprised; I can't wait to show you. I hope you like it."

"Oh, give me a hint." Please let it be the spice she was looking for in her life.

"No hints. But I think you're going to love it."

"So I just have to wait?"

"I'll be there soon."

Carrie loved surprises. She tucked her knitting into its own storage bag, placed Rob's favorite beer mug in the freezer, and brushed the loose cat hair from the couch. Next, she cleared the dining room table, so there was plenty of room for him to show off the new purchase. He didn't mention it was for her, yet her mind slid in that direction immediately.

As soon as she heard his car in the driveway, Carrie ran out the door. But the hug she'd been waiting for was replaced by Rob's double-handed high-five to the air above his head. Or was he having a spiritual awakening? She couldn't tell.

"I'm not sure I've seen this side of you before. You're almost giddy!"

"Oh, you'll understand why. Come here. Wait, cover your eyes first." Rob put his big, gnarly hand over her eyes.

Carrie got so excited, she felt her hormones firing on all cylinders. He took her hand and led her to the back of his SUV, and she wanted to scream, "Take me now!"

He took his hand away from her face. "Isn't it cool?"

She did like the bright blues and greens, but beyond that, she had no words. She blinked slowly and swallowed hard.

"A kite?" *Oh, shit*, she screamed on the inside.

"Well, not just a regular kite, but a stunt kite, and it's a lot like a sailboat, just without the water." He pulled out the kite and put it together so she could see it more closely. "There were some people on the beach on Saturday, and I walked down there after I was done helping my dad with the boat. Before I knew it, this guy let me fly one of his. It was incredible."

"A kite," she repeated, no longer a question, but rather a statement of disbelief. *Take me now* was replaced with her mother's knock on her bedroom door when she and her high school boyfriend were supposed to be studying for their senior exams. The mood was killed.

"I was there all afternoon; I bought one from a vendor who was there. I think you'll like it—it's a great upper-body workout."

"I was not prepared for you to say a kite, but yeah, sure. I'll try it sometime." She wasn't sure what would relieve the mundaneness of her life, but she was certain it wasn't kite-flying.

"What about now? We can walk up to the clearing in the park."

"Hang on. I hear my phone ringing. Let me run to grab it." Carrie ran back into the condo, saw it was Kyle, and clicked her phone off. She took a deep breath and rejoined Rob who was untwisting the kite's tail. Walking along the trail to the neighboring park, they filled each other in on their weekends, but Carrie's thoughts were elsewhere. She couldn't shake her mind off Kyle and wondered why he was calling. He would never be this childlike over a couple sticks and some colorful paper attached to a ball of string. Somehow, she missed when Rob told her about his plans to work in Chicago the next week.

"So, Thursday night, I'll make something delicious," she said. "Maybe my mom's meatloaf."

Rob stopped walking and looked at her with a confused expression. "No. I'll be in Chicago all week except for my class on Wednesday. Didn't you hear what I just said?" The agitation in his voice reminded her of a dull knife cutting through a tough steak.

"Sorry. Too much on my mind, I guess." Carrie bent over and picked up a leaf. "Look at this. Between the color and the shape, it's perfect."

Rob took the leaf and flipped it over. "You see those spots? Fungus. So much for being perfect."

Carrie clenched her jaw and started to walk. "Well, I think it's still beautiful." She dropped the leaf and kicked it into a small pile along the trail.

"You're right. Sorry. I can already feel the effects of working both places and teaching, and I hope you'll be patient with me."

"Of course." She let her chin drop. He took her hand in his, and kissed it. She couldn't stay irritated with him.

"I promise you'll have me all next weekend. How's that?"

"I'll pencil you in from Friday night through Sunday, okay? But it's starting to rain. Maybe we can find a better time and place to test out the kite. I'd really like to give it a try."

"Tell you what. I'll race you back to the condo," he said. Before the words were out, Carrie was gone and quickly built a 15-step lead. He caught up with her as they finished the quarter-mile run. "That's not fair. The kite was dragging me back."

"Excuses, excuses. Don't blame it on a kite." She gave him a quick jab.

"Hey, I hope you don't mind—"

"You go home. I know you have stuff to do before you head out tomorrow. We'll have plenty of other time together."

"You sure you don't mind?"

"Not at all. But if I finish second to a kite…."

Rob laughed and kissed the top of her head. "I'll call you later."

Carrie watched him pull away and smiled as he waved goodbye. She'd find another time to tell him about her job thoughts.

Stepping inside, she had a call to return. She closed her eyes and took a deep breath. She'd never been able to resist Kyle. Could she now?

"Hey, Kyle, I just got your call." Within five minutes, they'd made dinner plans for the next night after work. This time, he wanted to cook for her and show off his place, sort of an apology for taking so long to call her back.

"How about we just meet at Sparky's? Do you remember where that is?"

"Ah, you don't want any of my home cooking? I bought a special bottle of wine just for the occasion."

Carrie tried to keep her devilish chuckle to herself. "Oh, I'm sure you can find other special occasions. But I prefer Sparky's. 6:00?"

"I'll see you then," Kyle said, his words dropped like a bucket of wet cement.

Carrie usually felt fresh and relaxed at the start of the week, but Monday morning was different. She had thrashed all night while she tried to sleep, and when she looked at herself in the mirror, she wondered how her hair had so much fun during the night while she hadn't. The dark rings under her eyes confirmed she needed more sleep.

Kyle was everything Carrie used to hope for in a man, and when she ran into him in August, her heart had done cartwheels, and her stomach, back-flips. It was obvious, he was still gravitating toward flash and fun, but she could also tell there was something missing in his life, and she'd never be able to fill it. Despite his charm and dynamic personality, he'd never know the true joy that would come from an afternoon of kite flying. Later that morning, she called and canceled their dinner date. She suddenly felt refreshed.

It was after 9:30 that evening when Rob called. She loved hearing his voice before she went to bed. Her heart was at peace, and she knew patience was the best option for her.

"I know we're both tired, but I just want to remind you of my cousin's wedding coming up. Are you still willing to meet the rest of the Klamerschmidt clan?"

"Willing and able."

The time couldn't fly by soon enough, as far as Carrie was concerned. It would be the first big introduction with all of the family together at one time.

Chapter 17

The wedding would be a larger test for Rob. The entire Klamerschmidt clan would be there—her own family plus all four aunts and uncles, 15 cousins, and now, more second cousins than Carrie could keep track of.

Finally, it was the day of Dana's wedding. After Carrie and Rob pulled out of the city and passed the sprawling suburbs and bedroom communities, their route paralleled Lake Michigan as they headed north. The sky was overcast with breaks of sun, and one lone sailboat bobbed along the horizon, holding its own with the whitecaps.

It was a beautiful day for the two-hour drive, and Carrie had planned plenty of time so they could meet her immediate family for a light lunch before the 2:00 ceremony. They'd met Rob when he helped Carrie pick up the furniture, but that was a simple test. The next 24 hours would be a lot of family time, and all she wanted was for them to like him—and for him to feel the comfort and warmth of her family. As long as they arrived according to her schedule, Carrie could remain in a stress-free zone.

"That guy better be careful or he's going to get caught in the storm," Rob said, referring to the lone sailor on the lake.

"How do you know it's going to rain?"

"Sailors know that stuff. Those clouds, the smell in the air. And it feels heavier."

Carrie noticed Rob kept a close eye on the water until she reminded him that the traffic had begun to slow down.

"Earth to Rob. The traffic ahead is stopped."

He hit the brakes, causing the car to slightly swerve onto the shoulder. When he resumed driving in their lane, he turned to her and flashed a nervous smiled. "It's all good. Sorry."

Finally, they came to a brief stop, and Carrie remained calm. The traffic began to move and then stopped again, and she began flicking the tips of her fingernails. For two more miles, it repeated the starts and stops until they came to the next exit and were directed off by a state policeman. Rob checked the GPS in his car and, though most of the traffic turned right after the exit, he turned left.

"Do you know where you're going?" Only a residue of calmness remained in her voice.

"Not exactly, but if I just zigzag a bit to the west and then north, we can meet the highway up here," he said pointing to the map displayed on his dashboard.

One mile later, Carrie wasn't convinced. "I see a bar up there. Do you think we should stop and ask? You know, just to be sure?"

"No, we're good."

Several minutes later, after passing farmers getting the last of their corn fields harvested, the blue dot on their GPS indicated they were in a location where there were no roads. Rob's plan had gone off track.

"Really, please, stop and ask at this store ahead. Obviously, the GPS doesn't know everything. I don't want to be late." The anxiety in her voice should have been a warning to Rob.

"Honey, relax. I just have to get over to this route and it's a clear shot." Rob was trying his best to remain light and upbeat. "Hey, I've got a joke for you. Speaking of corn, what did Baby Corn say to Mama Corn?"

Carrie was not amused, glanced at Rob, then stared ahead.

"Where's my popcorn?"

"You're kidding me, right?"

"I've got another one. Why did the orange stop running? He ran out of juice."

Carrie moaned. By now, she wanted to open the door, jump from the moving car, and run through the field. Instead, she pulled an emery board from her purse and was working on a nail.

The tension in the car was increasing every mile they drove. Fifteen minutes early was late for her, and his attempts at humor weren't working. The cushion she'd built into their schedule had evaporated. Adding to the joy of the trip was the smell of the freshly fertilized field they passed.

"I've got one more for you. What did the right eye say to the left eye? Between us, something smells." Rob chuckled until he noticed Carrie blotting her eyes.

"I'm sorry, Carrie. There's nothing we can do about it now except to make the most of it. It will be all right. Just loosen up a bit, will you? Let's have some fun."

Carrie bristled at the suggestion, but bit her tongue. Finally, they came upon a small town, and Carrie could tell by Rob's sigh that he was as relieved as she was.

"Good deal. This is exactly what I was looking for. We just need to zip through town and reconnect with the highway. Don't worry, we're still going to be okay." He reached over and held her hand.

Carrie took a deep breath and checked her phone. They'd be pushing it, but she was still confident they'd make it on time. And then she saw the banner hanging across the road: "Beet Bonanza; Parade at 1:00." It was 12:55, the barricades were already set up, and the traffic was being diverted. Rob pulled into a mini-mart on the corner.

"What are you doing?" Carrie's high-pitched voice was frightening, even to her.

"I'm going to make a quick stop in here to confirm our route through town to make sure it's the best way. Plus, I have to go to the bathroom. And grab a pop. Do you want anything?"

She shook her head and let out a gasp. "Now you ask for directions!" She tried to control the volume, but didn't succeed.

Carrie texted Kim while waiting, knowing that they'd taken the same route. Kim's response was simple. "We're here. The detour only added five minutes. Where are you?"

Carrie looked to the side and saw Rob posing for a selfie with some young girls. "We got a little lost. Meet you at the church. I'm going to kill him!"

Rob was laughing as he handed her a KIND bar and a bottle of water when he got into the car. "You're not going to believe it;

that was Miss Sweet Beet and her court. I just had to take a picture."

"Just drive." Carrie wasn't sure what annoyed her more, that they were late, that Rob was still chuckling, or that he didn't know that times like this required chocolate. She ripped off the wrapper and ate the gooey dried fruit nut bar anyway. She closed her eyes and dreamed it was chocolate laced with caramel.

They'd missed the family lunch, and by the time they got to the church, the bells were pealing as they drove through the parking lot, searching in vain for a spot. Finally, they found a street-side parking spot in the next block.

"I know, I know. You don't have to say anything," he said as they ran to the old church. They each took the steps two at a time. Before they opened the door, Carrie stopped to take a long breath, smooth her hair and calm herself. She reached over and straightened Rob's tie, and brushed some hair over his ear. When they were both ready, they each gave the old double doors a yank and FLASH—just in time to photobomb the bride and her father who were standing in the church's narrow vestibule, and about to start their walk down the aisle.

Carrie quickly stepped to the side and gave Rob such a firm yank that he stumbled into the stand holding the guest book. Fortunately, the bride's father caught it before it fell. An usher quickly escorted Carrie and Rob to outside seats in the last pew, and Carrie wanted to slither out of sight, but just smiled at the woman next to her who was clutching her purse, perhaps fearful of the latecomers.

Rob leaned toward her. "I'm sorry."

Carrie pursed her lips and gave her head a slight shake until she scooched a bit closer to him and patted his knee, keeping her eyes focused in front of her. So far, the day had become as convoluted as a corn maze, and somewhere during the homily, she envisioned other potential snags.

While the priest led the congregants in prayer, she prayed Rob wouldn't launch into a story with her family about some medieval king from Prussia. And that her boorish cousin would lay off the stinging comments about women her age who weren't married. And that her widowed aunt wouldn't raise her Cruella Deville eyebrows and ask, "Is he finally the one?" Amen.

After the ceremony was over, Carrie and Rob joined the rest of her family in front of the church.

"So what happened? I thought you left before we did?" Kim asked.

Carrie took a deep breath and gave her eyes a slow roll. "It's a bit of a long story. You know, the one about the guy who knows a shortcut, gets lost, ignores his GPS and won't ask for directions. I'm sure you're all familiar with it. Then add the smell of fresh manure and the dust of the fields, and that explains our morning." She paused and began to chuckle. "Really, we just wanted to enjoy a more scenic route. You all remember Rob, don't you?"

He hung his head until the laughter and good-natured teasing stopped, then looped his arm around Carrie's neck and snickered. "Don't forget about Miss Sweet Beet."

"Since you missed us for lunch, let's head to Leo's, and you can tell us all about it," her dad said. "We've got plenty of time before the reception."

"Dad, not Leo's," Carrie said.

"But it's a family tradition. Every time we're in town, we stop there."

"Just a quick one, then we need to get checked in to the hotel so we can freshen up before the reception," Barb said.

"Honey, we've got a couple of hours," Carrie's dad said to his wife, to which the women all responded with groans.

Leo's was packed with mostly young men watching college football, shouting over the sound from the TVs to be heard. It was not the perfect location to impress anyone, but over drinks, the family gave Rob a quick rundown of family members he needed to be especially aware of.

"Just watch out for Uncle Ray. He can only talk two things, football and religion, and they are basically the same for him. If he even gets the scent that you don't know everything there is to know about the Packers and their history, you're trapped," Charlie added. Carrie's brother had learned this lesson at a young age.

By the time they sat down for dinner, Carrie was feeling a bit woozy. "I just remembered. It's been several hours since that KIND bar," she whispered to Rob. "I'm starving." Carrie was still embarrassed from the incident at the church, and just wanted to get through the evening without another incident.

The meal settled Carrie's head, stomach, and nerves, and she and Rob were having a great time dancing and being with her family.

"Where's Rob?" Maggie said.

"He just went to get some refills, but now that you mention it…" Carrie said.

They looked toward the bar, and saw Rob walking back to the table, looking like a worn-out, scolded puppy, with his head bowed, exaggerated pouty lips, and one shoulder drooping.

"I've met Uncle Ray. He even put his hand on my shoulder at one point, and it felt like he was driving me into the ground. It was like a death grip. I held my own, looking interested in the Packers, until he began talking about the O-line. My eyes must have glazed over. Some guy named Ted rescued me."

Charlie led the laughter. "I warned you."

"And to make things worse, you forgot our drinks," Carrie said to console her date, still laughing.

"I'll get this round," her father volunteered. "I've been handling Ray since he married my sister when they were still teenagers." He paused. "About five months before their oldest was born."

When it came to the portion of the evening Carrie dreaded the most, she headed to the restroom. "Carrie, you've got to come back. You have to be here for this," yelled her widowed aunt, from several tables away. "All the single ladies need to be up front."

Carrie hated the bouquet toss, but as her aunt pulled her by the arm, she had no choice. "Let's do this together. You know what it means if you catch it?" she winked as she asked Carrie. "By the way, your friend is pretty cute. Is he *finally* the one?"

It wasn't Carrie's intent to catch the bouquet as much as it was to guard her face as the flowers were hurled her way. She'd forgotten the bride had been a softball pitcher and, even when standing backwards, she could toss a bouquet with force. Carrie recovered and tossed it to her aunt like it was a hot potato.

"Oh no, we're not on to seconds until everyone has their first. And now, it's your turn." Her aunt tossed it back. Carrie bent down and tried to give the flowers to the flower girl who turned her back on her, then a cousin's 16-year-old daughter.

"Nope. Mom says I'm too young to get married." The rest of the women had formed a circle around Carrie and began clapping, as she stood under the twirling disco ball. She walked back to the table, not saying a word. Rob stopped her as they passed, since he was walking toward the front for the garter toss.

He bent down and whispered to her. "You were beautiful out there," then kissed her before she could respond.

She sat at the table between Kim and Maggie. "I can't bear to watch," shielding her eyes with the flowers.

"You two are so in love." Carrie snapped her head as Kim continued. "It just shows in both of your faces."

"She's right, you know, and you need to stop fighting it. Barb said the same thing. I can't wait until he joins us for Thanksgiving," Maggie added. "Uh oh. The toss is about to happen."

The music grew louder as the groom removed Dana's garter, and the drum-roll began, ending when the garter flew into the crowded dance floor.

Carrie looked up to see Rob extend his extra-long reach over two other guys so he could snatch the garter before it even started its downward flight. She lowered her glance to her lap. "Oh, my Lord. What just happened?"

Maggie reached over and gave her a gentle rub across her shoulders. "He's wonderful, and you're just fine. And thank heavens, he put it in his pocket and not across his forehead like Charlie did at my wedding."

The DJ followed the fun with a slow song, and Rob was quick to pull Carrie out of her chair. She offered no resistance. As they swayed to the music, he pulled her close. "I had to get the garter after you got the flowers. I love you so much."

Neither had uttered those words before and, for a split second, Carrie tensed, until the warmth of his hand on the small of her back melted all her anxiety away, and she leaned closer. She finally looked up at him, smiled, but said nothing. Instead, she squeezed him tighter, and let tingles run through her body. She felt like she was dancing above the floor. Now this was how this day was supposed to end.

Carrie smiled the entire trip back home on Sunday, and she was glad Rob didn't feel like talking. She rewound the past 30 hours, and had a new definition of perfect, despite the hiccups that popped up. She also knew what love felt like.

Chapter 18

Carrie returned to work on Monday and discovered her morning would be disrupted with an 11:00 meeting with Marta. It had been several weeks since Marta tried to upstage her over the marketing plan, and Carrie had avoided her as often as she could. Throughout the morning, she braced herself.

After considering a job search, Carrie decided to wait a little longer to see what happened at St. Hedwig's. A merger could work in her favor, as surely, they'd offer Marta a buyout. Carrie had no idea why Marta wanted to see her, but her goal was to make sure she didn't say anything that would be detrimental to her own position.

Marta was on the phone, but waved Carrie in and pointed to the chair for her to sit down. Carrie recognized Marta's phony laugh and wondered if the person on the other end knew it was insincere.

"Adam, I'm shocked. That couldn't be further from the truth. I meant every word I just said. Perhaps we can talk about this another time." Oops. Apparently, Adam, whoever he was, couldn't be fooled. Marta replaced the receiver on her desk phone with a force usually reserved for special ugly occasions.

"Carrie, come in and have a seat. I hope you had a good weekend." Marta remained seated behind her perch and looked at Carrie, but her voice had its usual crispness.

"It was wonderful. Thank you." Carrie had no interest in telling her any more or stretching out this meeting any longer than it needed to be.

"Well, I guess it's my obligation to tell you I'm retiring at the end of December. I don't know how Jack is going to divvy up my responsibilities, but I'm sure he'll inform you and the others as soon as a plan is in place. A general announcement will be made this afternoon, but I expect you to keep this to yourself until then."

"Absolutely." Carrie waited for Marta to continue, but she had already started to read one of the papers on her desk. "Is that it?"

"Yes. What more would you expect?" Marta looked over the top of her glasses and signaled the door.

"Okay. Good luck."

Carrie felt ten pounds lighter when she walked back to her office. She tried to manage the joy she was experiencing by keeping her eyes focused on the floor. She knew if anyone stopped her, she'd channel one of her favorite songs. *It's a new dawn, it's a new day, it's a new life for me, and I'm feeling good.* She wanted to dance—and Carrie never wanted to dance—but that's what this announcement did to her. Instead, she went out for an early lunch before her 1:30 meeting with a hospital sponsor.

Everyone knew Marta's retirement was not her own initiative. The relief of her impending departure was replaced by the fear of the unknown, producing as much anxiety. There was much scuttlebutt about her replacement, but the job hadn't been posted, which led everyone to assume another reorganization affecting the department was in the works. Rumors of a merger grew stronger. The good news for Carrie was with the time Marta had already scheduled out of the office, Carrie could easily survive the last of her work with Marta.

She scheduled coffee for the next Thursday morning with Judith at their favorite eastside coffee shop. She needed advice from her on how to proceed during this time with limited information coming from the CEO. She also wanted Judith's reassurance that she'd have her support for the promotion.

Carrie crossed the parking lot with more energy as she walked to meet Judith, and felt as cheerful as the shop's blue-and-white striped awning. Entering, she savored the smell of the freshly ground beans and looked over the case of homemade pastries. She always passed, but had to look each time. That satisfied her sweet tooth.

Judith was already seated at a table toward the back, looking at the newspaper. Carrie liked to plop into one of the over-stuffed leather chairs in front of the fireplace when she was there by herself, but Judith informed her those were too low and not made for curvaceous post-middle-aged women.

"Good morning, Judith." She greeted her friend with a hug. "Glad to see you're already settled. Do you mind if I get a cup?"

"Heavens no. It gives me more time to finish my crossword puzzle."

Carrie had to wait for two people in front of her before she ordered. "I'll have a grande latteccino, skinny, vanilla, whip, with a drizzle of caramel. And I like the milk extra frothy, please." She always ended her directive with a smile.

The wait for Carrie's drink took longer than expected. "Sorry for the delay. Seems they're training a new person on how to make a perfect froth."

Several minutes of conversation went by while they enjoyed their drinks and caught up with each other's lives. Finally, Carrie brought up the potential promotion.

"There's no question that you have the skills, and the volunteers enjoy working with you." Judith stopped to sip her coffee, and pushed the vase holding the single stem of alstroemeria to the side. Her eyes drifted across the room, and she waved to someone.

Carrie looked at her friend, waiting for her to continue.

"But I'm not sure it's the best fit for you. Now."

Carrie sat back in her chair, stunned.

"But others have said I'd be a shoe-in for the job. The only other person at the hospital who has the experience and background is Dwight. And he keeps a calendar in his office and crosses off every week toward his retirement."

"Carrie, I think the world of you, but it may not be your time."

"Why not?"

"Remember a couple of years ago, you almost lost Weymouth Medical Supply as a sponsor? They needed more time, and you were really pressuring them to make a decision."

Carrie grimaced at the reminder.

"I've seen the same thing on the board at Northside. Relationships take time, and you don't always have that patience to get the result you want."

Carrie struggled to find her voice, but feared it would break if she tried to talk.

"You're a perfectionist, but it's also important to always keep your eye on the big picture, and know when perfection is important and when it isn't. A written report should be perfect. But many times, we can still be effective in getting our message across without getting caught up with the fact that it has to be perfect."

There it was again. Her strive for perfection and her impatience had gotten in her way.

Carrie forced a smile and willed back the burn she felt forming in her eyes. She cleared her throat. "Judith, this has been tough to hear, but thanks for sharing. It gives me things to think about." Carrie had never felt this dejected in work.

"One more thing." Judith wrapped her hands around her cup and spoke in a hushed tone. "If you *committed* to *working* on those two issues, *there's nothing you couldn't achieve*."

"Thank you. That means a lot."

"Now, I hope you understand, but I have a meeting with LeRoy at Northside Center, so I've got to run. Are you going to be okay?"

"I'll be fine, Judith. Thanks for being so honest."

Carrie was glad she was in a far corner, her back to the front door. She stared at the wall in front of her, her eyes tracing the swirly pattern on the paprika-colored walls. An hour ago, she entered feeling like she was Carrie-in-Charge. She sat there now with her shoulders drooped. One more day until she saw Rob, and that's all she cared about. Rob always knew how to make her feel better.

Most of their Friday nights were nothing more than dinner and collapsing onto the couch to watch something on Netflix. This week, Carrie stopped to get some pot-stickers and chicken red curry on her way to Rob's place. His schedule hadn't improved his housekeeping skills, but she'd learned to step over piles of shoes. Tonight, she didn't even care about the dirty dishes that greeted her in the sink or the moldy food in the refrigerator.

"Madame Curie called. She needs more mold for her penicillin research and wondered if she could have this yogurt."

"Very funny." Rob wrapped his arms around her waist from the back. "But that would be Alexander Fleming. Madam Curie discovered radioactivity, and I keep that stuff in my bedroom."

"Speaking of radioactive, let me tell you about my conversation with Judith today." By the time she was finished with every detail, she felt like she'd been too close to an atomic blast.

"Maybe the time isn't right for you. Seriously, and it has nothing to do with your skills. I've seen you work—you can do the job."

Carrie wrestled with his words.

"Look, I know I have changes in my job coming, too. And I want you to be part of them when the time is right. I've been thinking," Rob said, his voice soft. "Why don't you come to the meeting in San Diego with me?"

Carrie was glad he couldn't hear her heart thumping. "You know exactly how to make me feel better."

"You can spend the entire week, but I thought it might be more fun if you came out Thursday, joined me for the big reception and dinner that evening, and then since Monday is a holiday, we can spend Friday through Monday sightseeing and doing whatever we want."

"That sounds perfect." She caught her words. "No, that sounds wonderful. I'd like that."

By the time she went to bed that evening, she had almost forgotten about the sting of Judith's words.

Carrie's holiday plans with her family were coming together, and they agreed they'd celebrate Christmas the day after Thanksgiving at Maggie's home in Birchfield. It meant an end to the tradition her mother had started of baking cookies the day after Thanksgiving, but Carrie was quickly learning many family traditions were coming to an end.

"Hey, I have an idea. I'm going to take the day before Thanksgiving off and bake cookies to take with me this weekend. Want to join me? Then we can relax and enjoy a nice meal before we head north on Friday."

Rob thought for a minute, then smiled. "Only if we can make biscotti."

Since they weren't driving up until Friday morning, Carrie and Rob fixed their own Thanksgiving meal at her place. After their post-dinner walk, Carrie turned on her gas fireplace, and poured a cup of tea for each of them. It was a typical cool fall night, and the fire set the mood for a romantic evening.

He stretched out with his feet on the ottoman, while she lay on the couch, covered with a quilt, letting him gently massage her head while she rested it on his lap. They enjoyed the silence, mesmerized by the dancing flames.

"Did you ever wonder why you never married?" Carrie asked, craning her neck to see his face. Instantly, she noticed him slipping his tongue under his upper lip. Men had asked her that before, but she'd never asked anyone. She felt safe with Rob, but suddenly realized she was entering murky waters.

"Well, I almost did once."

Carrie raised her eyebrows, but said nothing. Neither did he. She turned her head to face the fire again. She knew he would continue, if he felt ready.

"We grew up together, she was a good friend in high school, and then we parted for college. When we both returned home for work after school, we began to date, but of course, we'd known each other all our lives. She wanted to pursue her PhD, so after one year, she headed to graduate school while I stayed and worked for my dad."

There was a long pause. "Is that it?"

"Two years later, we planned our wedding. Our parents knew each other well, and everyone was happy for us. I had a good job with Dad, though I hated it, and she was finishing the classroom part of her degree. She'd do the rest in Ridgewood, at a couple clinics."

He paused again and lifted her up as he shifted his legs, drawing his knees up to his chest. Carrie sat up and lay her head on his shoulder as he cradled her in his arm. It was his story to tell when and if he wanted to, but still, she was curious. Had there been an accident? Did she die? What happened?

"Two weeks before the wedding, she called it off, told me she was moving to New York and was in love with someone else—a woman. She was in love with a woman. Here this person I'd known for all those years, I'd never really known at all."

"Wow." Carrie didn't know what else to say, so she continued to remain quiet, sitting as still as she could. The pause became uncomfortable.

"A few years later, she tracked me down. She and her partner wanted to have a child, and she asked me if I'd contribute the necessary ingredient."

"And?"

"Of course, I said no. But I've seen her since then when she was home, and she has a little girl named Alice."

Carrie stared at the floor before she looked at him. She placed her hand on his. "Thank you for sharing. I can't even imagine...."

"I've never felt a rush to the altar since." He raised his glass in Carrie's direction as if to salute. "Or even to get into another relationship. I've dated a little bit, but it was an awful time for me, and I never wanted to go there again."

Carrie sat so she faced him. "So, what did you do? I mean, how did you cope?"

"It was the most caring and generous I'd ever seen my dad. He told me to take any time off that I wanted. I went sailing for a couple of days—it was August, and I made the decision it was time for me to move on. That's when Phil helped convince me that Chicago could have some good opportunities. I ended up being offered a couple positions and moved within two months. My dad never forgave himself for giving me the time off. He was pissed I used it to find a way to leave the business."

There was a flatness in his voice, a controlled emotion. Finally, he lightened the mood and chuckled. "My mom got the best deal out of it. I gave her the honeymoon tickets, and she and her sister went to Ireland for 10 days."

"So, why now? Why get back into dating now?" Of course, Carrie knew she'd have to answer the same question, if he asked.

"My mother was in a bad car accident last year, and I saw how Dad took care of her. I wondered who'd take care of me if something ever happened. I know that sounds selfish, but I decided I didn't want to be alone anymore."

More time passed as they continued to watch the fire, and Carrie curled up around his shoulders. Finally, it was her turn.

"So, tell me about you.... Why aren't you married?" Rob asked.

"Truth is, I went through a period after college, and then again, after my mom died when I didn't make the best decisions. My mother was my best friend, and I had a hard time coping. I've had a couple other relationships since then that were serious, but I found out one guy was cheating on me. That was tough. Then another guy was transferred to Colorado, and I didn't want to move. That was Kyle."

Carrie's stories were less interesting, and she'd been close to an engagement once, before she moved to Milwaukee. He didn't need to know about all the past short-term boyfriends, or worse yet, the hook-ups with first-name-only men. And he didn't need to know the secret from college she carried that prevented her from the deepest level of emotional intimacy. At least, not yet.

"I think, way back, like when I was in high school, I developed a formula. It was my idea of advanced chemistry, what made a perfect mate for me. I kept looking for that relationship, and if there was something that didn't fit the formula, I moved on." Carrie shifted her position and hesitated before she continued. "I never factored in things like piano playing or kite flying or someone who tutored English to a couple from China so he could improve his Mandarin." When she finished her story, he was sleeping. After a few more minutes in complete silence, she nudged him awake. "Okay, Big Guy, the party's over. Let's go to bed. I'm going to assume you heard every word, so I never have to utter that stuff again."

The Klamerschmidt Christmas celebration, though a month early, was more fun than either Carrie or Rob could have imagined. Once the gifts were opened and the meal was over, Maggie encouraged Rob to play the piano.

"I just had it tuned. I was hoping you could play for us, and give us a break from the football game."

He slid onto the piano bench, and soon began to play a medley of Christmas songs, joined by the girls and women, who stood around the piano and began singing. On cue, Carrie's dad sprang from his recliner in the family room, and led them in "We Wish You a Merry Christmas." Charlie surprised everyone with his Elvis impersonation of "I'll Have a Blue Christmas without You," as he put his arm around Carrie. Maggie and her husband, Brad, demonstrated a lively two-step, as Rob kept the beat going with "Rockin' around the Christmas Tree." When the singing and dancing was over, the entire family laughed and clapped, which was the best welcome for Rob.

"Welcome to the Klamerschmidts," Carrie's dad said, as he reached over and gave Rob a soft punch in the arm. "By the way, Carrie, you're saved from representing all of us at Aunt Christina's Christmas Day party this year. She's moving it to New Year's Day, and it starts at 1:00 and ends when the last person leaves. And you're all invited," Carrie's dad said with a broad sweeping arm movement.

Carrie's eyes did a slow blink as she wiped her brow in mock relief. Continuing on before anyone else could talk about their plans for Christmas, she added. "Sounds like fun. Now who wants to play cards?"

"Continental rummy—I'll get the decks," Maggie said. In two hours, Rob realized he still didn't like playing cards, and joined Brad and Charlie, watching the second football game.

The next morning brought an emotional set of holiday goodbyes, and it was evident they were all going their separate ways for Christmas.

It was an hour into the quiet trip home before Rob brought up the subject Carrie wanted to avoid. "So, what *are* your plans for Christmas?"

"Well, there's a nice Presbyterian Church near me that has three different Christmas Eve services, and I'm always welcome at Judith's."

That was true. Sort of. Judith did normally invite her, but they were traveling this season and would be gone. Why is everyone traveling except me, Carrie asked herself.

Instead, she'd already planned her pity party. She had a new pair of holiday flannel pajamas, she'd feast on some ring bologna and macaroni and cheese, using her Great-Grandma Belle's recipe, and begin binge watching something on TV. For dessert, she'd break into the package of white-fudge-covered cookies between episodes. The celebration would carry over to Christmas day, except she'd splurge and have some pimento cheese spread and summer sausage. Ah yes, this was destined to be the Christmas of processed meats and cheese. What could be more festive? If she couldn't be with her family, the old-time junk food would be with her.

"Why didn't you tell me? You made me think you'd be with your family in Birchfield."

"I really don't have any plans," she said, turning her gaze toward the lifeless, brown fields, already hardened by the frost.

"I'd love for you to come to Ridgewood with me. I hadn't asked because I know your family has some holiday traditions that are important to you, and now I feel bad. But seriously, would you come with me? I'm flying over on December 23 and returning December 27."

Carrie put her head back and closed her eyes for a minute. All she could see was Rob partially obscured by the ficus tree the first night they met. "Are you sure it wouldn't upset your family's plans? How would your mom feel about it?"

"First of all, my mom would be ecstatic. I've said this before—the two of you share some similarities, and you'd be at ease with her right away. My dad? He'll be fine, but I've never taken a woman back home. I have no idea how he'd act, but he's probably not as bad as I make him out to be sometimes. We would go to church Christmas Eve, and you'd get to meet my sister, Shannon, and her family. Then you and I could spend Christmas together, too."

Carrie smiled and looked at her hands, fidgeting in the gloves. "I'd like to. You've convinced me, and it sounds like this would be a nice time. But what about…?" She looked at Rob.

He chuckled. "No problem. It's a four-bedroom house, and Mom has kept two guest rooms ready for when Shannon's kids spend the night. Plus, we'll have the whole upstairs, so there would be nothing awkward, if that's what you're asking."

"It sounds wonderful. Thanks." She reached over and held his hand, relieved she'd have a meaningful holiday, with much better food. She fought back a tear until it fell onto her cheek.

"What's the matter? Are you okay?"

"You've made me so happy. I'm better than okay, but sometimes the memories of Christmas can get to me."

"No problem. We'll make it through."

As they drove the rest of the way home, Carrie kept her hand on Rob's shoulder, every now and then, massaging the back of his neck. She didn't like spending Christmas away from her dad and siblings, and she longed for the time when she'd enjoy a cup of coffee and some fresh apple coffeecake around the kitchen table with just her mom on Christmas morning. Or how her mother would top the baked ham with her special root beer glaze, and everyone would fight over her sweet potatoes with pecans. Or when her father would lead the family prayer, ending it with a special blessing for her mother's health. But those days were gone, and she had to move on.

Chapter 19

After a month of holiday preparation, Carrie was ready to meet Rob's family. For a few days, she wouldn't think about work and the unsettled feeling of not knowing who her new boss would be, or how they'd reconfigure the assignments since Marta's job hadn't been posted. She'd refocus when she returned.

Carrie took a deep breath as she waited for Rob to pick her up. When she walked to the car, the crisp air made her eyes water. She knew lake-effect snow could blanket Ridgewood, and hoped she was prepared if a storm hit the area. It had been almost 10 years since she'd made an overnight trip to meet a boyfriend's family, and the anxiety was tearing at her. It had helped when Rob called his mother one evening when Carrie was with him, and Carol extended a friendly welcome.

Rob's dad picked them up early in the evening and gave Carrie a warm, nice-to-meet-you greeting, but turned his back as Rob reached out to him. "Let's get going. Your mother will be glad to see you," he said rather sternly.

As they pulled in to the driveway, Carrie let out a slight gasp and hoped neither of the men heard her. The house was stunning in holiday elegance. White lights intertwined with fresh evergreen garland draped the double front door, garage door, and lamp post. A wreath that framed a glowing candle decorated each window on the first floor and three dormers upstairs. Spotlights shone on the red-brick colonial, and Carrie wondered how long it took to create this Hallmark scene. From outside, she could smell wood burning in the fireplace and watched the wisps of smoke leave the chimney and float through the clear sky.

Rob's mother met them at the front door, and Carrie was astonished by her beauty. Short, shaggy black hair accented by natural silver streaks highlighted her face and her dark brown eyes. But it was the black pants and turtleneck, topped with a long, bold, contemporary-patterned vest that draped over her tall, slender frame that really caught Carrie's eye. This was not the mousy librarian who loved to knit shawls and collect rescue cats that Rob had described.

"Welcome to our home. I am so happy to finally meet you." She embraced Carrie. "And Robbie, my son, you can never come home enough, you know. You're looking good." She took his head in both of her hands and pulled him down for a kiss on the forehead, before she straightened his collar. "There. That looks better."

"Let the boy alone. He looks fine," Bob said, a bit aggravated at his wife's fussing.

"Please, please come in. Robbie, take your things and show Carrie to her room, then come back down for a glass of wine. How does that sound?"

Carrie shook her head and smiled in agreement. "That would be lovely. Thank you." She was glad they'd eaten at the airport in Milwaukee, or it wouldn't take too much wine to go right to her head.

Rob led her upstairs, where she was pleasantly surprised to discover she had her own bathroom, and his mother had left a note on her bedside. She turned to see Rob in the doorway, and knew she'd read the note later.

"Everything okay?"

"Very."

With that, he took her hand and led her back downstairs.

'We have Merlot, a Chardonnay, and a Riesling. Will any of those work? Bob is ready to pour you a glass." The whole bottle might be good, Carrie wanted to say. This was going to be a nice time, she just felt it.

"Riesling would be fine, thank you."

The glow from the fireplace bounced off the mocha-colored walls, and the wood's crackle almost drowned out the Tony Bennett Christmas music. A creamy white couch and coordinating loveseat anchored the room-size, dark Oriental rugs that reminded Carrie of the ones she brought back from her family home. Two wing chairs in a dark brown-and-ivory-medallion print completed the room. White crown molding framed the entire space.

On the walls hung two large, unframed, bold-colored paintings. Carrie couldn't tell exactly what they were supposed to be, but clearly the artist had an abstract vision, and the warm yellows and reds were in sharp contrast to the otherwise conservative feel of the room.

Carol caught Carrie looking at one of the paintings. "They are rather contemporary, but I love them. My mother painted them almost 50 years ago. She had an incredibly creative eye, and she had a thing for adding a dash of purple or chartreuse to everything. Lucky me, she added both to these two."

"This room is stunning." Carrie's attention shifted to the bookshelves. On each side of the fireplace, white, ceiling-high built-in cabinets and bookshelves stood tall, like protectors of the flame. The tchotchkes surrounding the books, with an assortment of holiday decorations, gave it a homey feel, and prevented the house from looking like it was off the pages of *House Beautiful*.

"I'm sure Robbie has told you we love to travel. It was always a priority as the kids were growing up, so we made sure they saw a lot of this country, and then the world when they were a little older.

Carrie cast a sideways glance to Rob, who kept his eyes focused on his fingernails. "No, I wasn't aware."

"My father was at a university in Berlin for two years, and we were there when the wall came down. Travel was the only way I could get Bob to take a break each year."

"Mom, Carrie knits, just like you. I told her about the sweaters you used to make for me." Carrie looked at Rob, and wondered why the sudden change in conversation.

"Oh, Robbie, that was back when you were a kid. I haven't knit in years."

The eyebrows on Rob's face shot up, and for a minute, Carrie thought his eyes looked too big for their sockets. "But I remember that sweater you made me in college."

"Yes, and that's the last thing I made. I still make prayer shawls for church, but I stopped knitting other things years ago." Turning to Carrie, she asked, "What kinds of things do you like to make?"

She described the wool felted slippers with the leather soles everyone in her family got this year, and the preemie caps she makes for the NICU where she worked.

Two hours of conversation went by over cheese, dried fruit, and tapenade from the gift box Carrie had sent.

"Where's that pimento cheese spread?" Bob asked. "What are we saving that for?"

Carol threw her hands up in disgust. "Bob, you know that stuff is just awful for you."

"It's no worse than your white-fudge-dipped cookies," he replied.

Carol smiled, shrugged her shoulders, and raised her hands as if to surrender. "What can I say? They are a once-a-year, holiday indulgence."

Pimento cheese and white-fudge Oreos? Oh, this was Carrie's kind of family. Carrie laughed at the gentle way Rob's parents bantered back and forth, though their reminiscing of travel stories began to get a little long. She was glad they asked about her family, and enjoyed telling them about the cottage by the lake and how her mom and dad had loved relaxing there. "It was perfect for my dad as it was only a half hour from town."

Carrie noticed Bob smile and let out a sigh, and she thought, based on the conversation, he, too, might have enjoyed some cottage time rather than schlepping through castles, cathedrals, and museums all over the world.

As the evening drew to a close, Rob assured his parents he and Carrie would clean up and put the food away so they could go to bed. Carrie was happy for the few minutes of time on the couch in front of the fire before they went upstairs. Rob pulled her close and kissed the top of her head. "I love you and I love that you came home with me. Thank you."

"I love you, too, Robbie," she snickered. He leaned over for a long kiss as the flames began to flicker.

The first few hours of her visit had been better than Carrie had anticipated, and she loved the closeness to Rob that she was experiencing, though she was frustrated he hadn't told her about all of the travel in his upbringing. He seemed so focused on the negative from his childhood.

"Your folks are lovely, and this house…. I think there's a few things you haven't told me, starting with your mother. She has such flair."

"She's my mother. What would you have expected me to say? Plus, I've taken my style points from my dad. I'm just not into corduroys and wool plaid shirts, yet." They enjoyed the moment as the embers slowly died, and the fire breathed its last hiss and crackle for the night. Tip-toeing upstairs, they said goodnight in the hallway.

As Carrie climbed into bed, she wanted to read from her iPad for a few minutes before realizing it was still downstairs in a bag near the door. She wrapped herself in her long robe, and using the light from her phone, she slipped quietly downstairs through the living room to get it. She was startled by the low voice from the dimly lit kitchen.

"It's me. Want to join me for a bit?"

The overhead kitchen light switched on, and it was Rob's father who was more surprised than she was.

"Oh my. I thought you were Rob," he said while putting his knife down to tighten the belt to his robe.

"That's not that pimento cheese, is it?" Carrie teased.

"Carol fell fast asleep, and it was my only chance."

"That's no different from my dad who loved to fix a cheese sandwich every night. Colby cheese, though, and the longhorn style. He liked the way it fit the bread. Then Barb straightened him out." They both laughed at the story.

Bob moved a chair out from the table with his foot. "Here, join me for a few minutes. I'm glad you came with Rob. He's grown into a good man and deserves the company of a nice woman."

Carrie wanted to say, *Stop, please repeat that again into my recording device so I can help your only son think you actually care about him.* "His interests are so varied and different from mine. I think we're good for each other." She picked up the knife and spread some of the cheese spread onto her cracker.

"Well, he's always been an inquisitive kid, I'll say that much, and just like his mom, he's a rescuer."

An image of Amy flashed in Carrie's mind. Rob was simply trying to rescue her.

"She used to bring home stray cats. I worried about him when he first started to sail. Frequently, he'd find an injured bird or animal and bring it in and try to nurse it back to health. Then he'd come home and tell us about a new cove along the shoreline he'd discovered. He had open water in front of him to go as fast as he wanted, but he liked the exploration of the coast, and I never understood it. He gets that from his mother's side of the family. Her dad was a philosophy professor and her mother an artist. That's quite a combination."

Carrie noticed the slight shake of his head, and wasn't sure if it was a slight tremor or his disapproval of their career choices.

Bob popped another cracker into his mouth before continuing. "Fortunately, they raised a fine daughter and were wonderful in-laws and grandparents, so that made up for their eccentricities."

"And what does he get from the Linder side?" She tilted her head and kept her eyes on Bob. This was helping her understand more about Rob's perception of his father.

Bob paused and looked at the table in front of him as if he'd never wondered how he'd contributed to his son. "His mother did most of the upbringing, but he's not afraid to put in some hard work, and he'll stay at something until the job is done. My dad was like that, and I'm like that."

"I've seen that in him."

"But he can be stubborn. You know, he could've gone to most any university he wanted in the country, and I hoped he would pick MIT, or maybe Stanford, but instead, he went to UP State, two hours away. I think he did that because he was just being obstinate and didn't want to go where I wanted him to." He put the lid on the cheese. "And I think he wanted to be closer to his mother."

"I think he's done well."

"You're right, he has."

Carrie let a few seconds of silence pass. "I just came down to get my other bag, but I need to get some sleep. Good night now. It's been nice talking with you."

Before Carrie slipped into bed, she read the note Rob's mother had left for her.

"Carrie, welcome to our home. I hope your stay will be warm and filled with great memories. You have brought so much joy to Robbie's life, and I've never heard him happier."

Carrie pulled the down comforter under her chin, and nestled under its warmth. It might have been the wine or the luxurious bedding, but mostly, she knew it was love. She was touched by the gentleness of Rob's parents, but darn, why couldn't his father share his feelings with Rob.

The next morning, Carrie was embarrassed when she was the last one to the breakfast table, and Bob had already gone to work. "Oh, he'll be home early afternoon. He still goes in at 7:00 every morning. I don't know what he'd do if he didn't have that place to go to in the winter."

Over coffee and warm muffins, they laid out their day. Rob and Carrie headed out for a local tour of the area and promised his mom they'd be back to help decorate cookies in the afternoon.

Carrie was surprised when the first place Rob took her to was the home of Linders Engineering, which sat on the south edge of town. They met up with his dad, who gave them each a pair of safety glasses before the brief tour of the operation. "There are just a few guys cleaning the equipment and stocking supplies, so it will be good to go when we get back after the holidays." He stopped and looked at their feet. "Good. I'm glad you have on rubber-soled shoes. They're an essential around here."

Still, the chemical, metallic smell reminded Carrie of an errant experiment in high school chemistry that confirmed the sciences were not her thing. Nevertheless, she was impressed with the size of the business, and how the workers were happy to see Rob. He responded by shaking their hands, greeting them by name, and wishing them a Merry Christmas. Obviously, he was still part of their work family, as well, after all these years.

"Not sure if Rob told you, but historically, we manufactured gizmos used in the shipping industry. Today, it's contracts with the Department of Defense that keep us going." Carrie learned Bob's grandfather was the inventor, and though most of his patents had had little success, several of them had served the family, employees, and community very well over the years.

"As much as I hate to say it, war is always good for Linders Engineering," Bob said. They walked a few more steps. "And this could have all been Rob's if he hadn't run off to the big city." The chuckle that followed told Carrie he still carried a grudge. She exchanged glances with Rob, who looked down and shook his head slightly. They finished the tour, and Bob promised he'd be home by mid-afternoon.

"See what I told you? Every time, there's a dig. He just doesn't get it," Rob said while opening the car door.

Carrie squeezed his hand, but couldn't find words to soothe him. "What's next?" she asked.

Following the visit to the family company, they swung by the waterfront, closer to the heart of downtown. "This is where the sailing began for me, in this little bay that spills out to Lake Michigan." Even though icy waves were crashing on the shore now, Carrie could see the natural beauty of it.

Shortly before lunch, they stopped at his sister's home, and it was clear that Shannon was in the final throes of Christmas prep. The dining room table looked like a gift-wrapping station. "We go to his parents today at 5:00 for dinner and gifts with his side of the family, and I don't even have everything wrapped yet, or a salad made that I promised I'd bring." She turned to Carrie who stood a half-step behind Rob. "Hi, I'm Shannon. Sorry about the mess."

Carrie waved off the apology, and before she could say anything, Emma, who was six and still in her Disney princess pajamas, emerged from the family room and jumped into Rob's arms. Soon, they heard the clunk, clunk, clunk of Noah running up from the basement. He was almost ten, and he immediately wrapped his arms around Rob's waist.

"Hi, Uncle Rob. I was down in our new man cave watching TV. That's what Dad calls it."

Carrie stepped back and felt a lump in her throat at the sight of this reunion. She had never seen this side of Rob, and he'd never spoken much about Emma and Noah.

"We can't stay, but I just wanted to come and say hi. We promised Mom we'd help her decorate cookies this afternoon. Well, actually, she promised." He nodded toward Carrie, and lowered Emma back to the floor. "She doesn't know it yet, but I'm going to be outside cutting and stacking some wood."

"Can I go, too? Can I? I can help with the cookies." Emma whined, but no one listened.

"Jeez, I'm sorry, I don't even have anything to offer you for lunch. The kids are getting Lunchables. How lame is that?"

Looking between Emma and Noah, Rob suggested the kids come to lunch with them, and then go to his parents' for the afternoon. This was the best gift Shannon could get this year, and she gladly offered to help Emma get ready.

"I've been after her all morning to get dressed. Sometimes, the six-year-old wins." Shannon followed Emma, who had already gone upstairs.

Noah was already by the door with his coat, ready to go. "Kid, it's cold out there. You're going to need a hat and mittens. And put your boots on. You're going to help me chop and stack wood this afternoon."

As they gathered at the door, Rob hugged his younger sister and said, "We'll all be over at Mom's after we find some lunch. I'll bring them back by 4:00, is that okay?"

"Super. You're the best."

By the time Rob drove his niece and nephew home after their fun afternoon, Carol was ready to start dinner. Carrie stayed to help and learn her secrets when she discovered they were having lasagna.

As Rob pulled out of the driveway, Carrie wasted no time. "Will you tell me how you make your sauce? Rob talks about it all the time."

Carol let out a loud laugh as she pulled a pan of lasagna out of the refrigerator. "Oh, those Linder men. They are so easy to fool. I simply use a jar of a good marinara sauce. I like Grazziella's, but really, any of them will do. Sometimes I mix two together. Then I add more tomatoes, garlic, and basil. Lots of basil. A few minutes before I serve it, I top it with some Parmesan. Rob's dad still thinks I work all day on it. As if! I stopped doing that the second month we were married, but they get an idea in their head, and that's it. Just like that knitting last night. Rob hasn't seen me knit in 20 years, but he still thinks I do. I'm going to pull together a salad, but let's sit down and catch our breath over a cup of tea. Or would you prefer coffee?"

"Tea is fine. Thank you."

Dinner was as delicious as Carrie expected, and the candlelight church service was remarkably soothing. Her family had been active in her home church while she was growing up, but as an adult, she had not seen the inside of too many churches, except for weddings and funerals. Tonight, it felt like home.

She didn't feel the same way about the repugnant eggnog Rob's father made when they returned home however, but this was all part of the family's tradition, and she was happy to be a part of it. "Here, you've got to dress it up a bit," said Bob, offering rum and cognac. "Name your poison."

"It gets better when you add more hooch to it," Carol joked.

Carrie took a wee sip and asked for a splash of rum. She took a second sip and summoned more rum. "Sometime, I'll introduce you to Tom and Jerry's. That's a bit of a Wisconsin holiday tradition, and it wasn't Christmas in our house without my dad fixing those for anyone who stopped by. Now that I think about it, maybe that's why we had lots of company."

The booze seemed to loosen their memories, and they shared stories of childhood Christmases. At midnight, Bob raised his glass in a toast. "To a beautiful Christmas Eve, and if we don't go to bed soon, Santa may never get here, and you won't see me on Christmas day, I fear. You kids stay up as long as you want."

Thirty minutes later, Rob followed Carrie into her room. She raised the blinds so they could watch the stars and the moon against the darkness. He stood behind her, massaging her shoulders.

"How did this happen? How did I fall in love with this wonderful man who is so different from me?" she said.

"I keep asking myself the same thing. How did you fall for me?" She turned and mock-punched him, until he grabbed hold of her arms to restrain her and started to move toward the bed.

"Not tonight. Your parents are downstairs."

"They'll never know."

Carrie had no response.

Chapter 20

An hour later, Rob walked back to his room. Carrie knew he was her match, and she was certain that before she fell asleep, she'd seen an angel outside the window.

The grass isn't always greener, Carrie, and once you find a good man, you can't let go. Don't be afraid to commit, as long as you don't lose who you are in the relationship.

Sometime during the night, clouds heavy with snow moved in. By morning, everything outside was a brilliant white, and it reminded her of her childhood when her family would gather around the table for her mother's Christmas breakfast casserole. That was her mother's name for it, so she didn't have to make it any other time of year.

Carrie inhaled deeply to smell the freshly brewed coffee wafting up the stairs, and she texted Maggie, Charlie, and her dad to wish them a Merry Christmas. She'd try to talk to each of them later that day.

She didn't smell the cinnamon until she got downstairs. "Good morning. And Merry Christmas. Robbie and his dad have gone outside and are clearing the driveway," Carol said. She wiped her hands on a towel to give Carrie a slight hug. "It's tradition that I fix this special breakfast for Christmas. Maybe you could help me fix the fruit? It's all washed, but I still need some of it cut, and then we'll put it into this dish." She handed Carrie an antique compote dish.

"I'd be happy to help." As if a switch had been turned on, Carrie's eyes welled with tears. She tried to turn away before Carol could see.

"How long since your mother has been gone?" Carol gently touched Carrie's arm.

"This is my 11th Christmas without her, and she had a dish almost identical to this one. It was passed down from her grandmother. It's crazy how just one little thing can trigger something. And now, I can't remember what happened to it."

"I know exactly what you mean, but it's good you have such warm memories."

The back door opened and let in a swoosh of cold air. Both Rob and his dad stomped the snow off their boots before taking them off, and hung up their coats. "It's a beautiful day for sledding," Rob's dad said.

Rob walked over to Carrie and gave her a kiss on the lips. "Merry Christmas."

She blushed.

"The toboggan is down and ready to go. What do you think, Carrie? Isn't it a great day for a ride?" his father asked.

Carrie looked at Rob for help, who stood there shaking his head, laughing as he rolled his eyes. "My dad thinks every day there is snow is a good day for sledding or skating."

"But I don't have...."

"That's okay, we'll fix you up. We have some clothes and a jacket and mittens you can borrow, don't we, Carol?" said Bob.

"Yes, and Robbie, you need a warmer hat, and a scarf around your neck. All of your things are upstairs in your bedroom. Breakfast will be ready in a few minutes."

A few hours later, Shannon and her family arrived with their plastic sleds in the back of the SUV. Noah said hi to his grandparents, but walked right past Carrie. "Hi, Uncle Rob. Grandpa said you'd take us sledding this afternoon."

"Whoa. Did you just walk right past Carrie without even greeting her?"

Carrie smiled and loved Rob's relationship with his niece and nephew, and how easy it was for him. Noah turned and wished Carrie a merry Christmas.

"Now that's better. And yes, Carrie and I are ready to go whenever you are. We're taking the toboggan, too."

"We are?" Carrie said.

"It will be a blast, I promise."

Carrie felt like an overstuffed snowman by the time she was dressed in one of Rob's jackets and an old pair of ski pants, and she tried to remember the last time she'd been sledding. She watched Rob and Noah take the toboggan down the first run, and when they hit a knoll and Noah flew off, she panicked, until he stood up and began to laugh.

By the time Rob and Noah got back to the top of the hill, it was Carrie's turn. "You two take your sleds, and Carrie and I will follow on the toboggan."

Carrie lost count of the number of runs she'd made on the old toboggan when she accepted Emma's invitation to try her sled.

"Take Noah's. It's a little longer," Rob said.

"I can't believe I'm going to do this," she said to Rob. "You are really bringing out the kid in me today."

She scooched into position on the sled, her knees bent close to her chin.

"I'm going right next to you. And hang onto the handles but let go if you fall off," Emma said. Carrie welcomed coaching from the six-year old.

With a good push from Noah, she was on her way, laughing and screaming with every bump. Halfway down the hill, she managed to turn the sled, now sliding sideways on her way to the wooded area. She rolled off to one side and let go, but not before she saw Emma fly by. Not sure how she ended up face first in the fresh white powder, she finally stopped laughing enough to stand and signal she was okay, but by this time, Rob and Noah were on their way running down the hill.

"I'm fine, really," she said, spitting out pine needles and wiping dried leaves from her hat.

"That was so cool," Noah said. He kept walking to fetch the sled that landed 20 feet further in some brush.

"Are you okay? Seriously?" Rob asked, his voice filled with concern.

"I'm better than okay."

"You were awesome," Emma said, finally making it up from the bottom of the hill. She rewarded Carrie with a big hug around her waist.

"I think that's it for the day. Let's go find some hot chocolate." Rob looked at Carrie. "Do you need any help back up?"

She returned his look of worry with her own smile. "This was a blast, but I can make it on my own to the top. Then you can carry me back to the car." She turned to whisper to Rob. "And I'll need a good massage tonight, too."

The next morning, Carrie was stiff and sore, but Rob wanted to take her snowshoeing. "Are you still up for it? I want to show you this place. It's really special."

She was happy to oblige Rob by trying this new outdoor activity, but she didn't know where or why he was making such a big deal out of it. When they stopped to borrow Shannon's snowshoes and poles, she handed Rob a small backpack.

"Everything is in there. Have fun," Shannon said as she handed him the pack.

"So where are we going? Are you going to tell me?"

"It's just a couple of miles out here," as Rob drove north of town to an area Carrie hadn't seen yet.

Suddenly, Carrie's mind spun into overdrive, and her imagination sped faster than it did when she'd flown down the hill on the sled the day before. Was he getting ready to propose? He'd been saying some obscure things, and maybe meeting the family was the final test, but she wasn't ready for this. She tried to remain calm, but knew she couldn't say yes, and then after they got home, tell him she wasn't ready. She loved Rob, but marriage suddenly seemed so remote for her. But why? She couldn't answer that.

They'd never talked about marriage or even living together, and wouldn't that be a natural next step? Maggie and Kim were right; she was afraid of committing. *Breathe, breathe, breathe,* she reminded herself. Maybe he is just taking me snowshoeing into some godforsaken woods.

Rob pulled onto the side of the shoulder at a what she could tell was a driveway with a small chain across it. They had made a gradual descent from the ridge, and Carrie took in the view to the west across the road. A handful of evergreens framed a magnificent view of Lake Michigan, though they were still too high on the hill to see the shoreline. On the right side of the car was a field that backed up to a wooded area. A family of deer in the distance looked up and then ran off.

Carrie and Rob sat in the car in silence, and Rob stared over the lake.

"This is pretty. Peaceful." That was all Carrie trusted herself to say.

Rob reached over and tightened his hand over hers. "This is my property. Fifteen acres. From the shore back into the woods," as he gestured with his hands. "It was a gift from my grandfather." He pointed out his side window. "Way out there is the Old Mariner's Lighthouse to the west, and if we walked to the edge, you'd see Sailor's Cove to the north. At least, that's what Phil and

I call it." He turned his head and pointed out the passenger-side window. "Then this field and my own private woods beyond in the back."

Carrie was stunned and continued to sit without saying anything.

"Shannon has the adjoining land, and when we start walking back there, you'll see how special all of it is."

He turned off the ignition and grabbed the backpack before he helped her with the snowshoes. "We could have cross-country skied back there, too, but this is easier on the new snow." Their snowshoes kept them on the surface, and they made new tracks along the protective stand of pines and cedars, then disappeared into the woods. Carrie looked back and couldn't see the road or the car.

Finally, Rob stopped, and the two of them stood in a clearing that opened into a azure blue sky, with wisps of clouds. Carrie was overcome by the serenity. The cold air burned her cheeks, tree branches creaked under their new coat of snow, and in front of them came the slight gurgle of a stream not yet completely frozen. A picnic table sat near the bank. Carrie looked around for the rabbits and racoons and maybe a fox to greet them, but there were none. Then, she heard a familiar bird cry.

"Shhh. Hear that? The cardinals are watching us," Rob said. Soon the tat-a-tat-tat of a pileated woodpecker joined the chorus.

She wiggled her fingers in her mittens to keep the cold at bay, and to remind herself that she wasn't a princess in a Hollywood movie. Then suddenly, the anxiety attack came.

Irrational thoughts filled her head. *Oh, my Lord, this is it. I've always envisioned my proposal happening in a lovely restaurant, probably Italian, because that's my favorite, and there would be violins, so that would have to be Italian. And he'd be in a well-tailored suit and get down on one knee, and everyone at all the other tables would put down their forks and clap for us, and then they'd raise a toast, and we'd drink wine. Really, that was my dream. And now, I'm in the middle of a forest, and it's 15 degrees and I have long underwear on, and he has a hunter orange jacket and wool plaid cap with fur-lined ear flaps. This wasn't my vision. Ever.*

With one large sweep of the hand, Rob cleared snow off the table. "I thought it would be fun to have a little picnic, so Shannon packed us a lunch. Let's see what we have here."

Rob started to pull everything out of the backpack, and just to make sure he had everything, he turned the bag upside down. Carrie began to giggle like a child.

Thirty minutes later, they repacked the rest of the whitefish spread, cheese, and crackers. Shannon had thought of everything for a wonderfully romantic winter picnic, including the peppermint schnapps for the hot chocolate. As they stood up to put their snowshoes back on, Rob pulled her close and they stood there, chins turned up, faces to the winter sun. She rested her head on his shoulder and laughed at how her breath glistened on the hunter orange. As he stepped back to walk, his shoe became entangled in hers and before either of them could catch themselves, they toppled into the snow, she landing on top of him.

"Hey, this is like the first time you took me sailing."

"Not quite. I didn't love you then as much as I love you now." They wrapped their arms around each other and kissed long and slowly.

"And I love you, more than I ever thought possible."

They laughed and made snow angels until the cold found their backs. Carrie would never forget this day, and the proposal that didn't happen.

Her first visit to Ridgewood felt like she was in a snow globe. And now it was time to go back to Milwaukee and face the reality of work. She was still happy that in three short days, she and Rob would have a few days to themselves over the New Year holiday, and she looked forward to spending some alone time with him.

Their flight returned on time, and they were anxious to get back before the snowstorm that was predicted to start any time. They rode to Carrie's in silence, her hand resting on his on the console of his car. Occasionally, they'd exchange a glance that expressed contentment and happiness. After a quick stop at the market near Carrie's house where they each picked up some food, Rob pulled into her driveway, and got out to help her carry her groceries.

"Remember Amy? he asked. "Would you like to go see her with me?"

Carrie's smile slid off her face, faster than the snow that was starting to fall. "What?"

"Amy texted me, and she can have visitors now."

"What? I had no idea she was still in the picture. And where is she? You better come in. We need to talk about this."

"Let me get home before the snow really starts to get bad. Then I'll call and fill you in."

"You're right," Carrie said. "But seriously, we need to talk about this. Later tonight, okay? I had a wonderful time with your family, and I don't want Amy to get in the middle of us."

"You're the best. I'll call you later. And trust me, she won't."

Carrie put her groceries away and freshened het cats' food and water, while Lila and Poppy let her know they'd missed her. "I'll play with you in a minute," she said as if they knew what she meant. When she scratched their backs, they rewarded her with loud purrs, and followed her as she dragged her suitcase upstairs. She peeked out her bedroom window. The snow looked lovely, and it was really starting to accumulate. She'd give Rob enough time before she called to make sure he got home without any problems. No, she'd just text him. This Amy stuff caught her by surprise, and she didn't feel like letting it ruin the warmth of the last few days.

Two hours later, she woke up to the phone ringing. It was Rob, and after 7:00.

"Hey, are you just getting home?" she said.

"No, the streets were still good. I've been home, and you'd be impressed. I am unpacked and put everything away, then, talked to my mom, checked my emails, and had some dinner. How about you?"

"I, ah, put the groceries away, gave the cats some fresh food, came upstairs, and plopped onto the bed. And your call woke me up. I haven't even opened my suitcase. I didn't even know I was that tired, but you know, we did stay pretty busy. It was a wonderful time."

"Well, my mother loved you. Dad, too. He told me how much he enjoyed your midnight snack together, which I knew nothing about."

"We both have our secrets, I guess. Mine involved pimento cheese and crackers. Now talk to me about Amy."

"Okay, but maybe this is more of a sensitive subject than I thought it would be. Amy's been in a psych hospital since October—shortly after the incident when you declared I was your boyfriend, and you both told me I look good in pink, remember?"

"Go on. Your attempts at being funny aren't working."

"Anyway, she texted me and told me she is making great progress and can have visitors, and asked if I would come and see her. So I thought maybe you'd go with me, that's all."

Carrie struggled to find the words, but couldn't, and remained silent.

"It's the holidays, and she has no one else. I don't know what the big deal is. She's not been able to have visitors, or a phone, or her laptop, so she must be doing better."

"Rob." Carrie paused for several seconds. "How do you know all of this?"

"Well, because I'm the one who took her there to be admitted. One day she called and asked me if I'd drive her to the hospital. Her doctor had made the arrangements. And occasionally, I'll drop off things like soap, toothpaste, and shampoo for her."

"Do you have feelings for Amy?" Carrie tried to hide her frustration in her voice, but the shortness of the question even took her by surprise.

"It's just Amy, Carrie. I had no idea you'd get upset about it. Look, she has no one else."

"Let me sleep on this tonight. I just can't believe you never told me about any of this. "

"It's nothing, Carrie. I just feel sorry for her."

"Look, I've got mail to go through, and I want to check my emails, then I'm going to shower and hit the sack. I haven't even thought about work, but I'll talk to you tomorrow night, okay?"

"Good night. And remember, I love you, my snow angel."

"Yeah. Good night."

Chapter 21

Carrie was disappointed that Rob had kept his Amy contacts from her, and since he was resolved to see her, she decided to go with him after work on Friday. She'd find a way to deal with her own discomfort. After a brief visit, they'd catch dinner at one of their favorite restaurants, and then settle in at his place.

The drive to the hospital was farther than Carrie thought, about 30 minutes north of the city. They left the highway and pulled onto a narrow county road.

"This reminds me of the first time you took me sailing, and last week when we had our picnic. I'm not sure where you're taking me, or exactly what your intentions are," she said in a teasing way. Rob slid his right hand over her leg and just smiled.

"Faith, Baby, faith."

"Man, it's dark out here, and a little creepy for me."

"Oh, this is some place. We're almost there, and trust me, I won't leave you." He smiled at Carrie, and she didn't know if he meant he wouldn't leave her there or wouldn't leave her at all. She preferred to think both.

With nothing but a small, well lit sign directing them to turn right, they may as well have been in a scary movie. She expected to see creatures jump out from the bushes. About a mile down a dark, narrow, curvy road through a stand of pine trees, they saw the massive stone pillars and wrought iron gates, lit with spotlights welcoming them to the Lakeside Center for Healing. Carrie squeezed Rob's hand for comfort. Upon receiving clearance to enter, they drove a short distance until they veered right and noticed the black horizon, lit by stars. "During the day, it has a spectacular view of Lake Michigan," Rob said.

The outside lights on the sprawling stone-and-wood building reflected a pale orange glow, and Carrie saw the warmth of its contemporary design. Small white lights twinkled under the snow on the ornamental trees and lower bushes that wrapped the building.

She felt the lining in her nose tighten from the bitter cold air as she stepped out of the car, and pulled her collar tight across her chin. Rob gripped her hand with strength she hadn't felt before, and she stayed close to his side as they approached the building. In the distance, the sound of the brittle ice cracking as the rumbling waves of Lake Michigan crashed onto the shore sent a shiver down Carrie's back. The low howl of the wind sounded like an animal in pain.

The welcome area of the Center felt like the lobby of a large, seductive hotel, without the bar and high-heeled patrons. Low light filled the space, and there were several semi-private conversation pits scattered around the open area. A massive stone fireplace on the back wall was ablaze with soothing warmth.

Thoughts continued to dance in her head, and Carrie knew there was so much more to this story. This place was not your psych hospital covered by your typical employee health insurance. "Her expensive shoes are starting to make sense now," Carrie said.

"What?" Rob said as they approached the welcome desk.

"I'll explain later."

"Rob. We're over here." Rob and Carrie turned to see Amy with a man and woman, sitting in one of the sunken areas. Rob slid his arm down around Carrie's waist, as she lagged behind.

"Hi Amy. You remember my friend, Carrie, right?"

By this time, Amy and her guests had stood. Amy smiled at Carrie. "I'm so glad you came with Rob tonight. Thank you." Turning to look at both Rob and Carrie, she continued. "I'd like you to meet my brother, Harrison, and his wife, Meredith. They're here from Boston for a few days."

"So happy to meet you, and I can't thank you enough for helping Amy out these past few months," Harrison said. "I understand she called on you between our visits."

Carrie saw a look of confusion on Rob's face as he raised an eyebrow, but she'd grill him in the car on the way home.

"You're welcome," was all Rob was able to say.

Harrison invited them to sit, and Carrie followed Rob's lead, leaving her coat on. In the next hour, the story of Amy unfolded—how she'd run away from her life in Boston and a mother who'd kept her hidden from society, refusing to get her the mental-health support she needed.

"And you traveled the country by bus for a year?" Carrie asked.

"Once I saw the lake in Chicago, I thought about staying there, but it was so busy, and people were rushing too much. I hopped on the bus to Milwaukee, and people were helpful right away that I decided to stay."

Rob and Carrie both sat there slack-jawed when they learned she was a wealthy heiress from one of New England's oldest families, and that Harrison and Meredith had devoted most of three years trying to find and care for her after the mother died. They both sat back and watched the conversation float between Amy, Harrison, and Meredith. Every now and then, Carrie would notice Rob peering at Amy when she spoke.

As the conversation came to a natural break, Rob stood and buttoned his coat. "Amy, I'm glad to see you doing so well. Harrison and Meredith, it was a pleasure, and if there's anything Carrie and I can do to help with her move back to Boston, just call on us."

"Meredith and I are headed back into the city now, as well. Have you eaten? Would you join us for dinner?"

Rob hesitated until Carrie gave him an approving nod.

Meredith gave Amy a long embrace. "I am so excited you're coming home. We've been waiting for this."

The hug fest continued with Carrie and Rob taking their turns, though Rob's was more of an awkward embrace. They returned to their car in silence.

"I had no idea." Rob sat and just shook his head before he started the car. "I'm really sort of pissed, but this proves to you that I never had any in-depth conversations with her, right?" Rob chuckled as he navigated the driveway. "And I had no idea about a brother or that he's been to see her and has been trying to take care of her for years."

"Yep, you've been played, Big Guy. But really, her mother sounds awful. Who wouldn't get their daughter the help she needed and ignore medical advice? Just because she was too concerned about what others would think? So instead, she just hid her. My mother had her own issues, but she always did what she thought was the best for us." Carrie squirmed in her seat. "I don't blame Amy for running away from it all, but taking the bus would not have been my ticket. She deserved a much better life."

"It's an amazing story, I'll say that. Can you imagine, just riding and getting off and staying in various cities around the country? And then picking Milwaukee because the lake reminded you of the ocean back home?" Rob maneuvered the car onto the highway. "On the other hand, she saw a lot of the country on her own terms, and she was always happy."

They drove without talking for a few minutes. "I can't believe she lives in The Commodore, so close to you. I remember seeing her get off the bus once as I was pulling in, and I saw her looking around. At the time, I thought she was trying to find you, but now I think she was just confused," Carrie said.

"It sounds like she'll have a great place to live in their guesthouse, and when she's better, there may be a job at the family's foundation."

They rode the rest of the way to the restaurant with nothing but the radio for sound. "You're awfully quiet." Rob said. "Something on your mind?"

"Ah…I'll tell you when we get home."

The place Rob had recommended was convenient to where Harrison and Meredith were staying and one of Milwaukee's old-time favorites, known for steaks and seafood, yet they managed to keep their menu fresh and contemporary. Carrie was starving by this time and gnawed on the homemade flatbread until her meal was served.

Carrie found both Harrison and Meredith warm, and they could be friends, under different circumstances. As they prepared to leave, Harrison handed Rob a check. "We'd like you to have this. Amy knows she wasn't her old self for quite a while. Well actually, she acknowledges she wasn't one of any of her old selves for a bit there." Harrison paused to raise an eyebrow, and they all chuckled. "But she also told us you're the only one who was nice to her. Thank you."

"It was nothing. I just picked up some toothpaste and shampoo for her a couple of times."

"Please, we insist. It's good to know there are great people in this world."

Halfway to their car, Carrie pulled Rob close under a streetlight still dressed in its holiday decoration. "You're a great man, Rob. I never doubted it, I just didn't want to share you with Amy." The warm kiss made her forget how cold it was.

"Thank you. Thank you for coming with me tonight. It meant a lot. I'm glad you're staying the night."

As they hung up their coats in Rob's condo, Carrie said, "I've got something I want to share with you." She took him by the hand, walked to the couch, and sat cross-legged, bringing her knees to her chest.

She could feel him looking directly at her, and wished he'd look away. Finally, taking a deep breath, she began. "When my folks picked me up from college after my sophomore year, I knew something was up. Usually, my mom would come alone, but my dad was there, too." She paused and sighed deeply, fidgeting with her hands. "They didn't take me home, but drove me straight to a camp in the woods of northern Wisconsin. Camp Hope is what it's called."

Carrie looked at Rob and felt an unfamiliar inner strength. "I was a classic college binge drinker, and I was losing control. Throw in some weed and my uncontrollable anxiety, and I was a mess, but I couldn't see it. One fed off the other."

She was comforted by Rob's arm around her shoulder. "It was an ugly scene when we got there, and I called my parents awful names. I don't know how they could love me after that." By now, Carrie began rocking gently. "I was there for a month, so going to Amy's place tonight took me right back."

"I don't know what to say. Was it hard?"

Her voice was quiet. "I was scheduled to do an exchange year in Spain that fall, but my parents told me I couldn't until I cleaned up, and that was the only reason I stayed, at first. It didn't take me long, though, to see how my choices were affecting my life and everything around me. My grades hit the skids, I lost a couple of friends, a boyfriend left me. I honestly don't think I'd be alive if they hadn't done that."

"But you drink now." Rob's statement was part question.

"I was never a chronic drinker—just binge drinking, and I was never identified as an alcoholic. That's why today, I always limit myself to two drinks. I can't say it's always been easy, but eventually, I grew up. The drugs? That was only at parties when I felt like I needed to smoke pot to belong, so that was nothing for me to stop. And I've never looked back." She spoke matter-of-factly.

Finally, she looked at Rob. "For me, it helped when I started to learn to manage my anxiety. After that, the rest was easier. I still see a counselor occasionally for support, and more often if I'm feeling really wound up, but I also work to manage that through diet and being physically active. You're the only person I've ever told. No one beyond my family knows about this."

As she unwound her legs and stretched them out in front of her, Rob removed his arm from her shoulder and withdrew from her physically. He leaned forward and placed both elbows on his knees, looked at the floor, and began to crack his knuckles.

"I have my own secret," he said.

It took him several seconds to begin, and she followed his gaze from the floor out into the dark sky. "When I was 13, I was assaulted at a camp I loved to attend."

"No!"

"Well, almost. The sailing instructor asked me to help put the gear away on our last sailing day. The next thing I know, I'm in a corner of the shed hanging up the sails, he's behind me with his shorts down, his hand is over my mouth, and he's reached into my swim trunks."

Carrie reached over and placed her hand on his arm. She swallowed the bile that had crept into her mouth, and winced at the bitterness.

"If another kid hadn't come in, I don't know what would have happened. The instructor told both of us that he'd report that he discovered us having sex if we ever said anything."

"What did you do?" she asked gently.

"Nothing. The next day, camp was over and my mom came to get me."

"You didn't tell anyone at camp? You weren't worried about how he might do that to someone else?"

"I was 13; I wasn't thinking about that."

"What did your parents do?"

"I never told them."

"What?" Carrie tried to keep the indignation out of her voice.

"The guy said he could tell I was gay. I didn't want my dad to hear that. I was never gay. And when Mom and Dad asked why I didn't want to go sailing when I got home, I just said I'd had plenty at camp."

"Oh Rob, I'm sick for you."

"Three weeks later, we got a letter from camp. They wanted us to know that sadly, the sailing instructor had been killed in a car accident."

"How did you feel?"

Rob sat back, held Carrie's hand and snickered. "Elated. The next day, I asked my dad if I could buy my first sailboat."

"You've been keeping that secret all these years? I don't even know what to say."

"It does feel pretty good to share that with you," Rob said.

"I never wanted anyone to know my secret and didn't feel I could trust anybody. I always felt ashamed. And now, for the first time, it's so liberating. I feel like this glass wall inside me has been shattered."

He laced his fingers between hers, and smiled at her. "Make that two walls that have tumbled."

When they held each other, she thought she could feel his heart beating in sync with hers.

Carrie couldn't get over how good it felt to wake up next to him in the morning. She enjoyed lying there listening to his gentle snore that mimicked the low rumble of the lake lapping against the ice-covered shore. The sun was lazily rising, and the sky was not yet blue. She searched the bottom of the bed for the comforter that had fallen off, and gave it a good pull, snuggling into him for more warmth before she drifted back to sleep.

An hour later, she woke to the smell of freshly brewed coffee. Wrapped in Rob's robe, she stepped over a pile of clothes on his floor and found him at the table, reading something on his computer.

"Good morning, Beautiful. I'm just reading the paper. How'd you sleep?"

"My smile doesn't tell it all?"

"Want to catch a movie today?"

"Maybe later." She let the robe drape to expose her bare shoulders.

"Well, happy new year to me, a day early," he said. "Coffee can wait."

By late-morning, Carrie had cleaned his kitchen for him, before making the drive to her place. Stepping into the shower, she let the warm water caress every nook and curve of her body. She was frustrated that he still didn't pick up after himself and was content to live in a messy home, but at least this visit, there weren't days-old dishes scattered about the place, and most of the shoes had found their way into the front closet. She knew he loved her, and she loved him, and she couldn't imagine a better way to start the new year.

Chapter 22

When Rob arrived at her place later in the afternoon, he brought a fresh baguette from his neighborhood market to go with the chili Carrie had made. In between football games on TV and packing up Christmas decorations, they enjoyed a simple New Year's Eve dinner, before they headed to her brother's for a night of music and dancing with about 20 other people. Carrie knew Rob was not looking forward to it and didn't like social gatherings like this.

"Just stay close to me tonight, and things will be fine," Carrie said. Maybe we can find a tech guy for you to talk with. There's bound to be one among their neighbors and friends. And don't forget, he has all those pinball machines. Charlie will be showing those off."

Rob had had fun when he helped Charlie rebuild the flippers and rewire the lights on his latest acquisition, an old Paul Bunyan two-player machine, and he hoped he'd be able to test it tonight. But Carrie knew it was the task of talking to new people that could induce his anxiety. She had done her best to help him overcome these social situations and feel more comfortable and more confident.

"Thanks. I keep telling myself, it will all be over in four hours."

"And the reward will be worth it," she teased as she reached up to kiss him. "By the way, you look great in that sweater. How does it feel?"

"I like it. It's so soft."

"Good, I have something else for you, too." She tossed him a black beret, followed by a flirtatious wink. "My mother was wrong. She said never trust a man in a turtleneck with jeans who wore a beret and liked jazz. But I think you look mighty fine." She adjusted the beret on his head so it slanted more to one side.

He looked in the mirror near Carrie's door. "I have to admit, I sort of like it. I'm not quite this jaunty, but tonight, anything goes, I guess. I'll be leaving it in the car, however."

"Oh, and one more thing before we go. I called my aunt today and told her we wouldn't be at her party tomorrow. We've just had too much going on, really. All I want to do is go home after the party, curl up with you, and bring in the New Year together."

Rob let out a long, low whistle. "Oh Lordy, thank you! Let's go. It's party time. The sooner we go, the sooner we come home."

Carrie had promised Kim she'd help fix the food, so they arrived an hour before any of the other guests. Her brother was not impressed when she took the time to arrange the plate of cold shrimp so the tails were turned in the same direction.

"Carrie, it's a party of our friends. You don't need to be quite so particular," he said, grabbing one and dipping it into the sauce.

"Let it go, Charlie. You know how she is," Kim said to her husband.

"I know, but I'm just saying that—"

Carrie flashed her sticky fingers in her brother's face. "It's a gift, Charlie. Attention to detail."

"Just tell me the meatballs aren't arranged by order of diameter." Charlie liked bantering with his younger sister, and she responded with a swat on the arm.

"Take Rob downstairs and play with one of your toys."

Rob helped Charlie carry the trays of cold food to the basement, where they'd bring in the new year. It was a perfect setting for a party, with music and dancing on one end of the room, and Charlie's video games around the corner of the only wall that divided the long, open space under their ranch home.

When the men could no longer hear, Carrie turned to Kim. "And what do you mean, 'You know how she is'? What are you saying?"

"Oh, it was nothing," Kim said, flipping her hand with her back to Carrie.

"Well, it must have been something. Do you think I'm too particular sometimes?" Carrie's voice sounded hurt.

"These are mechanics from Charlie's work. And our neighbors, who have three preschoolers, and my friend from work who has a 15-year-old daughter she's struggling with. None of them will care if the shrimp plate is meticulous. That's all I'm saying. In some occasions, presentation is important. Not tonight. That's all."

Carrie fiddled at getting the last of the beef-and-cheese sliders onto the heated tray. It was the same message Judith had told her, and Carrie had never seen her fussiness as an obstacle before.

"Now go downstairs and have some fun. I'll wait for the people to arrive," Kim said.

As she had hoped, Rob and Charlie were in the midst of an enthusiastic game on the Paul Bunyan machine. "Carrie, it's official. I've decided to turn my dining room into a game room," Rob said.

Carrie frowned and let her shoulders drop. He would take better care of the noisy pinball machine than he did her family's dining room set.

"Hey just kidding." He turned back to the game. "Lighten up a little and relax. Let's have some fun tonight."

Soon, Kim and Charlie's friends began to fill the basement rec room. Charlie greeted his guests, and Rob helped him fill drinks at the makeshift bar. *So much for worrying about Rob*, she told herself. Carrie was happy to see Kim's good friend, Stefanie, who she had met before on numerous occasions.

"Carrie, you look great. It is so good to see you again," Stefanie said, reaching in to hug Carrie. "I'd like you to meet my younger sister, Brittney. She's here from Chicago for the weekend."

Carrie and Brittney greeted each other, and the three women immediately began talking and catching up with each other. Carrie finally felt relaxed. She didn't know the others, and had worried about Rob fitting in. Suddenly, she was glad she had the other two single women to talk with.

By 8:30, the last of the people had gathered and the music had started. Carrie thought there were at least 30 people there, each having a good time eating, drinking, and talking. Neighbors exchanged holiday greetings with each other and talked about their kids and how excited they were for the holiday break to be over. They picked apart the antipasto tray and gleaned onto the egg rolls Carrie had brought from Wang's. Charlie's mechanic friends hung together and liked the sliders and meatballs the best. Their wives and girlfriends stayed in a group, and enjoyed the wine.

"You can tell the women who are dates from those who are wives. The single women will eat the shrimp and veggies now, but in a couple of hours, they'll be into the wings and pizza rolls, too, I guarantee it," Brittney said. Carrie laughed. She liked Brittney and knew exactly what she meant.

Rob caught Carrie's eye from across the room and motioned to dance, but she was enjoying talking to Stefanie and Brittney, and shook her head no. Rob looked dejected and remained behind the bar.

"Excuse me for a few minutes. It looks like I need to freshen up some of the trays. Who knew this would be a veggie-eating crowd?" Carrie said.

Returning several minutes later with more food, she moved through the dancing mass. "Coming through with…." She saw Rob dancing in the corner near the bar, but who was he with? She placed the food on the table and walked back to Stefanie.

"Brittney is sure having fun. She came back after the first dance and told me she really liked this guy she's dancing with." Stefanie's voice had the gentleness of a hopeful older sister.

Carrie craned her neck. "Is that her over… oh yeah, I see her now." Of course, Brittney was having fun; she found a willing dance partner in Rob. "Oh yes, they are having a good time." Had she been able to disguise the petty anger in her voice? She wasn't sure, but the picture of Rob and Brittney doubled over in giggles with Rob's hand on Brittney's shoulder was a scene she would remember a long time. A million scenarios ran through Carrie's head, and she settled on the easy one where no one would end up dead.

When the music stopped, she put a big smile on her face and walked to Rob and Brittney. "Brittney, I see you've met my boyfriend, Rob. Isn't he a good dancer?" She rested her hand on Rob's shoulder and was immediately relieved she hadn't said something ugly. She continued. "Rob, let's go play that Paul Bunyan game. I know you've been wanting to show me."

"We can do that later. I'm having fun dancing." It was apparent in the lightness of his voice and his goofy smile that he was going to be suffering a miserable hangover in the morning. And that he was totally unaware of Carrie's feeling.

"Nice to meet you, Rob. I think Stefanie wants me," Brittney said and walked to Stefanie.

"Another dance later?" Rob said, but Brittney kept walking.

Kim had been standing with her back to Carrie and overheard the exchange. She turned and stepped between Rob and Carrie, and spoke to Rob. "Really? Is this how you want to end this year?"

Kim gave him a wink. “Don’t screw this up. I’ve worked too hard to save you too many times already.”

Carrie laughed a few quick snorts.

“But she said she didn’t want to dance. I thought….”

Carrie grabbed him by the hand. “The music is getting started again. I’ll try not to step on your feet.”

Although it was good to see Carrie’s co-workers who had all returned from holiday vacations, it was nonetheless a long week at work, filled with chaos and tension. Marta was gone, still no word about what would happen to their unit, no reassignment of work, and no mention of a new vice president. Carrie had been doing her job long enough and didn’t need direction, but there were still logistical issues that needed to be resolved. She missed Rob when he worked in Chicago, and she was glad to escape the work grind on Friday to pick him up.

Slick roads made the drive downtown to the train station to meet him unnerving. An accident on the freeway left her rushed for time, and once she made her exit, she dodged snow piles on the streets, while the steam bursting up through the manholes obscured the view. She pulled in to a parking space as close to the front of the station as she could, but she still had to get out and flag Rob down. The wind snapped at her face. She didn’t care. His hug warmed her immediately.

They stopped at his neighborhood market to pick up a pizza before they settled into the evening at his place. While Rob changed clothes, Carrie cleared away a dirty glass that was stuck on the table, and wiped up some cereal crumbs. She’d learned to overlook his sloppy habits most of the time, but when she noticed the ring the glass left on her family's teak table, she was disappointed.

After four hours of unloading her ongoing work challenges and the angst she was feeling about work, she had to leave so she could get up to meet the singles' ski club at 6:00 am.

"I know I've been talking all night long, and you've been incredibly patient, and other than telling me your week was good, I didn't even give you a chance to say much," she said.

"No problem." Rob helped Carrie on with her coat. Turning her to face him, he placed his hands on her shoulders.

"You're so forgiving. This is just another reason why I love you so much."

"We're both going to have changes at work, and we just have to figure out how to support each other and get through whatever we need to. In the end, you'll be fine."

"Thanks. I won't be home until late tomorrow night, but I'll call you sometime during the day, and we'll have Sunday together."

Chapter 23

It had been a year since Carrie had enjoyed a long day of skiing and reconnecting with friends she'd made over time in the club. In the early morning darkness, she boarded the bus and found her seat near the front next to her friend, Melissa. She hadn't seen her for several months, and for most of the trip, they chatted about their jobs and recent holidays.

"So, you're going on the annual trip to Colorado, right?" Melissa asked.

"With the trip I'm taking to San Diego, I couldn't afford the time, so I had to pass this year."

"Who am I going to have fun with?"

"I'm sure you'll find someone, and I'll expect a full report," Carrie said.

"I'm ready for it. I hear there's a couple of new guys going," Melissa said with a wink.

By the time they got off the bus and waited for their skis to be unloaded, Carrie and Melissa had plotted out their plans for the day. Carrie collected her equipment and stepped away from the group.

"Hi Carrie. Planning on ripping up the slopes today?"

The voice snuck up behind her. Lorenzo. She hadn't seen him since their summer date, and she was still embarrassed for how drunk she'd gotten that evening. Even in layers of ski clothes, the man looked sinful.

"Oh my gawd. What are you doing here?"

"I kept waiting for you to invite me skiing, but then I found this group, and I've been having fun. Looks like we'll have the next 16 hours to catch up with each other. By the way, are you going to Colorado in two weeks?"

"No, it didn't work out this year. How about you?"

"I thought I'd give it a try. It sounded fun, and there's still room in case your plans change" Lorenzo said.

"Well, I'm sure you'll have a great time. My friend, Melissa, is going, and I'll make sure you meet her before today is over."

Carrie was relieved when she realized she'd be on the tougher runs, while he was limited to the starter hills.

"Who's that? He's cute," Melissa said, as they met and walked away.

"I'll tell you about him later. A class guy though, for sure, and he's going to Colorado," she said with a sly smile.

Carrie's thoughts had already drifted to Rob and their getaway to San Diego. She'd made these ski plans before she found out he was going to be in the Chicago office more often, or she wouldn't have tied up an entire Saturday. She kept thinking about what he'd said: "We're both going to have changes at work…." What did he mean? She assumed he was being pulled in to the Chicago office permanently. Chicago. She didn't like it, but could live with that, at least for a while. Maybe she *would* look for a job there.

It had been a perfect day on the slopes, with sunny skies and temperatures warming up to the mid-20s. And she'd avoided Lorenzo, which was fine, as well. She slept most of the four-hour drive back home, but knew she'd be tired in the morning. It was after midnight when they returned, and the next morning, her body ached with exhaustion, but she made herself get out of bed. She called Rob to see how he wanted to spend the day.

"Hey, how do you feel about a good brunch this morning? I know a place that serves a great one."

"Sounds perfect. What time and where?" he asked.

"How about 11:00? Here. I've got everything we need."

"Perfect. I'll see you then."

Carrie showered and put on her favorite jeans and a dark purple sweater. The wind had given her face a rosy look, as fresh and natural as any model's. She let her long, thick hair fall naturally over her shoulders, and its honey tones made her blue eyes pop, as her hair stylist liked to say.

Within an hour, the house filled with the aroma of the ham-and-onion quiche. She made a fresh pitcher of Bloody Marys. Now she just needed Rob, and then she'd toss the croissants in the oven to heat through.

"Jeez, Carrie, this is delicious. When did you have time to make this?"

She deducted a slight nervousness in his voice.

"That market of yours is a very good one, you know. They have all sorts of things in that freezer." Carrie laughed.

"Well, here's to a great brunch," he said, "and a beautiful, sunny winter afternoon, just the two of us." He raised his drink. Then he ran his tongue between his upper gum and teeth. Uh oh. That was usually reserved for an Amy conversation. They ate in silence except for the music in the background. Rob made little eye contact with Carrie and didn't offer any conversation.

Carrie hoped her inner voices stayed quiet. *I'll let him finish while the food is hot, then I'll ask. Oh please. DO NOT tell me this is about Amy again. What now? I thought she was gone for good. It's either Amy or a move to Chicago. I can handle the move. I can't handle more Amy. Carrie could feel her face turning red. Breathe, breathe.*

She got up from the table, walked to the kitchen, and returned with the butter, slathering it on her croissant. Croissants. She didn't care that they were made already laden with fat. She topped it with a spoonful of raspberry jam.

"Do you want to tell me what's wrong? We're enjoying a great meal and suddenly, it's as if you've become obsessed with your croissant," Rob said.

"Are you seeing Amy?"

"What the hell?" Rob put his fork down and pushed his empty plate away. "Where did you get that idea? Where did that come from?"

"The last time you were like this was when Amy showed up that time. So, I thought maybe…."

Rob planted both elbows on the table, laced his fingers, and stared at Carrie. It was several seconds before he spoke. "I've not seen or talked or emailed or texted or pony-expressed Amy since you and I saw her together. We've not exchanged smoke signals, used carrier pigeons, sent or received a telegram. Though I did try my hand at Morse code to send a distress signal, it must have been intercepted, because I never received a reply."

Carrie looked down at her plate and set her croissant aside. She returned his stare, this time with a smirk, acknowledging the scolding.

Rob leaned forward, reached across the table, and held her hand. "But I do have some big news, and I've been anxious to tell you."

"Let me take this stuff to the kitchen first, then I can focus." Carrie knew it. He was going back to Chicago. Finally, she sat back down to hear the news.

"When we're in San Diego, they are going to announce some major changes. And I'm one of them. I'm getting a great promotion that has thrown me for a loop, and they're moving me again."

"I am so proud of you." Carrie gave his hands a hard squeeze. "You deserve it, and I know how much you love Chicago."

"Well, you haven't heard the rest of it." Rob sat back, sliding his hand out of her grasp. "I'm not being transferred to Chicago; they're moving me to Tokyo."

Carrie sat back in her chair. The wind sailed from her lungs. She stared at him before she turned to look out the window, looking at him out of the corner of her eye. "Tokyo? As in Japan?"

"That Tokyo. I'm being named the Director of Operations for the new Pacific Rim Division. They seem to think my knowledge of Mandarin will be helpful, and they're right, to some degree."

Carrie pushed herself away from the table, stood, and walked into the living room, massaging her head with deeper and deeper intensity. Rob followed her, but kept his distance.

"When? For how long?"

Rob stood behind her and steadied her with his hands on her shoulders. "They want me there by May 1st, and they've asked for a two-year commitment.

"I'm thrilled for you, but what about us?" She turned to face him. "What's going to happen to us?" Her head dropped, and she faced the floor.

"And about us?" He reached down and lifted her chin so her gaze met his. "I want you to come with me."

"Japan? Japan? I don't speak the language. I wouldn't know anyone. I don't even like sushi. And I saw a piece on TV that showed their teeny, tiny apartments. What would I do all day when you're at work? I would never see my family. What about my job here?" Carrie shook her head and walked away. "I do not see myself in Tokyo." She looked around her condo and swept her hands in a broad motioning pattern. "What about all of this? And in three months? Are you kidding me?"

"Well, that went well." Rob made another Bloody Mary for himself. "I'm glad you're at least *open* to the idea," he said as he sat on one end of the couch.

Carrie sat on the end farthest from Rob, clutching a throw pillow to her chest. "Can you take your own stuff? What about my stuff? And really, what would I do?" Just then, Lila jumped up onto her lap and demanded attention.

"I don't remember all the details. I'll have a certain amount they'll ship, and I'll have a generous housing allowance. I just don't remember all of it now, but everything will work out."

"Do they have homes with wide front porches?" Carrie looked up, her eyes red with sadness.

"They have huge, modern high-rises with all the amenities in the building that anyone could ever want, geared specifically toward ex-pats. They've already sent me some information to begin looking at and learning more about the city." He paused for a minute. Carrie stared at the floor blankly. He took a long drink from his glass. "But no, they don't have homes with wide front porches."

"Can't you turn it down? What's wrong with Chicago? Or even finding another job here? Or your dad's business?"

"Carrie, I know this is hard. You have a job you love, but it's in transition with a lot of unknowns. You have a family you love, and they are also in transition, as Maggie's twins will go to college next fall, and Charlie's kids are getting older and into their own things, and your dad will spend more time in Arizona. But this is also a chance for you to spread your wings and try something really different, and for the two of us to have fun exploring another culture so different from our own."

Rob leaned forward and put his elbows on his knees. "Carrie, here's the deal. I hoped you'd be willing to give it a shot. To look at the positives. You have no idea how exciting this is for me, and how much I want you to come with me." His voice began to tremble. He reached over and took her hands in his.

"Or you can stay here, enjoy your family, which, by the way, is wonderful, and will still be wonderful if you move away. You can stay here and see what happens in your job."

She pulled her hands away, and Rob leaned back on the couch. Carrie shifted her eyes outside. He continued. "But an opportunity like this—not very many people get it, and I'm taking it. Can you imagine the adventure this will be?" He paused, but Carrie didn't respond. "And it's because of you that I got this far. A year ago, I don't think this could have happened, but you've helped me get so much more comfortable in social situations with people I don't know. They have confidence in me, and I'm not going to let them down."

"I don't know. I just don't know." She sighed. "I don't know if the timing is right. I don't know that I want to give up everything I have."

"What is it exactly you don't want to give up?" Rob stood and looked at her, hands on his hips, head cocked. "Dinner every night with your two cats? Shelves of old tennis trophies? A job you're not even sure about?"

Rob walked toward the kitchen window, raising the blind so he could focus his eyes outside. His hands were bony knots resting on the sink.

Carrie stepped in to the dining room so she could see him, but still couldn't find any words.

"You know why I like jazz? Let me tell you." He turned and began walking toward her, his voice almost quiet. "It's eclectic.

It's passion in music. It can be as smooth as fine bourbon, but it can also be messy and dirty and never the same twice. It can be out of control and take the listener to the edge of their seat wondering what's going to come next."

He stopped just short of her personal space. "It can be euphoric like a 15-year-old boy jacking off in his bedroom and come crashing to an end when his mother walks in. It can be impulsive and spontaneous. And it has a beautiful soul." He paused and took a deep breath, and lowered his voice. "I thought you were my jazz."

Carrie stood just watching him, her arms crossed at her chest, her hands near her throat.

"But you." His deep breath and flailing arms scared her until she backed away. "You're more concerned about the symmetry on the mantle instead of the fire in the hearth. Your ties to tradition are beautiful, but binding. And if you can't control it, you can't accept it: your mother's death, your dad's remarriage, the changes at work. Your condo is perfect, and it's a showpiece. Every time I come over, you're chasing me with coasters, telling me where I can't put my feet and where I can't move a chair. You have five pillows on your couch, and I can't put my head on any of them."

When it was clear Rob was finished, it was Carrie's turn. She lowered her arms and let them hang by her sides, fingers relaxed. Her weight was centered over her feet, calm and controlled.

"I've worked hard for everything I have," motioning with her hand to show off her furnishings. "And yes, I like nice things, I like clean, and I like order." She maintained her focus on him. "And I'm not ready to share them with a slob."

His eyes blinked and he raised his chin. She took a step closer to him. "You keep every pair of shoes you have in a heap right inside your front door. You can't even get them in the hall closet." By now, her hands were balled into fists.

"When I was there the other night, I had to unstick a glass from the dining room table. How long had you left it there? Have you seen the cup on your desk? You're too old for that kind of science experiment. How about that pile of nail clippings on your bathroom counter? Gone yet? This is way beyond putting the cap back on the toothpaste; you can't even get your dishes to the kitchen, much less into the dishwasher."

Carrie paused and walked away before she turned and squinted at him. "I am not your mother willing to pick up after you, and I can't live like that."

Neither of them spoke, and continued to look at each other.

"So now what?" Rob asked as he looked toward the dining room table.

"I'm not going to San Diego with you."

"Just like that?"

"I'm going to Colorado with the ski club."

"When did you decide that?"

"Right now. I found out yesterday they still had room, and if I can catch the flight, I'm going. We need some time apart. Then when we get back, we can talk."

Rob got his coat out of the closet. "I thought it was you. I thought you were the one for me, and I was the one for you." His voice broke, and he ran the back of his hand across his cheek.

Carrie grabbed his arm. "I didn't say *no*."

"Two weeks?"

"Two weeks. You'll be back from San Diego, and I'll be back from Colorado."

Carrie caught up to him as he opened the door. "I love you. More than you'll ever know," he said.

No sound came from her mouth as she mouthed the words, *I love you, too*, but he was gone.

She bawled. Grabbing a tissue from the kitchen counter and covering her face until the sobbing stopped, she gasped until she caught her breath.

Through tears, she cleared everything from the counter, wiped it multiple times, and put things back into place. She pulled out the bottle of wine he'd brought her and looked at it.

Moving to the cupboard, she alphabetized all her spices, then rearranged them in order of use. Next, she fluffed the pillows on the couch, aligning the prints in the same direction. She restacked a pile of magazines and papers on the coffee table, straightened the cords at her charging station, and replaced Valentine's coasters on the end table. Finally, she sat at the table, made a list of 11 things she needed to do, and immediately crossed three of them off as being done.

Shit. *What have I done and who have I become*, she asked herself? Maybe cleanliness wasn't next to godliness, as her mother had drilled into her, but she didn't want to test it now. As an adult, she discovered her mother's penchant for order was to keep others from discovering her bottles of booze stashed in her secret hiding places. *I have nothing to hide from him*, Carrie told herself.

Finally, she put the unopened bottle of wine back under the cabinet.

Later that evening, Maggie called, and Carrie unloaded on her, sparing the details of the ugly words she'd exchanged with Rob. After several minutes of nonstop talking, she finally let Maggie talk.

"First of all, you're all over the place emotionally, and I get it, because this is really big. You've had your first big fight. But I just want to know—did he ask you to marry him?"

"No, but…."

Maggie cut her off. "Let me get this right. He wants you to give up your career, your home, family, and friends—basically your entire lifestyle as you know it—and move thousands of miles away to a very different culture? But he's not interested in getting married?"

"Well, I don't know that he doesn't want to get married," Carrie responded.

"Did it come up at all? Has it ever come up?"

"No, but that doesn't mean…."

"Just talk to him and see how he feels. You haven't even known him for a year. What are his long-term plans? Does he want an international lifestyle? Carrie, you need to think about this and get some answers before you jump in with a big old yes. Two years isn't that long. You can wait for his return. Remember, Brad and I dated for almost five years before we even started talking about living together."

Carrie was disappointed with her sister's advice, but knew she was right. For her entire life, Maggie was the logical, pragmatic sister, and Carrie, the more emotional, sensitive, sibling.

"You're right, but we're going to take a couple of weeks off. We both said some things we probably already regret, so right now, I won't be asking him anything about marriage."

"Ah, okay then. Well, you guys have to figure that out. But remember what Mom always said: forgiveness is just as important as love in any relationship."

Carrie ended the call and walked over to a picture that had just been taken at Christmas: Rob, with his arm slung over her shoulder, and the stack of wood behind them in the fresh snow. They were a couple in love. What happened? Was it more than Japan?

Chapter 24

As soon as Rob left, she signed up for the ski trip and booked the flight. She wasn't normally this impulsive, but Rob's words stung, and he was right; she needed to be more spontaneous. After a fitful night of sleep, Carrie picked up the phone to text Rob as she did every morning, and then reminded herself, she was the one who suggested the two-week hiatus. Still, she needed to hear his voice, but decided it was just anxiety, and put the phone back down.

Upheaval at work. Rob's transfer. Nasty, pent-up words they'd thrown at each other, exploding like firebombs. She even regretted her decision to go on the ski trip, but also knew it would be good for her to get away, spend time with Melissa and other ski friends, and enjoy the mountain-fresh air. She'd managed to stay clear of Lorenzo on the one-day ski trip, and hoped her luck would hold.

Her mood became upbeat when she got to work, and Denise from the CEO's office called first thing in the morning.

"Jack would like to meet with you at 3:30. Will that work for you?" Denise asked.

"Absolutely. I'll bring updates on my projects. Do I need to bring anything else?"

"No. That will be fine. We'll see you then."

Carrie closed her eyes, smiled, and thought she could smell roses in the air, feel the wings of butterflies flitting around her head, and the warmth of the sun shining down. All would be right at work, now that she was getting the promotion, even if it was temporary. She sat through her monthly finance meeting and another with the newsletter production team, both with newfound confidence. After lunch, she finalized her post on the hospital's blog on winter health care challenges, until it was time for her meeting. She rarely freshened her lipstick throughout the day, but today was not like any other. Walking up the one level to Jack's office, she passed a member of the risk management division, who held his head low and didn't respond to her hello.

Denise greeted her when she arrived. "Jack will see you now," she said, in a flat voice, empty of its usual cheerfulness.

"Thank you." Carrie had grown very fond of Denise over the years, and had wanted to ask if she was all right, but thought this was not the time. Instead, she entered the office of her mentor and advocate.

"Carrie, it's good to see you. It's been a couple of weeks, but how were your holidays?" Jack motioned for her to sit down on the couch.

"Thank you." Carrie relaxed, but sat on the edge of the chair. She tugged at her skirt and cursed the low-sitting behemoth piece of furniture. "I had a wonderful time. And yours?" *Let's get on with the news and what my new salary will be*, she thought to herself.

Jack made himself comfortable in a leather chair at the end of the couch. She endured a story about how his wife lost her luggage on their way to Naples and how their youngest grandchild had to go to the ER on Christmas Eve because of a high fever, but he was fine, and just a couple days later, playing like the rascal he is. Seriously, enough of the chit chat, Carrie thought.

Finally, he launched into the meeting. "Carrie, I've been looking at your file. Ten years, and you've done a great job for St. Hedwig's."

Carrie smiled. She could feel herself sitting taller. "Thank you."

"I'm taking the time today to talk personally to you and members of the leadership team before others hear the news. St. Hedwig's has been sold to Metamora Health in Michigan, and at this time, they expect to utilize their own leadership team. As a result, several staff will not be retained, and that includes you."

Carrie gasped, but wasn't certain she'd heard him correctly. "I'm being let go?"

Jack nodded. "Effective the end of next week. You will be given a glowing letter of recommendation, a generous exit package, insurance for…."

Carrie didn't hear the rest of it. She accepted the envelope Jack handed to her that would describe the benefits of her dismissal, but sat in silence, glaring at the floor.

"I'm trusting you'll keep this quiet before the announcement is made tomorrow. Matter of fact, I'd suggest you take the rest of the day off."

It was 3:40. Of course, she was taking the rest of the day off. She worked to steady her breathing, feeling like she'd just been sucker-punched, and when she stood and tried to walk, it felt like her feet were stuck in cement.

"Carrie, I'm always available to be your number-one reference, and you have my cell number. And remember, this was a business decision. Don't take it personally."

She wanted to spit at him, but knew that would solve nothing. Within five minutes, she had gathered her purse and laptop, and was in her car, not sure where to go or what to do, but she wasn't going to have her breakdown in the hospital parking lot.

How she found herself lying on her living room floor was confusing to her. She vaguely remembered entering from the garage and going upstairs to change into her yoga pants, wool socks, and a hooded Marquette sweatshirt, but details from her drive home were lost in the emotion. Yet here she was, on the carpeted floor, hood pulled over her head, arms outstretched. She felt numb until her cats joined her, one on her left, anchoring her shoulder to the carpet. The other sniffed around her head and face before curling up next the warm fleece of her shirt.

Carrie flattened her back, wicking strength from the hardness of the floor. Inhale. Exhale. Long, deep breaths. After several minutes of stillness, she called Maggie. Then Kim. Both calls went straight to voicemail as she knew they would.

Her emotions fluttered among anger and sadness, pity and self-doubt. But she couldn't cry. After several minutes, she sat up and called Rob. She didn't care about the two-week ban that she had suggested. She needed to tell him, but as soon as she heard his pre-recorded message, she hung up.

By 10:00 that evening, she was ready for bed. She'd shared the news with everyone in her family, and her father suggested an Arizona vacation. But she still hadn't connected with Rob, and he was the only person who could make her feel better.

The next morning, Carrie attended her monthly breakfast meeting with her fellow Public Relations professionals. She listened for open positions in the area. None of them captivated her interest, though she wasn't sure she knew what would at the moment.

Two hours later, she walked in to her office, confident she would remain professional as the news broke. That was her goal for the day, just make it through without excoriating anyone. She didn't even know who else was being let go, and hadn't thought about her staff until she opened the door.

It was clear the announcement had been made when Dorie, the administrative assistant, was the first to jump out of her chair and hug her.

"Carrie, I can't believe it. Did you know?"

"Yes, I did. Thank you. How about anyone else from the team?"

Dorie shook her head. "Just you."

Several other members of the team gathered and, suddenly, Carrie felt like she was in a casket looking up at them. "I'm not dead. I'm not even gone yet, and I'll be okay, really." She laughed at their condolences and stepped in to her office. From the doorway, she turned and said "I'm here until next Thursday. Let's see what we can get done."

Dorie, a mother to the team, entered Carrie's office with a box of Kleenex. "I'm stunned, that's all I can say. I never thought he'd let go of you. Can't he see what you've done for the Foundation? For the hospital? I am just so sorry." She turned to leave and stopped. "Yet, he keeps that putz, Dwight. I don't get it." She left, leaving Carrie slightly confused.

Carrie opened her computer and read the email delivering the announcement. "It is with much joy that I announce the realignment of St. Hedwig's with…." Where is the part about the casualties? About me? "It is also with much sadness that I announce this will result in the loss of several valuable members of the St. Hedwig team." She read the list of seven names, including the man she passed in the stairwell. How did Dwight survive and I didn't, she asked herself? Then she read the final sentence.

"Determining which positions to eliminate to realign St. Hedwig's to fit the Metamora model was the most difficult thing I've had to do as CEO." There it was. Metamora Health hadn't decided to cut her position; Jack Stewart had.

Throughout the day, numerous employees called, emailed, or stopped by her office. She was flattered and felt validated. She held her head high and actually found herself helping to comfort some of the members of her team.

After she finally absorbed the news, she began to look at this as the new opportunity she was looking for. Meanwhile, she wanted to do whatever she could to make sure the Foundation staff was upbeat when the new posse rode into town. She knew how to put on a great game face when she had to. She'd relied on her mother's advice when she'd run into a bump in high school, and it was just as apropos today as it was then.

Caroline, you can take the high road, or you can take the low road. That's the easy way. Sling mud, spread gossip, do the least amount of work possible. I didn't let you pout when you didn't get the lead role in the sixth-grade play. There's no reason for you to start taking shortcuts now. Work hard, do your best, and when it gets tough, put on that game face.

Carrie left work on Friday with renewed anticipation about work, and at the same time, dread and doubt about her relationship with Rob. He had ignored her calls, and maybe that was a sign she needed to acknowledge. It had been a long five days since their fight.

Maybe it was all right she had time to sort through things and figure out what she wanted. After dinner, she plugged in her ear buds, pulled on her red fleece cap, wrapped her cherry-red scarf around her neck, and found her warmest fleece-lined mittens. She went for a short walk around the complex and out onto the trail. She let music from her playlist of favorites guide her pace. The sidewalks were clear, it was a beautiful winter night, and she stuck out her tongue to catch the light snow that was flittering about. If winter could smell fresh, this was it, and she didn't want to think about living somewhere else.

Just as she settled onto the couch, wrapped in her favorite quilt to catch up on some of her TV shows, her phone rang. Caller ID told her it was Rob.

"Hey, it's good to hear you. Are you ready for your big week?" she said with a sheepish tone to her voice.

"Wanted to let you know my dad had a heart attack, and I was in Ridgewood most of the week."

Carrie clutched her chest as if she was having a cardiac event. "Oh my God, what happened? When? How is he?"

"It happened early Monday morning, and he's home now. He's stable, so I drove back yesterday."

"That's good. What's the prognosis?"

"Good," Rob said. "Between diet changes and some drugs, they expect he'll do just fine."

"How's your mom doing?"

"She's remarkable. Doing well."

"I imagine she was happy you were there," Carrie said.

"She started to cry."

"So how about you?"

"I'm good," Rob said. "Frankly, I was glad to get back in the office."

Carrie paused before continuing. "Rob, I'm sorry."

"We'll talk sometime, but I'm headed to bed now."

"Can we get together this weekend before you leave for California?" Carrie asked.

There was a long pause before Rob spoke. "I have too much to do before I leave. And I think your idea that we take a break for two weeks was good. I'm just calling to let you know about Dad."

"Okay. Thanks for calling. And Rob," she wanted to tell him her news, but choked on the words. He had enough right now. "Good luck next week." Her words were barely above a squeak, trying to hold back the emotion in her voice.

With a quiet weekend alone for the first time in months, Carrie caught her nephew's basketball game Saturday morning, then went to her office to pack up her personal items. She had just three work days the next week before she left for the ski trip, and then her life at St. Hedwig's was over. For the first time, sitting alone in her office, tears began to fall. Finished with what she wanted to do, she walked to the parking lot, balancing a box, a tote bag, and her purse. She heard someone shouting behind her when she was almost to her car.

"Miss, Miss, I have to ask you to stop." The hospital guard was panting as he ran to catch up.

Carrie braced the box against the back of her car, turned, and glared at the guard.

"Miss Carrie, I didn't know it was you. But I can't let you take those things."

"But they're mine, Leonard."

"But we've been told. You and the others can only take things out during working hours."

"Who said that?"

"Jack Stewart."

"Screw Jack Stewart. You call him and tell him…. Just tell him I'm taking my stuff."

"But, Miss Carrie, I'll have to report this."

"Nope, nope, not going to stop, Leonard. Do what you need to do."

Carrie opened the hatch on her car, emptied the contents of her arms, closed it, got into her car, and started the engine. She opened her window. "You might want to move Leonard, 'cause I don't want to hit you as I back out."

Leonard stepped to the side, threw his hands up, and began to laugh. She'd never squealed her tires before, but she was entering new territory as someone who'd been "right-sized" out of an organization.

Sunday afternoon, Carrie began to lay out the clothes she'd take on the ski trip. She also called Melissa to carpool to the meeting point.

"Carrie, I'm glad you called. I'm not going. I had to cancel last week. My mother needs surgery, and I've got to help her."

"I am so bummed. Rob and I had a fight, and I was excited to hang with you on the slopes."

"Not to worry. Remember, your friend, Lorenzo, will be there."

Carrie felt a dull throb in her head when she hung up. How would she avoid Lorenzo the entire trip? On the other hand, maybe he could be a good diversion for her.

From the time the ski club assembled at the airport on Wednesday night until their final dinner Sunday evening, Carrie truly exhausted herself, and her path crossed Lorenzo's only a couple times. She physically attacked the slopes like she hadn't done in a long time, and avoided the younger members of the club, who were more interested in drinking and flirting than she was. After dinner each night with a couple other long-time members she'd known throughout the years, she'd hit one last run, then to bed. Despite the physical exertion and the thin mountain air, she couldn't shake Rob off her mind, and by the time she said goodnight to the group on Sunday, she was anxious to text him on Monday morning.

"Dinner Tuesday?"

A few minutes later, he responded. "I'll be in Chicago, and I teach Wednesday, then have to go back to Chicago on Thursday. How does Friday sound? My place?"

She had a lot of thoughts on her mind that she wanted to share, and had not told him that she was unemployed. She was eager to move her life forward. But was dinner at his place the right idea?

"I'd really like to fix a good meal for you there," Rob said.

He wasn't usually this insistent, so she agreed. She'd meet him at his condo after work. Well, at least after his work.

Chapter 25

When Carrie woke up Monday morning, she let her feet dangle while she thought about the day ahead. Jobless. She didn't know how to feel.

The hospital merger and layoffs had been in Sunday's paper, and when Carrie opened her phone, she was astonished to see all the unread emails, texts, and messages that had been left. Responding to all of them took the entire day, and resulted in breakfast, lunch, and dinner meetings set over the next two weeks. She was overwhelmed by the support she had in Milwaukee.

But anxiety about her dinner with Rob at the end of the week hung in her stomach like a heavy cloud. Would he feel the same way he did before the fight? Would he still want her to join him? Regretting all the crappy words she said to Rob in a fit of anger, and her own close-mindedness about starting their life together with a move to Tokyo had left her frustrated, even before her job loss. Move on, Girl, she told herself. What's done is done.

Tuesday morning, she enjoyed a leisurely jog in the cold winter air. Carrie fixed herself a cup of coffee, then sat on the floor of her living room, and opened a box of family items she'd unearthed from the basement. She hadn't remembered seeing this box until she brought it back from her family's home last summer, and was excited to see what she might learn.

On top was the old Belle family Bible, and she could tell by dates in the front it belonged to her great-great grandmother, given to her when she left England. As she flipped through the thin parchment papers, several news clippings and old letters fell to the floor. She'd read them later, she thought, as a large, worn, leather-bound book sitting on the bottom of the box caught her attention.

Joys, Sorrows, Regrets, by Rita Mae Belle Klamerschmidt, was part scrapbook from her mother's childhood, photo album from family gatherings, and finally, a series of writings. Carrie paused to consider the date, then realized it coordinated with the time her mother was in rehab when Carrie was just a little girl.

As Carrie read the essays, her face became distorted. This couldn't be true. Why didn't she know any of this? Who was this woman? It certainly wasn't her mother. Carrie's hands began to tremble. She closed the book, placed it back in the box, and called Maggie, but ended the call before it rang. What she was going to say? It was obvious by the dates, Maggie had to have known what Carrie was just now learning for the first time, yet it had never been spoken of. Perhaps this explained the coolness between Maggie and their mother over the years.

Carrie went to the window and watched a cardinal flitter around the bushes. Suddenly, the ringing of her phone captured her attention.

"Hey, did you just call?" Maggie said.

“I did.”

“What’s up? Are you okay? Where are you?”

“I’m at home and I’m fine. Well sort of. Just really confused.”

After a long pause, Maggie continued. “Well…are you going to tell me?”

“I found letters Mom wrote as part of her therapy at that rehab camp. Let me read one to you.”

“I don’t know why I ran off with Joe Don and his sister, Bethie June. I sat next to them at the counter at Lou’s Café where I’d stopped after a doctor’s appointment. It was a cold, February day, and I helped them figure out how to find their aunt’s house. They were in town for a funeral, and I gave Bethie June my hat and mittens. When they told me how pretty Arkansas was, I asked if I could ride back with them. Two days later, they picked me up after Maggie and Charlie had gone to school. I just needed to get away. I had just had my third miscarriage, Ed was working long hours, and I knew Katharine could take care of the kids.

“Once we got to Memphis, I caught the Greyhound bus back, and Ed drove to Madison and picked me up. It’s the greatest regret in my life, and for a long time, I felt just as guilty for making Ed take a day off as I did for leaving my kids.”

Seconds ticked before Maggie spoke. “That was a long time ago, and Mom wasn’t in a good place when it happened. I was seven, Charlie was five, and Dad was at the hospital all the time.”

“But Arkansas? With two strangers?”

“I don’t remember much about it, except she came back in a few days, she had a fight with Aunt Katharine, and life went on.”

"I always thought she was the perfect Mom. Now, I'm not sure I even knew her that well."

"She was a good mother to you, Carrie. By that time, she'd gotten good medical care, and life was better."

"Yeah, until she had to go to rehab when *I* was five. Maggie, she left her children and husband to go away with some strange guy she just met at a diner. Who does that? My mind has been flooded with memories of her lately and all the advice she gave me along the way, and I'm not even sure I can trust that she knew what she was talking about. And I finally figured out that she was an obsessive neat freak so she could stash her bottles around the house, and no one would stumble upon them. And now I'm a neat, control freak, because I thought she was perfect, and I wanted to be like her." Carrie's voice broke as she talked.

"Carrie, Mother loved you more than anything else. She loved me and Charlie, too, and suffered tremendous guilt the rest of her life for leaving us. Living with her when I was a kid wasn't always easy, but I always knew she loved me. Then when I was ten, you came along, and our whole family adored you. I never saw her as happy as she was when she would just hold you. You, my dear sister, brought great light and joy to the family.

"Thanks. I needed that."

"She was a good woman, Carrie. She had her flaws, and she wasn't perfect, but none of us are."

Carrie felt better when they hung up, but calls to Maggie continued throughout the week, as she uncovered more family history. She marveled at the new information, and for a couple of days, she forgot about the growing anxiety of her dinner with Rob on Friday.

Carrie arrived at Rob's promptly at 6:30. Rob buzzed her in through the gate and met her at his door as she walked from the elevator. She was nervous and wasn't sure how the words would come out, even though she'd practiced.

"Hello."

"Hi."

She took two steps into the condo before she discovered the pile of shoes was gone. And the dust bunnies had vanished. He hung up her coat in the closet, but she hung onto her tote bag.

The table was set, including placemats, with a large vase filled with red roses. The glasses sparkled. The kitchen sink and fixtures glistened. Stacks of books, magazines, and papers were neat and orderly on the desk. Ironically, there was a set of coasters on the coffee table from the San Diego Zoo.

"Hmm," was all she could say as a slight smile crossed her lips.

"You were right, and I needed to hear it." He hung his head in shame.

"And you were right about me," she said. "I'm trying to let go. I've had a lot of time to think, and I'm finding out that a little disorder and even chaos in one's life is probably a good thing." She laughed nervously, but he did not.

"Will you join me? I asked Chen to pull together a sampling of their best." Chen was the hostess at Wang's, and Rob and Carrie frequented it so much, they knew each other's first names. "I think she added some extra shrimp just for you." Rob poured two glasses of wine and motioned for her to sit at the table, but she moved to the couch.

"Maybe we can talk a bit first. The food will be fine in a few minutes, anyway."

Conversation seem stilted at first, reminding Carrie of their early dates. "Tell me about your dad, and then I need to hear about the meeting in San Diego."

"You know, I haven't always loved my dad, but it was rough to see him lying there connected to machines and tubes, and hearing the constant sounds and buzzers. This is a man in phenomenal shape for 67. It made me think about the inspiration he's been to me over the years and what he taught me about working hard."

"But he's going to be okay?"

"I think so. You know, he woke my mom up about 3:00 Monday morning and was having a hard time catching his breath. He was gripping his chest, and I guess his color was awful, real grayish, so she called, and EMS came right away. I now know that more heart attacks happen Monday morning than any other time, and in the winter."

Carrie got a lump in her throat as she listened. She could barely contain her news.

"Anyway, that morning when I got to his hospital room, I had to turn and step back into the hallway. It was tough to see. Finally, when I went back in, he woke up and seemed really upset at first. 'Where's your mother?' he barked. Not 'Hi son, thanks for coming,' or 'How was your drive?' or 'It's good to see you.' I was probably expecting too much. I was sort of pissed after I'd driven all that way."

Carrie was desperate for him to finish, but waited patiently.

"I never felt I lived up to his expectations, but I'm not even sure I knew what those were. When I was eight, he scolded me in front of the workers for failing to adequately clean the floor around the stamping press at work. As I got older, my love of jazz, books, and foreign languages was always in stark contrast to his love of hockey, classic rock, and racing of any kind—boats or cars. Of course, when I moved out of state and left the engineering firm that bore the family name, he took it personally."

"I lost my job," Carrie said, but Rob was in his own world. She could tell it was cathartic and was sorry she'd interrupted.

"I really stopped sharing my accomplishments with him somewhere back in college, maybe even earlier. He always treated Shannon differently, and she'll say the same thing. He still had high expectations, but showed a gentler side toward her. Then when Shannon married Greg, and he joined the law practice in Ridgewood, and then when she gave him grandchildren to spoil, well that only made the distance seem...."

Rob paused and looked at her with a confused expression. "Wait? What did you just say?"

"I was laid off. Let go. Down-sized. No, I believe the term is right-sized. I'm sorry; I didn't let you finish."

"When? Why? How?"

"The hospital was bought out by a health system in Michigan, and seven of us were let go. Dead on arrival."

"Why didn't you call? Or text?"

"I tried calling you several times the day I found out, but didn't want to leave a message. Then when I found out about your dad, I didn't want to—well, the timing wasn't right."

"Jesus. I had no idea. How are you doing? What are you going to do?"

"I've been unemployed for a week, so I've had time to think about it. I'll tell you my thoughts in a minute. Finish telling me about your dad, and the trip."

"No, that's enough about my dad, except he finally thanked me for coming. Then he asked how long I was going to stay. Before I knew it, I said 'as long as I need to.' He gave me a thumbs up and a big smile."

Carrie dabbed her eye.

"Are you crying?"

"No, not really. But that's a beautiful story, Rob. He does love you. He's just never been able to control you or even understand you, so he doesn't know how to respond to you."

They each sat holding each other's hand across the table, as if words weren't necessary.

"So how did the big meeting go?" Carrie asked. "Did everything work out well?"

"Everything went as planned. The CEO is excited I'm going into this position. When it was all done, I went back to my room and thought of you. Thought of us. Wondered if we could still make it."

"I'm so sorry." She paused. "The break was good for me, though. It helped me think through some things. Brought some clarity into my head. But this job stuff has thrown me. I really thought I was safe."

"So what *are* your thoughts?" he asked.

"Let's eat first, then I'll share some ideas. I'm ready for an egg roll. How about you?" As they took their first bites, the crunch of the crispy wrap was the only sound in the room.

She reviewed the details of her severance package and Rob was impressed.

"Not bad. It gives you some breathing room, right?"

"I've looked into some vacancies, but nothing appeals to me. To be honest, I'm not really sure what I want." After several seconds of silence when they were both finished eating, she pushed her plate away and walked to retrieve a box from the tote bag she'd brought with her. "Except this. I know I want this, and I hope you do, too."

He looked at the chocolate layer cake, covered with ganache, and his eyes grew wide with excitement.

"I haven't had this since the first time I came to your place."

"I was trying to win your heart then." She looked up and met his eyes. "I'm trying to win you back now."

He stood to meet her and wrapped her in his arms. The kiss was longer than they'd ever shared. It was clear, they were both still in love with each other.

"Let's sit down and save the cake for a few minutes. Chen sent some sherbet and cookies, and I want to eat that first."

He returned from the kitchen with the frozen dessert in sparkling glass bowls that Carrie hadn't seen before.

As they finished, Rob got a bit childish, which made Carrie chuckle. "Ohhh, fortune cookie time. I'm going first."

"Go for it. You're just like a kid."

He ripped off the cellophane and broke open the cookie. He gulped a bit of air. "You will go far with someone you love."

"It does not say that. Let me see." Carrie ripped the fortune from his hand.

"You open yours now. Maybe it says the same thing."

Carrie wrestled with the wrapper until she used her teeth. Finally, she broke open the cookie, read the fortune, leaned to the back of her chair and sat there, her mouth wide open, her eyebrow furrowed. She finally looked at Rob who was on one knee.

He pulled the ring box from his pocket. "Will you?"

She couldn't believe it. Her fortune said, "Will you marry me?" Suddenly, she placed her hands over her face and started screaming.

Scrambling out of her chair, she knocked Rob to the floor and bent down to join him.

"Carrie, I think I got things in the wrong order a couple of weeks ago. I needed to ask you to do this before I asked you to move to Japan."

"Yes, yes, a thousand times yes." The large, emerald-cut diamond set in a simple platinum band dazzled on her long, slender finger.

"You decide the when, where, who, and everything else. We can make it work. So, I just need you to tell me when I need to show up and what I need to wear."

They both stood and moved back to the couch. “Are you kidding? I’m ready,” Carrie said. “I mean, I’m really ready for Tokyo. I’ve studied and researched, and I’m ready for the next chapter. Mostly, I just want to be with you.”

“You amaze me. You don’t have any reservations?”

“None.” Carrie paused. “Well, just one. Do they have dishwashers? My mother always said it saved marriages.”

“I would have loved to have known your mother.”

“Well, in me, you sort of do. And I have faith that whatever we run into, we can work out together. And I’m working on my spontaneity. But really, May 1? On the other hand, I have some free time now.”

“No actually, the new date is July 1, so that should be better.”

Chapter 26

Carrie calmed herself, and needed to know more about her future father-in-law. "So how did it go when you told your folks about Japan? What did your dad say?"

Rob regurgitated the story of breaking the news of his promotion and move while his dad was in the hospital. He joked with his dad and said he wanted to make sure there was immediate attention should his heart fail again. "My mom gasped and reached over and held my hand. She was just so excited, but my dad didn't say anything at first."

"Nothing?"

"He was sitting in the chair in his room, and said to me, "Get over here," and then he gave me a big hug. This was followed by, "I'm so damn proud of you," to which I responded something cheap about his heart attack making him a new man."

"You said what?"

"Anyway, then they both wanted to know if you were going with me, and I said that I hoped so. But I did promise both of them that I'd go back there for a few days in the next few weeks. And

I'm hoping you can go with me, with skis this time. By the way, for the first time on this visit, I really became aware of how much my mother waits on me. It drove me nuts."

"Planning a wedding, selling my condo, and moving to Japan. In just a few months. Good, no pressure, but yes, I would love to go back to Ridgewood with you. I don't think I will be eating any more pimento cheese with your dad, though."

"I have one more surprise for you." Rob led her into his bedroom where laid out on the bed was an exquisite dark purple kimono with white, orange, and fuchsia flowers. "I found this in California, and I hoped you'd say yes, because I can't return it." Carrie laughed at the suggestion and wrapped herself in the luxurious silk.

Later that night, they celebrated as many newly engaged couples would, and for more than an hour after Rob fell into his low snoring, Carrie was still restless. Thoughts bounced around her head like commuters running to catch trains, and sleep seemed half a world away. Living in Tokyo would be an adventure, but she still worried about the time she'd have alone, and how she'd meet friends, since she was not part of the mommy crowd. She knew the dynamics in her own family were changing, and she loved Rob, and wanted to marry him. There was no doubt in her mind.

By the end of Saturday, she'd spoken with her dad, her sister, her brother, and her aunt. It was with her call to her dad that she learned Rob had already contacted him before he asked. She loved when Rob's old soul snuck out and met hers.

The weekend went too fast, and it was clear, as she armed herself with wedding planning magazines and websites, Rob meant what he'd said. He would not be much of a participant in the planning, and Kim and Maggie had assured her, that was not only the norm, but probably the best.

Fortunately, they also knew they wanted to keep it simple, with family and close friends only. Rob had insisted on inviting Phil's entire family, including the parents who still lived in Ridgewood, and Carrie didn't argue. She knew how they'd been his extended family since his childhood days. He'd celebrated weddings with Phil and his brothers, and now, it would be his turn. Phil and Maggie would be their attendants, and that would be all. This was all getting very real, very fast.

Monday morning, she took a deep breath and called Judith. Though Judith's words several weeks ago had been hard for Carrie to hear, she still trusted her more than anyone else, and had confided in her immediately when Jack had broken the layoff news. Judith was furious that he hadn't found a place for Carrie in the new organization.

"Judith, how are you? Do you have a minute?"

"For you, Sweetheart, I have all the time in the world," Judith said.

"Well, what do you want me to tell you about first, that I'm getting married, or that I'm moving to Japan?"

Judith let out a high-pitch shriek. Oh good, Carrie had the melodramatic Judith today. When there were others around, Judith was more often the picture of composed elegance, but she and Carrie had such a bond that, often, she let her guard down with her like an old college friend.

"And I almost forgot. I owe it all to you." After reminding Judith that Rob was one of The Professors who played at the garden party, Judith let out another shriek.

"Oh Lord, I can't wait to tell Richard. I'd tell him now, but he's out golfing. Carrie, I just couldn't be happier for you. Tell me all about it. Do you have a date yet?"

"No, but we'll be in Tokyo by July 1. It all depends on finding a venue. We're planning something small, just our families and a few close friends. Of course, you and Richard will be included. I'd like mid-June, so it would also be one big goodbye party."

"Ideally, where do you want to have it?" Judith asked.

"Well, to be honest, this is when I really wish I had a local church affiliation, but neither of us do. I've thought about having it at our family's lake home, but it will be too buggy then. And if I keep it in this area, it will be so much easier on me and most everyone else. I just have to get creative, because most places will already be booked. I called Hillman Garden first, but they don't have any Saturdays or Sundays, and Fridays, they have their concert series. I'm just not sure yet. Do you have any suggestions on good places?"

"I do have an idea, and it would be really beautiful, and as unique and special as you are," Judith said.

"I'm holding my breath, Judith. I'm never sure what's going to come out of your head."

"I would love to host your wedding at our house. You know we've had large receptions here, and we can easily seat as many as you need; it's a perfect location."

"Oh Judith, I couldn't."

"There's nothing I'd love to do more than this."

Carrie had been to parties at Judith's home in the summer with dressed-up cocktail tables surrounding the pool. Overlooking Lake Michigan, her flower beds added splotches of color throughout the yard.

"We've got all that lawn space for tents in case it rains, and the patio is perfect for the food, or even dancing. It would be my greatest joy." Judith's voice cracked as she spoke. "I always dreamed of having Rebecca's wedding here."

"Oh Judith, it's an incredible offer. Let me talk it over with Rob, and I'll get back in touch in the next couple of days. But you're absolutely right; it would be spectacular and special."

She knew Judith would stop at nothing to make it a grand affair and was certain Rob would be grateful for her offer.

"I'll even throw in my brother-in-law to perform the service. He's a retired Lutheran minister, you know." They laughed when she offered and thought maybe they should ask him, and then meet him first.

As she got ready for bed Monday evening, the cats continued the nesting ritual in the comforter. The wedding was all going to come together, but she still had doubts about the move, which included selling her condo, arranging for storage, and sadly, letting go of Poppy and Lila. How could she find a perfect home for her cats? Even without working, how would she be able to get everything done? She peeled back the bedroom blinds to check the snowfall one last time. I wonder if they have snow like this in Tokyo? She knew they didn't and smiled. Maybe it won't be so crazy after all.

The next morning, she had a breakfast appointment with a long-time professional friend, who sounded eager when he spoke with Carrie. Carrie wasn't in the position to take on a full-time, permanent job, and she should have called him. Yet she knew she'd function better with some responsibilities besides packing and wedding planning, and she wanted to see him. With her severance package and extended health insurance, all the practical matters were in place, yet she still had a calling to work and leave Milwaukee feeling positive about her skills.

The winter weather gods were threatening Milwaukee again with a major storm, and for the first time, Carrie was glad she didn't have to battle rush-hour traffic. Arriving at the restaurant 15 minutes early, she began to worry when the time slipped to ten minutes past her meeting time. Did she have the right time, the right place, the right day? Her head had been filled with self-doubt since she was laid off, and she was hopeful that after meeting with people throughout the week, she would feel better. Finally, with a whoosh of the door, he arrived, and her self-confidence was restored.

For the first 15 minutes, she filled him in on the plans for St. Hedwig, at least those she knew. Finally, he had a proposal for her.

"The university needs somebody to head up donor relations, and I'd love to suggest your name. They haven't gone public yet with the announcement, but it should be out by the end of the week. What do you think?"

"It would be perfect, except for the one thing—I'm getting married and moving to Tokyo this summer."

"That's incredible. Congratulations! How did I not know?"

"It all just came together and hasn't quite sunk in yet. But the job really does sound like a great fit, and thanks for thinking of me. If you have anything short-term, let me know."

"Carrie, you're well respected, and I'm sure someone can use your talents here."

With that, he wished her well, paid the bill, and with the same whoosh as he entered, he left.

Carrie had a refill of coffee and pondered what might be if she stayed, but couldn't let her mind drift too far. The university brought its own set of challenges, but the rewards far outweighed them.

Appointments with colleagues during the next two weeks followed the same routine.

"You're great, it's been fun collaborating with you, I've enjoyed working with you, no one can ever replace you, they made a big mistake, and keep me posted." The messages were the same, yet Carrie felt hollow when each wished her luck. One week later, she received a call that moved her in a different direction, and challenged her to stay calm.

"Hello Carrie, this is Marcella Sampson, from Metamora Health."

Carrie held out her phone and looked at it.

"Hello. This is a surprise."

"Yes, I doubt you thought I'd be calling you, but I have something for you to think about. I heard wonderful things about you last week when we visited the staff at St. Hedwig's, and I've learned you will be getting married and moving to Tokyo. Is that correct?"

"Yes. I guess the word is out there."

"Metamora is recognizing that more of our customers are traveling and even moving overseas for work, and we want to figure out how to serve and retain them. Would you be interested in writing a monthly online newsletter that addresses issues in accessing health care internationally? It would be a contractual position with Metamora Health and would not interfere with your severance package from St. Hedwig's."

"Marcella, I'm not sure. I'll have to think about it."

"I know. It's a broad scope and I can send you our thoughts. We'd love to have your input as well."

"I really have to think about this. Can I let you know in a few days?"

"Take a couple of weeks. Does that sound good?"

"Yes, that's fine. And Marcella, thank you."

Chapter 27

Carrie was eager to make the return trip to Ridgewood with Rob, even though she had much on her mind. Before he picked her up, she knew there was one more thing she had to do.

"Hello, Marcella…."

"So, how did the call go?" Rob asked as he drove toward the airport.

"It was awkward, but good. Marcella sounded truly disappointed, but was also excited for me." Carrie turned to look at Rob. "I just want to focus on us right now."

For the past 17 years, Carrie had worked full-time, paid her way through life, and forged her own identity through her career. She'd read about the challenges others felt when they left the work force and relied on a spouse for total support, and feared the adjustment, yet she was confident things would fall into place.

"Carrie, I know you're sacrificing a lot for me. I know how much the prospect of the job at the university excited you. This means so much to me. Making this trip home with me—making this move with me—I'll make it up to you some day, I promise. I just want you to be happy."

"It's all good, and I'm looking forward to spending the time with your folks. But the first time I see your mother trying to wait on you again…."

"That is over, trust me." They both laughed. "But she'll always be my mother."

When Rob and Carrie sat down for dinner on Saturday at his family home, they'd had a full visit. Carrie loved his folks, but four days had been enough, and she was ready to return home. She prayed his father would not bring up the unknown future of the family company a final time. If they could get through the evening without that stress, she'd be happy. Over dinner, his father opened up about Rob's work transfer. "You know, I am a bit envious of you right now. Your mother and I both are."

"Why's that?" Rob said.

"For one thing, you've always stood up to me when I tried to pressure you to stay here with the company. Along the way, you inherited my stubborn streak and used it against me." Carrie's shoulders relaxed when he started to chuckle.

"But there's more. I never wanted to be an engineer or stay in northern Michigan, for that matter."

Rob jerked his head back as his mouth fell open.

"My brother, Will, was going to do that. That was always the plan. But when he…." His voice trailed until he composed himself. "It was Christmas of his junior year at State when he came home and told our parents he was leaving school to join the

Air Force. He threw away a student deferment out of loyalty to his country, despite the unpopularity of that war. There were protests on every campus. It was ugly.

Eighteen months later, I had just gotten home from baseball practice when I saw two military officials talking to my mom and dad at the door. His plane was shot down in a jungle. No presumed survivors, but they couldn't be certain. Anyway, we never saw him again."

"I knew he died in Vietnam," Rob said.

"No. We don't know that he died. He's still listed as Missing in Action."

"Dad, I never knew the whole story."

"We didn't talk about it. Your grandfather's way of dealing with Will's death was to tell me I was going to State to become an engineer, just like Will. And when I was done with college, I'd come back here and work. He brought home the college application one night from work a few months later. Mother was supportive at first when I told him I didn't want to go to college to become an engineer, and calmly asked me what I did want to do after high school."

Carol adjusted her position in her chair and let a smirk crawl over her face. It was obvious she'd heard the story before.

"I sat tall and told them I was going to move to Florida, find a job in a sail shop, and I'd figure out the rest."

"What?" Even Rob was shocked and began to laugh. "You said that to Grandpa?"

"Mother rolled her eyes, looked at me, and told me in a tone I'd never heard her use before that I was going to State to become an engineer, and she kindly reminded me that her oldest son had not given his life in some jungle in 'Nam just so I could bum around Florida. So I plugged away at school and then came back home. I started the Monday after graduation. My dad wasn't big on celebrations, and he was ready to begin the training."

"The best thing that happened to him during that time in college was that he met me." Carol tried to lift the somber mood. "Of course, we both knew he could still be drafted until he turned 26, so he refused to get married until the day after. I wasn't waiting an extra day."

Rob's father continued. "The world's a different place than when I was your age. Maybe you can even learn some things while you're in Japan that might help the business here in the long run. Who knows, maybe your mother and I will even come visit sometime," he added during the dinner conversation.

"We'd love that, wouldn't we, Carrie?"

Carrie responded with a broad smile and a nod of her head.

"Dad, I've got an idea. When we're over there, would you like to go to Vietnam together? Would that interest you at all?"

Silence filled the room while Bob looked at Carol for an answer, his eyes filling with tears that refused to drop.

Carol spoke quietly. "Why don't we start with a trip to Milwaukee first. Sometime later this spring, but before the wedding. In the meantime, your father and I can talk about your suggestion."

Finally, it was Carrie's turn. "Rob and the band he's in are playing with the Milwaukee Symphony at the end of April. You should come to hear them."

"A band? I thought you ditched that in high school," his dad said.

"We're called The Professors, and we play three or four times a year.

"The Professors? How'd you come up with that name?" His dad reached for the butter until his wife pulled it away.

"Well, everyone's a professor at either UW Milwaukee or Marquette."

"So how did you get in there?" It was apparent his dad was totally oblivious to Rob's life.

"Pop, I've been teaching a class at Marquette ever since I landed in Milwaukee. So, though I'm only an adjunct professor, they're happy to have me.

"Hmpf. I had no idea."

"I think you'd really enjoy this concert. We have a great symphony," Carrie said.

Rob's dad rested his silverware on his plate and furrowed his brow, sat back and crossed his arms as he looked at his son. "The symphony? What kind of music are *you* playing with them?"

"We're a jazz band, and I play the piano."

"Interesting." His father kept his eyes on Rob and nodded slightly.

Rob's mother rolled her eyes, took a good look at her husband, and let out a heavy sigh. "Excuse me while I get the dessert." She stood to leave.

"What did I do?" Rob's dad shrugged while looking at his wife.

"We'd love to come to Milwaukee to hear you. Rob. It would be a thrill. Just let me know when and the rest of the particulars."

"But Carol, I don't know if I can…."

"Yes, you can, and yes we are going. We can drive, but I'd much rather fly." Turning to look at Carrie, she finished. "And maybe I can do a little shopping and find a dress for the wedding."

"I'll make sure you have a great time, I promise." Carrie stood to help. "Here, let me finish clearing the table."

When the two women were alone in the kitchen, Carol turned to face Carrie, and put her hands on her shoulders. "Rob's father is paying the price for ignoring him all these years. I hope it's not too late. Somehow, you have opened the door. I don't know how or why, but thank you."

Carrie was excited her future in-laws would visit Milwaukee and attend the symphony to hear Rob and the group. As an added bonus, Carrie's dad decided to return from Arizona and stop in Milwaukee for the weekend to meet them for the concert. It would be the first meeting of the parents.

For the next several weeks, Carrie spent as much time as possible sorting, packing and tossing stuff out. One Saturday when Rob came over to help, she found the cherry-red scarf she'd made as her mother lay dying.

"Let me tell you about my mother, this scarf, and why I can never get rid of it."

Carrie had never really talked that much about her mother, and it felt good to share with Rob.

She slid off Rob's lap and cozied up alongside him on the couch. "The devotion my parents had toward each other until the day she died was special, just like your folks. My mother always said, "The best thing you can do for your children is love your mate." I think our parents were great role models for being married."

Carrie enjoyed the moment, and for whatever reason, she didn't tell him about what she'd learned about her mother in the last few weeks. She also left out the part about her mother's treatment for alcoholism. What mattered to Carrie was that as long as she could remember, her mother was loving and attentive to her.

Before Carrie's dad arrived, Rob had helped her clear out her extra bedroom and pack the items for storage. He had to admit, her obsessive/compulsive nature for orderliness had been an asset during this process, and boxes were neatly labeled and organized.

When her dad got there Friday afternoon, he and Carrie enjoyed a couple hours together. "Thanks for coming, Dad. It's been too long since we've had time together."

"You're looking as refreshed as I've seen you in a long time, Carrie. I'd say love agrees with you."

"Well you're looking a little thin, Dad. I hope everything is okay."

"Barb wants me around a long time, so we eat lots of leaves and sticks, as I like to say."

"Good. As long as it's nothing more."

"I'm just fine, Kid. Now let me look at the list of projects we're going to tackle this weekend."

Carrie didn't want to take advantage of her dad too much, but was grateful he and her brother had agreed to do some repairs on

Saturday while she spent time with Carol. But first, they had to go meet Rob and his folks for dinner. Carrie tried not to be nervous, and hoped the conversation would move more smoothly.

The first meeting of the parents went so well, Carol suggested they meet Saturday prior to the concert. When Rob suggested the Beau Thai, Carrie gave him a sharp look. “Really? Maybe something a little nicer?”

“I want them to experience the finest Milwaukee has to offer. What can be classier?”

Carrie burst out laughing and added, “Okay, but I hope you’re taking your clothes to change into. We wouldn’t want any stains on your suit.”

“I agree. She’s sounding like me now,” his mother added. Carrie hoped no one saw her roll her eyes.

“Well, I can see why you won Carrie’s heart by bringing her here,” Rob’s dad said. The group responded with a hearty laugh.

“I’m all class, Dad. Learned it from the best.” Rob winked as he gave his dad a quick point of the finger.

After they enjoyed their meal, they rejoined at the Symphony Hall, and wished Rob luck. Carrie, her dad, Bob, and Carol enjoyed a glass of wine before they took their seats. Carrie chuckled as she overheard Bob ask Carol, “Did you know he was in a band? How did I miss this?”

Carol responded with a slight wave of the hand, and Carrie smiled. She did have much in common with her future mother-in-law.

About a third of the way through the concert, The Professors were introduced. They played a jazzed-up version of Beethoven's "Moonlight Sonata," featuring Rob on the piano before the other instruments joined him. But it was when the full orchestra moved into a medley of smooth jazz sounds that The Professors really stole the show with their improvising.

When they returned for a second set near the end of the concert, members of the audience were so moved, they even stood and began dancing to the beat. Soon, two violinists from the orchestra joined the movement.

Rob's dad sat in stunned silence. His mother applauded like a mad woman.

"I had no idea," his dad said.

They met after the show at the bistro in Carol and Bob's hotel for drinks and dessert.

"Son, you were outstanding. When can we come back to hear more?"

"That's it, Dad. I'm sure glad you and Mom were here. You, too, Ed. What an evening."

"Here's to our son and his wife-to-be." Rob's dad held his glass high. "To Rob and Carrie. And what a wonderful weekend this has been."

When Carrie's dad left on Sunday, she rounded up all the clothes she was donating to the Women's Resource Center. As soon as Rob arrived, they'd finish planning for their apartment-hunting trip to Tokyo in three weeks. Making this trip ahead of their actual move would relieve the last of Carrie's anxieties. After all, it would be home for the next two years. In addition, she was going to connect with three ex-pat wives she'd met through a chat room, who offered to show her some local sites. She hadn't wrapped her head around the title of wife yet, but she knew that would be her identity.

Carrie was on the last load of putting clothes in her car as Rob arrived from dropping off his parents at the airport.

"Perfect timing," she said. "My work is done here, and we have the rest of the afternoon. Time to relax and snuggle. That's all I want to do today."

"Let's go on in. I've been waiting to tell you about a call I got on Friday morning."

"Do I even want to know about this?" Carrie grabbed two cans of soda from the refrigerator.

He braced himself against the kitchen counter, and faced her. "A headhunter called me about a job in Washington, DC. They're really eager to talk with me. Some guy heard me at the bank's annual meeting, and they've checked out my credentials."

She stopped what she was doing and gave him her full attention. Her mouth fell open. Finally, she spoke. "Washington, DC? Really? What kind of job?"

"Well, he was a little evasive. But they're interested in my work in cyber security and the fact that I speak multiple languages. Beyond that, not a lot more."

"What did you say? I presume you said no, right?" Carrie leaned against the opposite counter and crossed her arms over her chest, feeling her shoulders stiffen.

"My phone interview is Wednesday at 2:00. It never hurts to talk to them."

"What about Tokyo?"

"It's a phone call, Carrie. I don't even know who their client is, but I suspect it's connected to the government." Rob waited for her response, but she turned to grab some ice. "I have to talk to them; I just have to. I have to know what else is out there for me. For us."

She gave him a hard stare. "I've worked hard at adjusting to a move halfway around the world, I'm excited to meet a couple other wives when I'm there, and I've made peace with the fact that I'm leaving Milwaukee and my family."

She sat on the couch, and he cozied up next to her, careful to place his can on a coaster on the coffee table. "It's just a phone call. I will never make any kind of decision like this without us talking about it first. You have to trust me."

"Okay. I trust you. But figure it out fast. I'm getting rid of a lot of stuff, and I'm listing the condo by the end of the week."

Rob's phone call went well enough that he was invited to a face-to-face interview the following week, on a Friday. He asked Carrie to go along for the weekend, but she stayed home. She didn't want to give him any false encouragement, and she had wedding details to finish.

"Just promise me you'll call me as soon as you can, to give me an update."

All day Friday, Carrie kept her eye on the time and was disappointed Rob hadn't called, much less sent a text. As she drove to the airport to pick him up, she was concerned, but this lack of communication was typical Rob. Didn't he know she was anxious to hear how things had gone?

She sulked at the prospect of a move to DC now that she wanted to move to Japan. Three months ago, she wouldn't have ever imagined life beyond Milwaukee. Rob walked out of the airport just as she pulled up, and her anger subsided at the sight of him.

"Hey, I'm sorry I didn't call. I've been rushing the entire day."

"I love you, and you're forgiven. Now tell me, how did everything go?"

"I don't think you have anything to worry about. Their client is an agency in the federal government. Rob filled her in on all the details. "But at the end of the day, I don't want to work for the CIA or even the FBI, or the Department of Justice or Treasury or anyone else in Washington."

"But why are you so giddy then? You seem really excited."

"Ya know, Carrie, I think it was the prospect of a new adventure that excited me. Just like the move is going to do for both of us. But I just had to meet with them. And I needed to know you really wanted to go to Japan. Speaking of...."

"What now?"

"We won't be making an advance trip in May as planned. They need me here to finish the project—which means we won't be able to find our new home until the move. Instead, they'll put us up for a few weeks when we get there while we find a place and our stuff arrives.”

Carrie’s shoulders sagged, and the nerves in her stomach started to sing.

“There’s nothing we can do about it, Carrie. It’s out of our control.”

Chapter 28

Throughout the rest of the spring, Carrie had tightened up all the details of their wedding day. She amazed herself when she realized how much easier life was when she let go of the minutia. Her condo had sold, she'd found buyers for her furniture, and moved in with Rob. Her grandfather's desk, the family rug, and other possessions not being moved were safely packed in storage. Finally, it was Memorial weekend. The entire family would descend upon the lake home, and in Klamerschmidt style, they'd celebrate her nieces' high school graduation, and Rob and Carrie's move to Japan.

Maggie had offered to take Poppy and Lila, so by 4:00 on Friday, Rob and Carrie loaded up her car, along with both cats, and headed north.

All weekend long, the skies were sunny and bright, and invited everyone outside for walking the trails around the lake, kayaking, and boating. Charlie and Brad were intrigued when Rob got his kites out.

"We'll be back in a bit. We're going to that clearing at the end of the channel," Brad told Maggie.

"I never dreamed my husband and brother would be so enthralled by kites," Maggie said to Carrie and Kim.

As expected, the family had a big family dinner Sunday night, where they officially initiated Rob into the family. Over ribs and steak and too many glasses of wine and bottles of beer, Charlie and Brad did their best to embarrass Carrie until Maggie intervened. Stories of her life were regurgitated and enhanced with each version. "I'm just happy the quest is complete." She turned and smiled at Rob, who quietly sat, seemingly enjoying the family banter, even though it did paint a rather salty picture of his wife-to-be. A rosy hue filled his cheeks.

"None of that matters now, does it," Maggie finally said. "She couldn't have found a better mate. Rob, we love you, and we welcome you to the family."

"And thank you for taking her off our hands," Charlie added to a roar of laughter from the men, and boos from the women. "Seriously, to the two of you. You are the best, and we wish you nothing but a lifetime of happiness."

Glasses and bottles clanked with toasts of "we love you," "we will miss you," and "we can't wait to come visit you."

Rob pulled Carrie close and planted a big kiss on her lips. "I don't know who's luckier, but thank you. I love you and your family."

"Pure joy—my heart is filled with pure joy right now," Carrie said.

Rob headed back Monday afternoon with Charlie, Kim, and their family, but Carrie was spending the entire week up north. She wanted to be there to help Maggie with Emily and Kate's graduation. Mostly, she wanted to fall asleep in the pine-scented fresh air and arise to the early morning call of the loons. This would be the last time she'd have this experience for a long time, and she wanted to savor every moment of it.

Carrie wasn't sure how it would be spending several days with just Barb and her dad When she last saw her father, he looked drawn and thin, and had only mentioned Barb briefly. In her weekly calls, his words were halting and tentative. She worried his marriage to Barb might be in jeopardy, and she didn't want to be in the middle of tension that might await her after everyone left.

As soon as the others drove off, she started her familiar jog along the lake. Half way, she took off her shoes and dipped her toes into the cold water. Finally, she walked in until her ankles were covered. With every detail of planning and moving taken care of, she was overcome with the grief that came from missing her mom at this momentous time in her life. The tears began flowing from a spout she couldn't turn off.

This wasn't her family's refuge anymore, and things weren't like they used to be. Even the shoreline was different, and most of the neighbors she'd grown up with around the lake were gone. For the first time in a long time, she heard her mother's words.

Time changes everything, and you have to be able to go along with it, or you're going to be left behind. That's just life. Embrace it and be happy. Ignore it and be miserable. The choice is yours.

Bending over and resting her hands on her knees, her tears fell into the water, creating tiny ripples. Moments later, she laughed at the minnows weaving figure eights around her feet and felt her mother's presence from when she was a child. Even after she'd learned more about her mother, she couldn't shake the love she felt for her, nor did she want to.

She shook her head, stood up straight, assumed the tree position from her yoga class, drew a deep breath, and felt her face relax into a smile. The lake was full of boats, as people welcomed summer, yet she still found solace in the moment. A year ago, these transitions would have been harder. With Rob, she was at ease with letting go and moving forward. Japan was looking better and better.

The workout had cleared her head, and when she returned feeling fresh and energetic, she joined Barb and her dad on the deck under a full, early summer sun. A budding maple tree provided shade on the west side.

"How was your run?" her dad asked.

"It felt great. Thanks. I sure will miss this place, though."

"And we will miss you, too. We might see if we can come for a visit sometime." Carrie was encouraged by Barb's interest.

"I would love that, and I'm hoping we'll have an extra room."

By now, Carrie had taken her shoes off and was sitting on the edge of a lawn chair. "By the way, Dad, you look like you've put on a little bit of weight since I saw you. You're looking better."

Her dad cast a sideways glance at Barb and smiled sheepishly. "Barb and I have come to an agreement. There's nothing wrong with a little pasta or a good burger once in a while. I'm working out several times a week, I try to stay pretty active between swimming and riding my bike, along with golf. I've also mastered an afternoon nap. Life is great." He reached across the side table to Barb and held her hand.

"I'd been spending so much time trying to help my daughter save her marriage, and was worried about being Super Gram to my granddaughter, that I hadn't realized how much stress I was carrying and transferring to your father. We're both eating better, and we're both happier. I love your father and don't ever want to put anything between us again."

"Ah, that's so beautiful. I'm happy for both of you. You both look great."

"And I love spending this time up here," Barb said. "I only regret that I didn't return with him earlier this spring to meet Rob's parents."

"Your daughter needed you, and you'd made the commitment to help her," Carrie's dad responded.

"I finally figured out that she and her husband have to pull together to make it work, or not. But I can't do that, even though I was making it my mission for a bit, but they have to find their own way as a family."

"I hope things work out for them. Every now and then, I worry about Rob and me, because I know so many people who are so much in love when they get married, but somewhere along the way, that love fades. I'm sort of glad we're making this big move to Japan together. It will be the two of us in a totally different environment, and it will be fun to explore and discover together."

"You and Rob are going to be just fine. I'm so proud of you, and your mother would be, too. Love truly and with all your soul," her father said. "That's what she would be telling you."

Carrie picked up a white napkin from the table and waved it in the air. "Stop, I surrender. Please don't get me started," as she dabbed at her eyes, but started to laugh at the same time. "She's been on my mind a lot lately, and I know she's watching, so I'm good. But really, let's change the subject. Any other plans for the rest of the day?

Now it was Barb's turn to laugh. "This is pretty much it. You can do whatever you'd like."

"I'm going back to the guesthouse for a bit," Carrie said.

"Take your time honey," her dad said. "We'll probably be right here."

The week was perfect for Carrie. She played a little tennis with Maggie, and enjoyed taking Emily and Kate for lunch on Wednesday. Afterward, she drove to her old neighborhood to visit the Munsons, and was surprised to see the house for sale.

Carrie pulled into the driveway and saw the car with the Connecticut plates. She assumed it belonged to the Munsons' daughter. Since their daughter was almost 20 years older, Carrie had never known her well. Connecticut had been her home for 40 years, and it seemed she didn't have much time for her parents.

Carrie got out of her car, crossed the lawn, and was surprised to hear the loud music playing in the background. She knocked on the glass storm door.

"Hi." A woman in her early 20s answered the door. She wore short denim shorts, a tank top, and a sneer.

"I'm Carrie, and my folks lived next door for a long time. I hate to ask, but I knew the Munsons well. Are they all right?"

"Yeah, they're fine, I guess. Sort of." The young woman's phone rang, she turned her back on Carrie to answer it, and walked into the living room. Carrie stepped in to the house and looked around until the 20-something returned. "You must be who Gramps was talking about. Do you live in Milwaukee? And your dad moved to Arizona?"

"Yeah, that's me."

"Well," she shrugged her shoulders. "I guess they're okay, but I haven't seen them yet. They live in Sunset Gardens, this nursing home, and that place depresses me, so I don't go. Mom's with them now, but she couldn't remember your name."

Twenty-something looked around the room and walked into the dining room, where boxes stood three deep, with some odds and ends still in the built-in corner hutches. "I think they wanted you to have…" Carrie followed her. "Here it is. Gram's hard to understand, but I think she said it was a gift from your mom for their anniversary. I'll tell them I gave it to you, but they won't remember anyway."

Carrie took the porcelain figurine from her and held it close to her chest. It was a woman's hand clasped in a man's, and Carrie remembered her mother describing it to her over the phone. *It's just the picture of true love. You're never too old to hold hands.* Carrie bit her lower lip while she scanned the rest of the house.

She wanted to ask about the old railroad bench that had been in the foyer, but couldn't trust her voice.

"We're just packing the last of their junk, some to take back, but most for the thrift shop or to toss. If there's anything else you want, help yourself. Mom wants it all gone, and we don't have any connection to what's left."

"Thank you. This is all I need, and I'm touched your grandmother remembered." Carrie walked slowly back to her car and tucked the figurine between the folds of a blanket in the back seat, as if it were an infant. For a moment, she looked at her old childhood home and the Munsons'. She looked up and down the street of nice lawns, dotted with pots of pansies, a child's bike in the driveway two doors down, and a new craftsman-style façade and porch on the house across the street. Even the neighborhood had changed.

Instead of getting in to the car, she walked back up the steps of the porch and rapped on the door again. "One more thing," she said to the granddaughter as she opened the door and walked in to the entryway. "There used to be an old railroad bench that sat right here. Do you have any idea what happened to it? My mom and I were with your grandmother when she bought it at an old antique shop out in the country."

"Oh yeah, it's in the back here ready to go. Do you want it?"

"Were you taking it home?"

"Oh no. It's not my design aesthetic. That's for the people who are picking up the rest of the junk."

Carrie shook her head in frustration. Design aesthetic. She wanted to laugh in her face and tell her she'd been watching too many home decorating shows on TV when she should have been calling and visiting her grandparents. Instead, she walked through the house, in to the kitchen and to the back porch, a route she'd walked hundreds of times as a kid. "Then if you don't mind, it's going to go back home with me." It was awkward, but Carrie picked it up herself, navigated the steps of the back porch and rearranged the things in the back of her SUV to make room for it. She slammed the liftgate hard and turned to find the granddaughter had followed her out.

"There's one more thing I spotted in the kitchen. I'll be right back."

Carrie returned from the house waving Mrs. Munson's rolling pin. "That's not all junk; that's your grandparents' lives, and yes, you do have a connection to it, because they're your family. I get that you don't want it now, but it's still not junk, because your grandparents aren't junk. They are the most loving and kind people I've ever known, and your grandmother was constantly baking pies for people who needed a little cheering up. I'm so sorry you never had the time or opportunity to find that out for yourself. Good luck with the trip back home."

Carrie got into the car, started it, and backed out before she could even look in the young woman's direction. She didn't know exactly where her outburst had come from, but it felt good. Knowing she had one more stop, she did a U-turn, and headed toward Sunset Gardens.

As she entered and inquired at the front desk, the receptionist flagged down Ellen, the Munsons' daughter, who was walking down the corridor. She remembered meeting Carrie many years ago and was happy she'd stopped by the house and had received the porcelain gift. And the bench. And the rolling pin. "Now if you'll excuse me, I need to go back and finish packing."

Mr. and Mrs. Munson were thrilled to see Carrie, though she wasn't sure Mrs. Munson knew who she was. Carrie thanked them for the figurine and wished them well. Mr. Munson's eyes had lost their luster, and the lower lids hung well below the sockets, exposing a pale sadness.

"Thanks for stopping by. The days get long, but you just made this one shorter. Won't you stay for a few minutes? Lorraine's a bit tired, but I'd love to talk if you have the time." He stood and straightened the small blanket over his wife's shoulders. She had already fallen asleep, hunched over in her chair. "She gets a draft easily."

For the next 45 minutes, Carrie told him about the upcoming wedding and the big move. He told her about the sale of their house, and how he was sad he couldn't play golf anymore. They laughed at the time she'd tried golfing in her family's backyard and sent a ball through Munsons' garage window just as he was pulling in. She recalled how it wasn't a holiday for their family without an apple pie from Mrs. Munson, and how he'd taught her to play dice, much to her mother's chagrin. By then, she could tell that was enough time, and they exchanged goodbyes. He pulled a neatly folded handkerchief from his back pocket and tried to blink back the tears.

Returning to the guest cottage, she received a text from Rob. "Call me as soon as you can." Uh-oh. This wasn't like Rob. Was it his dad? Carrie was managing the stress as well as she could, but was near her breaking point. Lord, please don't let it be his dad, she prayed.

"Talk to me. What's going on. Is it your dad?"

"Huh? Oh no, he's fine. But DC called me again this morning. They've got another position, double what I'm making, and I can work remotely."

"Are you serious?" A confluence of relief and frustration washed over her.

"I don't know what to do. There are so many reasons to go to Japan, and for every one, I come up with a reason to stay and take the job."

"I'm sure they don't need to know today." Carrie was actually a little upset that he was still wavering.

"I told them I'd let them know next week."

"Rob, I'll be home Friday, and we can talk about this. I don't know what to tell you. I love you, and will go wherever you go."

"Something else has come up, too." Rob paused for several seconds.

"Well?"

"Do you ever think you'd be interested in living in Ridgewood?"

"Seriously? And you'd go to work for your dad? Where did this come from? You're really messing with me now."

"You're right. I'll see you Friday night, and I'll bring you up to date."

Chapter 29

As she drove back to Milwaukee on Friday, Carrie's head was swirling. She emptied her suitcase in Rob's spare bedroom and sat on the balcony with a glass of wine. She watched the sailboats glide across the lake effortlessly. When Rob arrived, he seemed a bit rattled, and Carrie became concerned. His face was flushed, and he ran his tongue over his upper teeth repeatedly, something she hadn't seen for months now.

"Don't worry. It's just work stuff. Where do you want to eat?"

"We'll eat here. I have a good salad from across the street. Now I think you need to sit down, relax, and talk to me about Ridgewood. How did this come about?"

"I had dinner at Phil's Wednesday night, and his youngest brother Tommy and his wife were there. You remember them from the weekend in Chicago? They're expecting their first, and they'd really like to move back to Ridgewood to be close to both sets of parents, who still live there. Anyway, we started to talk about job opportunities for Tommy. One thing led to another, and it got my wheels turning. He could help me run the business. We even started to talk about ways to make it more sustainable. He's dynamic in sales, but misses the opportunity to use his engineering background."

Carrie sat tall, leaned in to the table, and reached toward Rob's hands. She cleared her throat and turned her head from one side to the other as if she was stretching her neck. Her speech was slow and deliberate as she looked into his eyes. "This is what I know. I'm getting married in two weeks. We're scheduled to pack out the week after that. I have spent the last five months getting psyched about moving to Tokyo. I've become adept at using chopsticks, and I'm ready to tackle their subway system. But I need you to follow your heart, and I will follow you. We have big plans to travel and see that part of the world, though we can do that anytime.

Rob took a deep breath. "You're right. Then I think of the opportunity the feds gave me. That's a lot of money, Carrie. I never thought I'd have these three choices."

"The bank in Japan, the federal government anywhere, Linders Engineering in Ridgewood—you have to make a decision."

"There's one more thing." He stopped to take a long drink from his beer. "Amy's brother called as I was driving here. They found a note from her and she's on her way back to Milwaukee. They think she's looking for me."

Carrie almost spit out her wine. "Then that solves it. To Japan!" she said. "Surely, she won't find you in Tokyo."

"You are right. To Japan!" Rob raised his bottle to clank her glass. "To us, and our life together, wherever that takes us."

She settled back into her chair. "But Rob? I think Ridgewood could be home someday. I saw nice homes with wide front porches there. Maybe in two years?"

Carrie was glad she'd included her sister, sister-in-law, and her nieces in the planning, but none of them knew the final decisions she'd made. Only Judith knew, because she was coordinating everything at her home. And now, it was time for the big reveal, but instead of a new home makeover, it would be the details of the wedding.

Maggie let loose with a little squeal when she saw Carrie's dress for the first time as the two sisters got ready at Judith's. "Oh my gosh, I won!" she exclaimed.

"You won? What do you mean?"

"Kate, Emily, Kim, Liesel and I had bets. Would it be long or short? White, off-white, or a pale color? Strapless or not? This is gorgeous."

Maggie kicked some shoes out of the way so she could give her younger sister a hug. "I never thought I'd see the day when you'd take this plunge, but Sister, I am beyond happy for you."

"That's enough," Carrie said as she waved her off. "My hair and makeup are perfect. You cannot make me cry!"

"I'll wait until after the ceremony then."

Maggie helped Carrie with last-minute adjustments getting into her dress, when Carrie opened her purse and pulled out a small, silver flask. "Here, you want a swig?" she said as she offered it to Maggie.

"The tradition continues!"

There was a gentle rap on the door. “Are you girls decent?” their dad said, as he slowly opened the door. “Everything is in place, and the groom is ready to go. Are you all set?”

Before they could answer, he burst into laughter and took the flask from Maggie. “This all started at your wedding, didn’t it?”

“Actually, it started at your wedding, Dad. Mom had this, and then gave this flask to me. I passed it to Charlie, and now it’s Carrie’s turn.”

He finally caught a good look at Carrie and began to go in for a hug.

“Thanks, Dad, for everything. But I'm wound a little tight right now.” She snorted a little chuckle. “Well, a little less than I was two minutes ago.” It was the laugh they all needed.

“I get it. But tick-tock. Let’s go. Time to start the best chapter of your life.” Before they could leave the room, he wiped the tears from his eyes.

“Really, Dad, don’t start,” Maggie said. “I promised her we’d wait until after the pictures.”

“I'm ready, just one second,” and Carrie slipped on her shoes. “I swear, I keep tripping on the carpet. I should have practiced outside on the lawn in these heels.” She looked up at her dad. “Just promise me you’ll be hanging on to me real tight as we walk down that aisle. Judith forgot to cut the irrigation last night, and that ground is soft.”

No one needed to be told when Carrie appeared at the back of the lawn, ready for her walk to the gazebo. All they had to do was watch Rob as he smiled and took a deep breath.

The breeze gently played with the long folds of her silk georgette skirt that shimmered in the sunlight. The lace top of the dress hugged her body and gave way to a delicate, wide neckline that framed the gentle lines of her collar bone. Gracing her neck was her mother's pearl necklace, another tradition that began when her mother had worn it on her wedding day and had been passed on to Maggie, and now, Carrie. She carried a simple bouquet of white calla lilies and blue hydrangeas.

Carrie stopped and gave her brother, one of the ushers, an embrace before she started down the aisle. As she feared, the heel of her shoe became entangled with the runner that had been laid down over the grass, and she was about to do a header into the lap of Judith's husband until her father and brother caught her. There was a slight gasp from the guests, and the string quartet stopped playing until she stood, straightened herself, kicked off her shoes, and gave a thumbs up to Rob, whose smile and nod returned the gesture.

During the reception, the guests were entertained by The Professors. Rob joined them for a special set when he sang a song he wrote for Carrie.

By the end of the day, Carrie and Rob were relieved they'd expanded the invitation list to include more family members and friends. She'd lost some control in the process, but realized it didn't matter. This truly was a celebration.

Following comments delivered by their best man, others chimed in with their stories, best wishes, and endless clanks of glasses. Rob sat tall and confident when his father asked to say a few words at the reception. Under the tablecloth, Rob gripped Carrie's hand as he accepted his father's gratitude and blessings.

Finally, it was Carrie and Rob's turn to say something. Carrie took the microphone.

"Of course, this is the best day of my life, and Rob's, too, I hope." She looked at him with an inquisitive look on her face, and paused until the laughter died down. "Both of us are so excited you've been with us during this last year and, of course, today. Thank you—for joining us, for supporting us, and to our families, for never giving up on us." She handed the mic to Rob while the group continued chuckling.

"You're the best. We're so excited to start our next chapter. In closing, we just want to say *doumo arigatou.* That's 'thank you very much' in Japanese."

Acknowledgments

This book would have never been written if it were not for the support of numerous people. I am truly indebted to them

Many, many thanks to –

- Kathy Lindahl, whose unwavering support enabled me to finish this lesson in lifelong learning.
- Judy Bates, for her ongoing interest and encouragement, especially during the rough patches.
- Barb Robson, Dr. Carolyn Brown, and Theresa Bizoe for their technical advice in health care and sailing.
- Friends who shared relationship advice their mothers had given them: Ann Morrow, Barbara Dieterichs, Cynthia Shipley, Leslie Johnson, Mary Levad Lovstad, Retta Parsons, Susan Mutty.
- Readers throughout the process: Anne Sievers, Elaine Maylen, Eugenia Hogan Sandy, Jenifer Thomas, Josie Fentress, Julie Breunig, Kathy Bruno, Kim Reynolds, and Laina Melvin.
- My critique group: Ray, Esther, Bob, Paul, Terry, Wing.
- Linda Chamley Johnson and Susan Finlay for publishing support.
- Crescent Rose Photography
- And finally, my editors, Teresa Crumpton/ Author Spark, Inc., and Mindy Hoffbauer/ Write Angle Consulting.

About the Author

Pam Sievers is a recent transplant from Michigan to the Phoenix, Arizona area. Her roots however, are in Wisconsin where she spent countless holidays visiting her grandparents in Milwaukee. When not writing, she enjoys quilting, and fun road trips exploring her new state. She maintains a blog at www:mypatchworkjourney.com

Made in the USA
San Bernardino, CA
26 May 2020